8.11.17
$26.00

117

D0090850

HOW *to* BEHAVE
in a CROWD

HOW *to* BEHAVE *in a* CROWD

A NOVEL

Camille Bordas

TIM
DUGGAN
BOOKS

NEW YORK

Copyright © 2017 by Camille Bordas

All rights reserved.
Published in the United States by Tim Duggan Books, an imprint of the Crown Publishing Group, a division of Penguin Random House LLC, New York.
crownpublishing.com

TIM DUGGAN BOOKS and colophon are trademarks of Penguin Random House LLC.

Library of Congress Cataloging-in-Publication Data
Names: Bordas, Camille, 1987– author.
Title: How to behave in a crowd / Camille Bordas.
Description: First edition. | New York : Tim Duggan Books, [2017]
Identifiers: LCCN 2016023941| ISBN 9780451497543 (hardcover) |
    ISBN 9780451497550 (softcover)
Subjects: LCSH: Brothers and sisters—Fiction. | Domestic fiction. |
    GSAFD: Humorous fiction.
Classification: LCC PS3602.O678 H69 2017 | DDC 813/.6—dc23
LC record available at https://lccn.loc.gov/2016023941

ISBN 978-0-451-49754-3
Ebook ISBN 978-0-451-49756-7

Printed in the United States of America

Book design by Anna Thompson
Jacket design by Christopher Brand

10 9 8 7 6 5 4 3 2 1

First Edition

For Marie Cordoba

If speaking for someone else seems to be a mysterious process, that may be because speaking to someone does not seem mysterious enough.

—STANLEY CAVELL

Contents

The Stain

THERE WAS A darker brown stain on our brown suede couch. If I swept it one way with the palm of my hand, it almost blended in. I could squint and forget it was even there, but then a swipe in the other direction, and the stain reappeared, darker than I remembered, like I'd just fed it.

Everyone had a different story about the stain. Simone said I'd pissed the couch as a toddler, after running free from our mother's bundle of towels, just out of my bath. "You went straight for the couch, stood right there on the armrest, grabbed your half-inch wang, and aimed," Simone said. "I saw it, and Aurore and Jeremie, we never understood what came over you, Dory. It's like you were on a mission."

It didn't, indeed, sound like me at all. First, the number of decisions that was implied, all of them transgressing my mother's law (running naked and barefoot on the cold living room tile, grabbing my penis in public, pissing on the couch). Add to that Simone's choice of words: *went straight, aimed, mission.* Hers was the least believable story. Aurore and Jeremie didn't even back it up.

Other stories of the stain incriminated my siblings in turn: coffee stain (Berenice), nail polish (Aurore), jism (Jeremie), tomato sauce (Leonard), paint (Simone). Each initial stain was, in every account, made worse by our mother's attempt to clean it with unfit detergent. One story was actually based on the premise that there had been no stain to get rid of in the first place, that our zealous mother had just wanted to bring a new shine to the couch and had ruined it with a single spray of the wrong thing.

The stain on the couch made me uneasy. It made me think I was the only one to notice things, to care. "Why do you care so much about the stain?" my mother once asked, and the thing is, I couldn't understand why no one else did.

I loved my family, I believe. Even though I'd known no other and couldn't really tell, I thought they were all right, decent people. But oblivious. They got lost in their thoughts. They had no sense of the other—of anyone outside our family, sometimes even me.

One point every story of the stain converged on: the stain was at the very least nine years old. That was a long time to keep a stained couch, I thought. We were not poor.

I knew we weren't poor because we went to the beach every summer, and I'd learned in school (fourth grade) that being able to go to the beach was a privilege not everyone had. There had been a national campaign to raise awareness of children who didn't get to go away at all during summer. Our teacher, Miss Faux, had shown us clips of kids seeing the ocean for the very first time thanks to the money collected the previous year by the Let Them Sea charity. Some of the kids in the Let Them Sea videos hadn't even believed the sea existed before. They thought it was just a fairy-tale word, "like magic wands, or castles," one of them told the camera. Some of them were older than me. I remember one girl in the video—her name was Juliette, the caption said— who'd looked more happy about her little brother's walking on a beach for the first time than about her own discovery. She kept looking at him, his reactions. She barely glanced at the water her-self. It had made me teary eyed a bit. After the clips, Miss Faux had put a tin jar with the Let Them Sea logo on her desk and encouraged us to put whatever we could in it, even just a penny or a dime. It was important, she'd said, that we realized that the smallest of our sacrifices could make a big difference in another kid's life. A couple of the boys in my class had lied and said they didn't get pocket money at all and sadly could not donate to the cause. During break, though, I'd heard them talk about all the candy they'd buy later, and why should they pay for poor people's vacations anyway, and how those of us who gave money were suckers who fell into the guilt trap like shit into the toilet bowl. I'd put the whole of my monthly allowance in the Let Them Sea jar. I had waited for a moment where Miss Faux would see how much I tossed in, but either she didn't pay attention or she didn't think my generosity was worth commenting on.

At home, I was always first at the dinner table. My siblings would come down the stairs only at our mother's insistence, and then like drops from a leaking faucet, one at a time, at painful intervals. I had to wait for them all to get there to start eating.

"The father won't be coming back tonight," my mother said one evening as she and I were waiting for the others. I thought she meant he was dead, but he'd only been kept abroad by a conference and had missed his connecting flight home. She called him "the father" to give him extra substance, I thought. We saw him so little.

Mom ate from blue plates and bowls because she'd read that blue tableware cut your appetite, and she always wanted to lose four pounds. That night, she'd made whitefish, and whitefish you could eat as much as you wanted and not gain an ounce, she said, but still she'd set a blue plate in front of her.

"The father won't be coming home tonight," she repeated to Simone, then Jeremie, then Leonard, as each showed up. No one asked for details.

Aurore was particularly hard to lure downstairs at the time, or to even see outside of her bedroom. She studied permanently. She and Berenice were both writing PhD dissertations, on different subjects and in different cities. Berenice lived in Paris and didn't come back home too often.

"Will someone see if Aurore plans to eat with us tonight?" my mother asked, and she was looking at me.

"Aurore," I said through her door.

"Is this a life-or-death matter?" Aurore asked.

"It's dinnertime," I said. "We're all waiting for you."

"Don't," she said. "I can't be interrupted right now."

"Do you want me to bring up a plate for you?"

"You're an angel, Dory."

When I went to bed that night, Aurore still hadn't touched the whitefish and potatoes on the tray I'd left outside her door. The potatoes had started turning purple-gray. I ate a couple. I wasn't even hungry.

Sometimes, Mom hooked me up with a blue plate too.

———

Every August, Berenice came home from Paris and our parents put the six of us in the van and crammed suitcases in between our seats and at our feet. The van had no trunk. We used the suitcases as ottomans and armrests. The drive to the beach was about three hours, and we usually listened to the traffic news radio station the whole way. It was pretty repetitive, but at least when they played music between bulletins, it was songs we all knew, which my mother thought was nice—not that we sang along to them or anything. It brought the generations together.

I don't know why we went to that beach every summer. I don't think anyone had particular affection for it. None of my three sisters would leave our bungalow (the same one every year) before five p.m.—they were all very light skinned and feared getting sunburned—and when they did go out, it was only to keep doing what they'd been doing indoors, which was reading or, when their eyes got tired, talking to each other about what they'd read. Leonard looked at people and took notes all day. Jeremie liked digging holes in the sand and lying down at the bottom of them. Summer after summer, the holes got deeper. At some point, it became impossible for Jeremie to get himself out of the holes without outside help, but he didn't seem to mind. He knew someone would come check on him eventually. He just liked to lie there on his back and look at that rectangle of sky he'd framed for himself, and once, when our mother informed him he could lie on the beach with her and me, at sea level, and see exactly as much sky, more sky, even, she believed, Jeremie agreed with her but added that he would also have to see a bunch of strangers in bathing suits.

The father and I were the only ones to actually go in the sea. He swam while I threw myself at oncoming waves, not too far from the shore, waiting for him to swim back to me. That's as close as I could get to sharing something with him, even though I was scared to go far out like he did. I wasn't exactly sure what the father did for a living but he did it away from us. Germany, China, Spain. Some sort of engineering. When teachers in school asked what our fathers' jobs were, I said mine traveled, and it seemed to be accepted as a valid occupation. Like any kid whose father didn't have a cool-sounding job, I assume, I hoped that mine was actually a spy. It had to happen sometimes that these fantasies turned out to be true, and I believed my chances were in fact higher than other kids' because my father traveled abroad a lot, so there was, at least, potential for covert missions and secrets, whereas the spydom of other fathers was unlikely, given that they worked in town, where nothing much ever happened.

We didn't see the father much, but when we did, on weekends, or in the summer, it seemed he couldn't wait to get away from us again. He swam a little farther every day. I'm not making that up to sound dramatic or anything. He did have this device he wrapped around his wrist that measured his progress, and he would announce a new record distance to us each morning.

My siblings loved swimming at the pool back home. They were all great swimmers and had bodies that proved it, athletic and lean, but the idea of swimming in the sea disgusted them. My mother claimed she couldn't swim, and it worried me. I wanted her to learn. "What would happen if I started to drown?" I'd ask. "Would you just watch me *die*?" She'd say that if I started to drown probably one of my siblings would go in the water to help me out. She'd always rush the pronunciation of the *probably*, but never once did she forget to say it.

Simone was the one who disliked summer holidays the most. My other siblings were already in college or grad school, so it didn't really make a difference to them where we were: they always had "research" to work on. But Simone still needed to be assigned work, and was of the opinion that school breaks were a waste of time. She'd skipped any number of grades over the years (she was only thirteen, a year and a half older than me, and already in high school) but she would've done the rest of her curriculum nonstop if that had been an option. She always got strangely nostalgic, though, when the time came to pack the car and go back home. Any other time, she was fine being in the middle, but she demanded a window seat for the ride back. She said looking at the seashore fade away through the window was a good way to get a grasp on her melancholy, and that being able to pull from a store of melancholy was what made great artists. "Car trips make great artists?" I asked, making sure I understood what my sister had said. "Car trips *back*," Simone specified.

The summer after I found out about kids who never got to see the ocean, I tried to be less bored, to look around me through their eyes and be amazed like I'd seen them be in that video. I found it hard to marvel at the water, though, and the waves, without encouragement. I wondered if a person needed to be looked at while enjoying something in order for that person to really enjoy it, and whether that was why that girl Juliette had only been looking at her little brother looking at the sea when they both saw it for the first time—to make sure he understood he had to enjoy it. I watched Simone being melancholy all the way home, but it didn't seem like she needed an audience.

My parents didn't look very much in love to me, and I thought it was my fault. I guess it's what happens when you're the only one to notice a thing: you feel responsible for it. They didn't really kiss, just a dry smack on the lips in the mornings when the father left for somewhere. They only seemed to exchange practical information about appointments or taxes, sometimes us. I thought they were waiting until I was old enough to move away to get a divorce.

I once went a whole week without seeing Aurore. Our bedrooms faced one another, but she rarely left hers. When she had to, for mandatory family dinners (one birthday or another), she looked out of place. I won't say much about our house because I'm really bad at picturing three-dimensional spaces, let alone describing them. I could never tell whose bedroom was the one right over our kitchen, for instance. I'm not good at drawing either. But basically: we had a living room, a kitchen, and a dining room we never ate in on the first floor, and then four bedrooms and one bathroom upstairs. I shared a bedroom with Simone. My parents' was next door. My brothers' and Aurore's were across the hall from us.

I missed Aurore's bedroom. When I was smaller and she was writing less important papers for school, she'd let me sit under her desk for hours. It was a panel desk, so I was enclosed on three sides. The fourth side opened onto Aurore, who worked with her legs up and folded half-lotus. All I saw of her was knees and bare feet, and I had all the space beneath the desk to myself. She never asked what I was doing under there. She had total respect for my privacy. I was so silent she sometimes forgot about me, though. She'd start stretching her legs for blood flow and I'd say, "Hey!" and she'd apologize and fold her legs back up.

Most of the time, I did nothing at all under there. I'd started drawing a mural in Crayola on the underside of the desk, but I only worked on it sporadically. I could never really see what I was drawing anyway, it was so dark. One day I started adding boogers to the mural, for texture. I felt guilty about it, but I couldn't stop.

When Aurore decided I'd gotten too big to sit under her desk, it hurt. I begged for one last afternoon, mainly so I could scrape off all the dried boogers from the mural. At the end of the day, Aurore could tell I was sad and she said, "I'll get a bigger desk for us one of these days," but she never did.

———

I believed if I ran away from home, it would make my mother happy. She always complained we weren't adventurous enough, and while my siblings usually met her remark with the same indifference they granted statements of personal opinions in general, I, the youngest of the six of us, took it to heart. I didn't want to be blamed for the others' quirks. I wanted to be my own man. To be different. I mean, I had no choice but to be different (I wasn't as smart or as good-looking as my brothers and sisters), but I had no particular idea what kind of person I should be either. I thought I could at least try what my mother had in mind and be adventurous.

It was unclear, though, what an adventure was. Jeremie, the younger of my brothers, had been offered chances to tour Europe with two different philharmonics: those would've been adventures, according to our mother, if Jeremie hadn't declined both opportunities, stating he preferred keeping cello a hobby. But when my other brother, Leonard, had begged my parents to let him go spend the tenth and following grades in boarding school, my mother hadn't thought it qualified as adventure, even though Leonard had tried hard to sell it as such. He'd said boarding school was actually the *ultimate* adventure, that Flaubert had written that whoever had known boarding school at a young age knew everything there was to know about society, and that Bourdieu backed this up entirely, and that Flaubert and Bourdieu were the two smartest men who had ever lived. I was four when Leonard made that speech, and the reason I remember it is because I hadn't really been aware that anyone existed outside of our family before that, and hearing that there not only were other names than ours (Flaubert, Bourdieu) but that they belonged to smarter people than my parents, that no one around the table—not even my parents—objected to it, made me panic and I started crying. My mother took advantage of my tears to seal her refusal.

"See," she'd told Leonard. "You're upsetting your little brother. Dory doesn't want you to leave us. No more of this boarding school nonsense."

Almost eight years had passed since then and I still wasn't sure what an adventure entailed, and whether Leonard resented me for crying that day. He'd just graduated from his master's program with all possible honors, but he was still sore and regularly reminded our mother that he would've been a better sociologist had he not been denied the boarding school experience.

———

Judging from the movies I'd seen, it seemed adventures were things that occurred outside of home or school, and that they merely made you meet people if you went on them alone, whereas at least one crew member had to die if you went out on an adventure with a group. So I decided to go alone (I didn't have friends anyway), and one night, on my sister Simone's bike, I ran away from home. The plan was to go to Italy, because it looked like a good life. I hadn't thought about how crossing the Alps on a bicycle might be a challenge. Not a mile out the door, I got tired and decided it would be easier to just go to the big city three miles west and hop a train from there.

By the time I made it to the train station, around two a.m., the place was deserted save for a few bums sleeping in corners and two travelers in shorts and hiking boots, each reading to the other from a different hard-sounding-language-to-French conversation guidebook. There was no train scheduled for any time before 4:55, so I just sat on a bench by the "Departures" board, where all the platforms started or ended, depending on how you looked at it, and I waited. I could see lines and lines of shiny black train tracks ahead but no trains anywhere. I wondered where they were spending the night.

"What do you have there?" one of the bums shouted from the corner he occupied. He was eyeing my backpack.

"Garbanzo beans," I shouted back. "Bears of honey. Canned tuna. Underwear." I was trying to remember everything I had packed and give the bum an exhaustive list. I think he was interested in the canned tuna because he started walking toward me after I said I had some. "Soap." I kept going while he approached, lowering my voice as he got closer. "A flashlight. Orangina."

"Orangina?" the bum said, appalled.

"That's all we had," I said apologetically.

"Wait 'til your mother just refilled the pantry next time you decide to run away, kid," the bum said, and he sat down next to me. He didn't smell as bad as other homeless people I'd seen. He smelled like damp cardboard.

"So you don't have any kind of weapon in here," he said after I was done with listing what I had. "If you're going to be on your own, you'll need a weapon," he said. "You can't just walk around like that, a little boy like you. There are some crazy motherfuckers out there. Fucked-up shit happens to cute little boys like you."

"I'm not cute," I said, and I wasn't fishing for compliments there, but trying to see if my being a little chubby might protect me from potential killers. The homeless guy took a closer look at me.

"You're cute enough for a psychopath," he said.

"Don't they prefer little girls, though?" I said, hopeful.

"They go for anything, kid. Anything that bleeds, all kinds of children, it doesn't matter, animals, women—anything."

He started scratching a wart on the back of his hand.

"You should put duct tape on that and leave it alone," I said. "Just cover it with duct tape, a new piece of duct tape every day, until the wart disappears."

The homeless guy looked at me and repeated, "Duct tape!" and laughed, I don't know if at me or at an old joke he might've heard before about duct tape.

"It really works," I said. "My brothers and sisters, they're big swimmers. They all caught warts on their feet at the pool when they were kids, and my mother tried everything—nothing works better than duct tape."

"That is disgusting," the homeless guy said. "Public pools are disgusting."

"Now we all wear flip-flops when we go," I said, so he wouldn't think I was disgusting too.

"Flip-flops won't help you any against fungus . . . the foot-bath thing they make you go through before you get in the pool? Ugh. I don't know that flip-flops protect you any against all that footbath fungus."

"People say they do."

"People say strawberry is the best flavor of ice cream," he said.

I thought that was a clever answer. I thought he might know where the trains came from in the morning.

"There's a depot that way, by the stadium," he told me. "I went there a few times, sneaked inside empty train cars for the night."

"Sounds cool," I said.

"I prefer being outdoors, actually. A train depot is not such a great place to wake up in. I keep it for when it's real cold out."

I thought I was stupid for saying spending the night in a train depot sounded cool, but the homeless guy didn't give me a hard time about it. He knew I had a lot to learn, I suppose.

"Did you say good-bye to anyone before you left home?" he asked me, and I said I hadn't, that it would've ruined the whole thing.

"Ruin how?"

"If I'd said good-bye to my sister Simone, say, she would've told my mother right away and my mother wouldn't have let me leave," I explained.

"Well, sure," the bum said. "You don't say good-bye to a family member. But you have to say good-bye to *someone*. Someone who can tell the police it was your decision, you know? So your poor mother doesn't freak out even worse and believe you've been abducted and killed when she finds out you're gone. Don't you have a little girlfriend or something?"

I gave it some thought. I liked the Juliette girl from the Let Them Sea video, but we had never met. I guessed Sara Catalano was cute. I'd thought about her many times at night, before falling asleep. Maybe I was in love with her. She was too popular for me to have a conversation with at school, but I knew where she lived; I could probably go say good-bye to her. Thinking about what I would tell Sara, I realized I was relieved I'd forgotten to do something important before running away, something I would have to go home to fix, and that I would get to have a good night's sleep in my bed before fixing it. The homeless guy seemed to be someone whose advice I should listen to. There might've been a flaw in his reasoning, though.

"But if I say good-bye to someone," I said, "and people worry less about me, then what happens if, on top of running away, I actually do get abducted? If I'm made prisoner? No one will come looking for me if they think I'm happy living my adventures somewhere."

"Well you can't have your cake and eat it too, buddy," the homeless guy told me.

"I don't see where the cake is, in that situation," I said.

"The cake is your freedom," the homeless guy said. "Eating the cake would be to have people worry about you. You can't have both."

He raised a sad arm and I thought he was going to point at something but the arm fell back on his thigh right away.

"The rest," he said, "not knowing what's gonna happen to you, if you'll get abducted or raped or killed and whatnot, or if people will leave you alone and you'll get to be happy, well, that's like not knowing whether the cake will be good or not."

He sounded like he knew a lot. I tried to remember if I'd ever disliked any kind of cake. I knew he'd been speaking of figurative cakes, of course, but I guess I was hungry. None of the foods I'd brought with me sounded appealing.

"So, you're going home?" the bum said after a minute. I'd been staring at emptiness, thinking about cakes, but the sound of the bum's voice made me focus on the first thing ahead of us. It was an ad for a brand of ice cream, Carte D'Or, more particularly for the strawberry flavor. "Voted Best Flavor by YOU!" it said.

"Well, yeah," I said. "I guess you made it clear I was unprepared."

"Good," the bum said. "Now go home, get a weapon, and say good-bye to someone."

"I will," I said, and I got up and extended my hand to shake the bum's.

"You're not gonna need your cans of food back home," he said. I left him everything.

———

Daphné Marlotte had always been the oldest person in town, but she became the oldest person in the country that spring. My mother congratulated her on her achievement when we bumped into her on our way to get groceries. It wasn't unusual to bump into Daphné. She only lived a couple streets from us, and she went everywhere so slow you could see her once on your way to the store and then again on your way back, only a block or two from where you'd first seen her.

Daphné didn't scare me like she did other kids, who thought she was ugly and a witch. I knew she didn't have superpowers or anything. She was just lasting a long time, and there was nothing more to it.

"I read that article about you," my mother told Daphné that day. "I didn't know you'd been married *five* times, my goodness! Talk about live and learn!"

Daphné laughed at this, but it looked painful and she shifted down to a smile.

"I've always been a slow learner," she said. "After the fifth one died, I thought to myself, You know what, Daphné? Maybe that's not for you." She paused to salivate. "Mostly, there aren't that many eligible bachelors over a hundred years old now," she said. "And I wouldn't go for anything younger. I need someone who's got the experience."

"The article listed some pretty old guys," my mother said. "There seem to be quite a few in Brazil, actually."

"That sounds nice," Daphné said. I knew she'd never left France.

She looked pensive for a moment and I started actually picturing the things we'd talked about—century-old guys in Brazil—something I never really did unless there was a pause in the conversation.

"Oh! Let me show you what I got!" Daphné said, interrupting her own reverie.

Whenever we saw her, Daphné would show us what she'd bought at the market. "Let me show you what I got," she'd say, like she'd found something extraordinary. She opened her caddy for us and we leaned over to see. "Carrots," she said, "potatoes, parsnips." Her fingers were all crooked at different angles, which is why people thought she was a witch, but it was really just arthritis. Sometimes I caught myself wanting to put rings around her fingers just for fun (the rings would have to follow all the sharp turns; it'd be like navigating a maze), but then I'd realize it was a weird thing to want to do. Daphné shifted things around to show us a piece of beef shoulder for her pot-au-feu. "I cook it for so long it just melts into your mouth," she said. "It's the last meat I can manage to eat, 'cause I can't really chew anymore."

"Sounds good," my mother said.

"Even the pot-au-feu meat is too much, actually. I just let it sit in my mouth and press the juices out and spit it out."

"Sounds really good. I might go for pot-au-feu myself."

My mother often pretended that Daphné's sharing of her caddy's contents inspired her meal ideas, but she never bought the same things that Daphné had. She designed her meal schedule a week in advance.

"And look," Daphné said, all excited (she always saved the best for last). "These beautiful oranges . . . They gave them to me for *free* today! Because of the article in the newspaper!"

She was really happy about the free oranges. I personally didn't understand how people liked oranges, even less how they could talk about oranges like they were candy. She gave me one. It was amazing to me that she'd think I'd like it.

"Thank you so much, Mrs. Marlotte," I said. "I hear oranges have lots of good vitamins."

"But mostly, they're delicious," Daphné said.

She was going to say more things about oranges but my mother congratulated her again on being the most senior citizen in the country ("Third in Europe!" Daphné said), and then we split. My mother's enthusiasm about Daphné's old age deflated the second we made our turn around the block. "Poor old Daphné," she said, lighting a cigarette. "All alone in the world. These oranges are her last pleasure. She has to rely on a storekeeper's kindness to decide a day has been good. Did you know her *three* sons moved back to town one after the other to take care of her and all of them *died* of old age before she did?"

"That's sad," I said.

"That's horrible, is what it is. To raise all those kids and still end up alone."

"Well, you had six," I said. "I'm sure one of us will survive to take care of you and Dad."

"What are you talking about? All of you will survive me and the father, and well beyond. Maybe even forever."

I didn't worry about it too much, but it was still comforting when my mother said there was a chance we wouldn't die.

"As for taking care of me and the father, when we're Daphné Marlotte-old and can't chew our meat, or even follow a TV movie anymore, I can't imagine your brothers and sisters stepping up to help. No offense to them but . . . they're not really good at caring for anyone. Not too sensitive. The opposite of you, really."

I knew my mother thought that of me. That I was kind, and good at reading people's emotions. What I didn't understand was why she thought it was a good thing. "A gift," she even said. To me, all it was was I had a good memory for things the rest of my family didn't pay attention to or had trouble with—people's names, their kids' and grandkids', the relationships and the diseases they'd had. I could always make small talk in place of my mother if she got trapped in a conversation with someone I knew she didn't remember a thing about, or take the reins when she ran out of juice. I don't think it meant I cared, though, remembering all these details about people. But maybe it did.

My mother turned to me and pointed her cigarette at my face. I assumed she meant it to be an extension of her index finger.

"Don't go and repeat to your brothers and sisters what I just said," she said, "about them being insensitive."

"Of course not," I said, though I was pretty sure the news wouldn't much upset them.

———

The second time I tried running away, I'm not sure it counted. I did leave at a moment when I should've been home, but like the first time, no one noticed, and I didn't meet anyone new. I got disheartened before I could.

I decided to take the bum's advice and pack better food, and a kitchen knife for self-defense, and to say good-bye to someone outside the family unit. And so on my way out of town forever, I knocked on Sara Catalano's door. Her father answered.

"Is Sara home?" I asked.

"Who the hell are you?"

"We're in school together," I said. "Isidore." I said I believed Sara had accidentally packed my math book at the end of our last class, which was a lie. We'd never sat side by side in class, even by accident.

"You could've called to make sure," her father said, but he still went in to get her.

I assumed Sara didn't know I liked her. We'd never spoken, so it was a reasonable bet. I hadn't considered she might not know who I was.

She came to the door and I rolled out the heartfelt speech about my feelings and my decision to leave, a speech I had spent three nights writing and two more memorizing. I sped things up toward the end, because I could tell I was losing her attention. When I got done, I had to announce I was done so she would turn her gaze back to me. I don't want to believe that I thanked her for listening, but I'm pretty sure that I thanked her for listening. "Have a good one," she said, and smiled, and shut the door on me.

I went back home. That weekend, I tortured myself over how stupid I must have looked. Over what Sara would think of me on Monday when she realized I hadn't run away like I'd said I would.

She didn't seem surprised to see me back in school the following week, though. In fact, nothing in our relationship changed.

———

I was brushing the stain on our couch the way it showed less. I'd petted that small part of the suede so much over the years it had become the smoothest thing I knew—and I'd tickled babies' armrolls before, and fishes had brushed past me in the Mediterranean. Leonard combed the stain the wrong way, just to mess with me.

"What are you now? Goldfinger?" he said, and he sat right there on the spot, between me and Jeremie.

"Yeah, stop fondling the couch, Dory," Simone said. "It's obscene."

Jeremie said to leave me alone, that maybe I had a compulsive disorder of some sort.

I said nothing. In a few seconds, I'd been made ashamed of a thing I'd been doing as long as I could remember, a thing I thought no one really noticed and about which everyone, it turned out, had a joke to make, an idea, a diagnosis. Maybe they talked about it when I wasn't around. I crossed my arms high on my chest.

We were watching this one spy show where the spy lady keeps her feelings for the spy gentleman to herself, and the spy gentleman does the same, because they work together, and a romance between them would jeopardize the quality of their spying team, and they're both very professional. As a result of their professionalism, though, they're lonely at night, in between missions. Many of the shows we watched, I'd noticed, made a big deal out of the professionalism issue, out of the wrongness of people who worked together having romantic involvements (the same thing as in the spy show went on in the cop show and in the political show, for instance—in the medical shows, however, the doctors could all sleep together and it didn't affect their work). My mother explained to me that it was because the shows we watched were American that they talked about professionalism so much, that Americans had a different culture and that the work environment was more important to them than anything else.

"I'll light us a fire," the spy lady said to the spy gentleman on TV (they'd gotten lost in a forest in Eastern Europe and night was about to fall).

"Well, I'll light a fire right in your pussy," Leonard said, impersonating the spy gentleman as his face appeared in close-up and he tenderly admired the spy lady for her ability to light a fire with just two logs and a handful of twigs. We all laughed a little, not too long, because we didn't like to miss actual dialogue.

Dubbing shots of meaningful looks and—better yet— meaningful silences with obscene lines was one of my siblings' favorite activities. I liked it, not only because the gap between a character's composure and Leonard's or Simone's or Jeremie's coarseness was funny, but also because I integrated the lines into the story, and it made all the characters seem more human. It was as if the spy gentleman, no matter how gentlemanly and well educated he presented himself as, could really be thinking this, *I'll light a fire right in your pussy*, as the spy lady labored for their survival, and it looked like he felt ashamed about it, like he'd been exposed again, had failed to hide his true nature from us. My brothers' and sisters' dubbings were, to me, as much a part of the show as the explosions and the twists, and so were their comments on the set, or on a character's clothes or features ("Do you think Ralph thinks about how pointy his ears are every morning?"). All in all, they were a nice crew to watch TV with, except for their habit of making prognoses about the plot.

"What do you think, guys?" Leonard asked. The spy lady and the spy gentleman had gone to sleep by the fire with their clothes and shoes on. The TV now showed the villain and his wife having dinner. "He murders his wife, or the Mafia takes care of her?"

"I'd say he does it," Jeremie said. "He poisons her."

"I say he chokes her," Leonard said.

"Either way, she has to die in this episode," Simone said.

The problem with my siblings' predictions was that they were always right. It ruined the surprises for me. I never saw anything coming. Never made guesses. Sometimes, Simone tried to force one out of me. I'd say, "I don't know, I'm not really following this," but the truth was I was always following, I'd been following for weeks, for months, yet I still never knew who *had* to die, what *had* to happen, and why, and when.

"Why does she have to die in this particular episode?" I asked. I usually didn't speak, but I happened to not care too much about the scenes with the villain's wife.

"She's of more use to the plot dead than alive now," Simone explained.

"Is there only one possible plot?"

"Sort of."

"It's always the same stories," Jeremie said. "Only a few variations. Since Aristotle."

"Aristotle's *Poetics*," Simone specified.

Leonard sneezed inside his cupped hands and looked closely at what had landed in his palms, as he always did, and for way too long before he'd get a tissue. No one ever gave him a hard time about that.

On-screen, the villain and his wife picked the haricots verts from their plates with great care and ate them, one at a time, which struck me as highly unrealistic.

"Did Aristotle write about what happens to villains' wives?"

"Not exactly," Jeremie said. "But you can always transpose."

The villain's wife did die by her husband's hand a few minutes later, right before the closing credits. The villain smothered her in their bed with a pillow, just when she was thinking they'd do the monkey business.

"This show sucks it," Leonard said, and he turned the TV off. He got up and locked himself in the bathroom with a book about medieval England. Simone disappeared into our bedroom shortly after that, to read something unappealing as well, I assumed. Leonard had left a butt print on the suede, the stain at its center, as visible as possible. I was waiting for Jeremie to leave the couch and the room, so I could resume brushing the stain (or at least so I could brush it once more) back in the direction where it blended in. I'd kept my arms crossed the whole time since they'd made their remarks on my obsessive/obscene/sickly behavior, and I didn't know how much longer I'd be able to stay this way when the stain was the only thing I could think about. But Jeremie didn't seem to be in a rush to go to his room. Jeremie was more contemplative than the others. He liked to read, like the rest of them, sure, and to be alone, and think, but there was less of a sense of urgency with him. He could do nothing but stare at a wall for hours and not blame himself for his idleness.

"I might stay here awhile, Izzie," he said. Jeremie was the only one who called me Izzie, which was really what I wanted to be called, not Dory. "You shouldn't hold back for me."

"Hold back from what?" I said.

"From doing whatever you do with the couch," he said. "I really don't mind."

I said I was okay.

As a kid, I thought actors had to be the smartest people. I believed they spoke all the languages and dubbed themselves in all the countries that aired their shows and showed their movies. I believed they spent their lives traveling around the world to act again, in a new language, what they'd already acted elsewhere. Actors had to speak at least twelve languages, I thought (I'd only come up with that number because twelve different languages were as many as I could think of), and so they had to be geniuses, given that the father only spoke four and people already said that meant he was smart.

But I never thought actors were inside the TV, as I hear that lots of kids do growing up, and as Simone, who resented explaining to others what they'd missed, used to try to trick me into believing so I'd come downstairs in time for shows' opening credits. "Hurry, Dory! The actors inside the TV are not going to wait for you to start the episode!" Her logic seemed flawed to me. If the actors really were inside of our TV, it meant they couldn't be in anyone else's TV at the same time, and therefore, they were only performing for our household, and I represented an eighth, a sixth, sometimes even half of their total audience: of course they were going to wait for me.

———

We lived on a block that went meat market, funeral home, custom-made closets. I'd only ever been inside of the meat market. My mother took me there on Saturdays, because the father usually came home on weekends and he liked a good steak.

For a while I thought my mother and the butcher were having an affair. She spoke at a higher, dumber pitch when he was working instead of his wife. She laughed at his jokes about meat. Once, I found it unbearable. She laughed too heartily at something the butcher said that I didn't understand but knew to be dirty (something about tying up the joint real tight). Her laughing too hard was not unusual, but I got extra embarrassed for her this time because her lipstick had left a red mark on her front teeth. I couldn't watch. She didn't usually wear makeup, except on Saturdays, and I thought it was for the butcher, when I could as well have thought it was for the father. I left the shop to sulk outside. I thought my mother would come check on me right away, but if she worried, she didn't show it. She took her time at the counter. I looked inside the funeral home's window while I waited. Between the "Always in My Heart" and the "Eternally Lamented" decorative stones, there was a crossword-themed tombstone on display. They'd engraved nice words about the deceased person, what she'd been like.

	W		A		■	S		■			G	
	I	■	D	E	N	T	I	S	T	■	R	
	F		O			R		W			A	
■	E		R	■	L	O	V	E	D	■	C	
D			A			N		E			E	■
A			B			G	■	T			■	F
U			L		■		R	■		H		U
G	O	N	E	■	T	O	O	■	S	O	O	N
H			■				M			N		■
T	■		C	A	M	P	E	R	■	E		
E						■				S		
R	■	D	R	E	A	M	E	R	■	T		

"Do you get the feeling the word *fun* shouldn't be where it is?" my mother asked, looking over my shoulder. I hadn't heard her come out of the meat market.

"Yes," I said. "It's quite unfortunate."

"*Unfortunate*," she repeated, "now, that's one they should've put on there."

I didn't even smile. I was still mad at her for flirting with the butcher.

"That's one grim list of words," my mother said as she inspected the stone some more.

"You have lipstick on your teeth," I said.

My mother lit a cigarette and only after taking a couple of puffs did she attend to the lipstick trace, as if rubbing her front teeth with her finger was part of the act of smoking.

"Don't blow your smoke in my face," I said, even though she wasn't blowing her smoke in my face and I wouldn't have minded if she had been. I usually didn't give her a hard time about smoking, the way Simone did. She said she needed it and I believed her. When Simone complained about her addiction, my mother blamed it on journalism school. "It's the first thing they taught us back then," she would say, to defend herself. "They told us we had to be able to smoke a lot and hold our liquor. 'Go smoke with the people, with your informers: that's when you get the best quotes.' That's what our teachers said." "But you're an accountant now," Simone would respond, and add "for a *local* newspaper," in case she hadn't been hurtful enough. "Well that wasn't always the plan," my mother would say. No one ever asked what the original plan had been. I would have, but it looked like it might make my mother sad to think about it.

"Is the stain gone?" she asked me, showing all her teeth. I felt bad she'd thrown away her cigarette because of what I'd said.

"You're all good," I told her.

On the Sundays the father wasn't at home, my mother went to church. She wasn't a believer, but she said that being surrounded by Christians made her feel at ease. She couldn't explain why. I went along with her once. We couldn't tell anything about it to the father or the others, she had me promise, because they wouldn't understand. Simone particularly had a thing against religion. She was furious when people assumed we were Catholic, which happened a lot because of how many we were. My mother said we couldn't blame people for thinking we were Catholic because we did fit some of the clichés, but Simone countered that if they really wanted to reason in clichés, they could at least assume we were Jewish, given how smart we were. Promising my mother I wouldn't tell about Mass made me nervous I would witness something terrible there. People always made you promise before you knew what they were getting you into.

What followed, though, was not really surprising to me. I didn't understand what the priest said, but that wasn't unlike most of my classes, and I'm pretty sure my siblings would've managed to make sense of it, contrary to what my mother had said. Unlike the kids I went to school with, the adults in the church looked friendly, and sad, and all in all it was a good experience. I'd always thought I was the saddest one in my class (except for Denise Galet), and to see that sadness might become a normal trait with age left me feeling hopeful.

After the service, my mother talked to old Daphné and a small group of people she called by their first names.

"This one here's Isidore," she told them, and the women showed admiration.

"So he's the youngest one, right? The little prince?" one of them said.

"They're all little princes and princesses," my mother said, and everyone nodded.

"How many more do you have already?"

"Five more," my mother said. "Two other boys and three girls. All by C-section."

She always specified C-section, which I didn't know how to feel about.

"Dory is the worldliest one," she added, and she smiled at me. "He's the only one who'll come out with me in the open, not entirely ashamed of his old mother."

"Not yet!" someone said, and all shared a laugh.

My mother had her hands on my shoulders, and little by little, she dragged me closer, placed my body in front of hers, the way villains do in movies with the hostages they take for protection as they retreat. I don't think my mother liked people as much as she said she did.

The father rarely said anything to us, or me, at least. Sometimes at dinner, after Simone or one of the others had given a lecture on how they envisioned their future, he'd ask what it was *I* planned to do in life. It made me nervous when he asked. I'd mumble something about not being quite sure yet. I thought I only had one shot at the answer, that coming up with the wrong one could loom over the rest of my life.

I tried to get serious about coming up with a vocation, for the next time he put the question to me. At the school library, I went through a guidebook that listed all the professions in existence. It actually said "all the professions" on the cover, but then there was a warning on the back, in small print, that said new professions were invented on a regular basis and that others disappeared, but that the reader should nevertheless rest assured the ones listed in the booklet should at least have a good twenty years of existence ahead. The list was four years old already. It bore 443 items, I counted, in alphabetical order. I tried to guess which ones would expire. Cartography sounded like a doomed business. Anthropology did too. I thought places and groups of people only existed in a limited number, and that once you'd studied a particular land and mapped it, or spent some time with a tribe and written about it, there was nothing to add, you'd done the job and crossed something off the list of places to map and people to study, and that the list had to be extremely short by now, if there was anything left on it at all.

Each professional title appeared in italics and was followed by a brief description of what it entailed, what kind of education you needed, how many years. I imagined the longest descriptions had to be for the most impressive jobs, and I skipped them.

I wanted to come up with something conceivable, not too showy, something my siblings wouldn't right away try to discourage me from pursuing. On the other hand, too modest a pick would expose me to their mockery. They despised salesmen and politicians, as well as anything too useful (like plumbing, for instance) or concerned with precious things (flowers, jewelry, stationery, babies).

I thought I would read the whole booklet and find a vocation in one sitting, but by D I got bored and headed home. I didn't see the rush in making a decision anymore. I was still pretty young. I could wait for the booklet with the new professions to come out.

———

The only thing I was good at was holding my breath. In fact, I'd had a brief taste of what the rush of athletic performance might be during gym class when I'd held my breath underwater for the whole length of the pool. It impressed my classmates, I could tell. When I resurfaced at the other end, they all stood small in the distance and didn't say anything. All of them had gone up for air midlength. Though I hadn't saved anybody's life or done anything of importance, and though I'd always despised those who stuck out their chests, I walked back to them like a hero, in my flip-flops (I left a different pair at each end of the pool), and, halfway there, realized that, had I been gifted any real talent, I would probably have been a terrible person.

By the next time we did free-diving exercises, however, my classmates had come up with an explanation for why I was good at holding my breath: I was on the fat side, so I had to have bigger lungs than them, and a bigger asshole as well, and bigger feet that must have worked as fins, bigger everything, in fact, but the one thing boys wanted to have bigger than everyone else—they wouldn't grant me that. That was in fact made smaller than average by the bigness of everything else, they said. I wasn't usually paid this kind of attention.

The following weeks, I started going up for air before I needed to.

———

The third time I tried running away, there were no good-byes—I left a note. Just a couple of miles from home, though, I realized I'd forgotten my helmet and turned the bike around to get it. The whole way back, I felt vulnerable to injury. If I died in an accident, my mother would begin a road safety campaign in my name, I thought. I made it home all right, of course, but was too tired by then to attempt leaving again. I tore up the note I'd left on Simone's nightstand and fell asleep in my clothes.

———

One Saturday morning, my mother was stuck at home waiting for a call and sent me out to run the weekend errands by myself. I went to the meat market first, because I hated the butcher and wanted to be done with it. Old Daphné Marlotte was there standing in line behind another woman who ordered veal ribs and chops authoritatively. Daphné turned to me and shook her head in silent disapproval of the woman's attitude.

"Will that be all for you, ma'am?" the butcher said.

"If you don't forget to pack the duck-fat beans like you did last time, yes, sir, that will be all."

"I am, again, really sorry about that, ma'am," the butcher said.

"Sure you are," the woman said.

The atmosphere lightened the second she left the shop.

"Some case of a stitched asshole on that one," the butcher told Daphné.

"You're supposed to—what?" Daphné said. "Slit your wrists over her duck-fat beans?"

The butcher smiled. It's true the woman had been sort of

snappy and rude, but I always believed people had reasons to behave the way they did, and so I wasn't ready to side with the butcher. The fact that Daphné did, though, it made me wonder. Being the oldest person in the country, she had to know something about how to judge people.

"Shopping on your own like a big boy, Dory?" the butcher asked me.

"Yes, sir," I said.

"What can I get you?"

I glanced at Daphné. I thought they were trapping me into being impolite.

"Oh, go ahead, kid, I'm not in line," Daphné said. "I'm just looking."

She was looking at a pork roast wrapped in bacon behind the counter window. When I asked the butcher to pack it for me, she said, "Excellent choice, kid," and moved a couple inches to her left to stare at another piece of meat, hands clasped behind her back.

"Hey, Daphné?" the butcher said as he was wrapping my roast. "You know the sixty-eight joke?"

Daphné looked up at him and readjusted her glasses on the bridge of her nose.

"Let me readjust my glasses," she said, "I'll hear you better."

"So. Husband and wife are in bed, right? And the husband goes, *Hey, honey, you up for a sixty-eight?* And the woman says, *Sure, babe, but what's a sixty-eight?* and the husband says, *You blow me, and I owe you one!*"

Daphné laughed, and I understood that the butcher didn't only tell dirty jokes to my mother, but to anyone who'd listen.

"Are we making this kid uncomfortable?" Daphné asked him.

"Nah," he said, looking at me. "You got the joke, kid?"

"Not really," I said.

"See?" he told Daphné.

I knew what a sixty-nine was (in theory), but it still took me a few months to make sense of the sixty-eight. Sex jokes in general, I didn't get. All I got was that they were dirty, the same way I understood racist jokes were racist, but nothing much beyond that. Arabs were the butts of most of the racist jokes around here, and I thought maybe it was because I didn't personally know any Arabs that I didn't understand the jokes about them. Also, maybe it was racist of me to think that there could be a way for those jokes to make sense in the first place. Maybe all kids are racist, as a side effect of wanting everything to make sense.

"Did your mother tell you that you could keep the change if you went grocery shopping by yourself?" Daphné asked me.

"Yes," I said. "For my efforts."

"What else is on your list?"

I showed her.

"Skip the greengrocer," Daphné said, after analyzing the list as if it were a complex document. "No one will miss those Brussels sprouts. Tell your mom they were out of them, or that they were all brown and mushy. You'll get to keep an extra euro or two."

The butcher asked if I wanted anything else and when I said the roast was all, he turned to Daphné.

"Instructions for the pork roast, Daphné?"

"How heavy are we talking?"

"About three pounds of it?"

"Forty minutes in the oven, three hundred fifty degrees," she said, eyes closed.

The butcher turned to me and nodded deeply.

"What a great memory she has," he said.

———

One night, it came up again, "What about you, Dory? What do you want to be when you grow up?" and it struck me right then that the answer should be that I wanted to be a German teacher. It was Sunday, and the father had just spent two hours helping Simone with her German homework. He'd helped all my other siblings with their German over the years, not that they were bad at it, they just weren't as good as they were at everything else. When they'd had papers to turn in, they'd always run them by the father. He was happy to help, and since German was the thing with which he felt he could be of most use to his children, he discussed every little translation choice they made in more detail than my siblings were comfortable with. Only because my father excelled at it was German mandatory in our family. He tried to make us believe that German was important—the language of Hölderlin and other people like that—but I think what he liked about it was really that he understood it and that it was more impressive than English or Spanish—which he spoke as well—because everyone spoke English and Spanish. German teacher was the perfect answer, I thought. An achievable goal. Respect would pour forth from all around the table.

I'd yet to start studying German—I would only have my first class the following year—but I had the hope that I could be good at it, and I looked forward to spending time with the father discussing German subtleties on Sundays, like the others had done before me.

"I know what he'll be!" Simone announced before I got the chance to share my last-minute vocation. "He'll be my biographer!"

She wasn't being sarcastic.

"People will fight to write books about me one day, but yours will be the only authorized one, Dory, I swear, we can make a pact about it right now."

The father thought it was a great idea.

———

Simone's plan for the future was unclear, but it involved changing the world without making a big deal about it. None of my siblings were too interested in taking part in society (they all wanted to be hermits and think), but our father was the opposite. He would get upset about wars and epidemics and elections like there was anything one could do about such things, and though Simone didn't believe there was, she still wanted to make him happy and find a way to save the world from all its problems while working on her novels (which would be her most important task), so the father could stop feeling sad about the news.

It had only happened once that the father hadn't been made upset by the news: the night Jacques Chirac had announced on live TV he'd decided to dissolve Parliament. That had kept the father laughing for a while. I couldn't understand why he thought it was so funny, but I laughed with him anyway.

The father was an idealist, though. He said there should only be Buddhists in the world, "and chiropractors," he added some days, when his back gave him a hard time. He voted for other idealists who had no shot at winning any election and was still disappointed when they didn't. Leonard once asked him why he didn't vote for one of the parties that always won, for a change, just to see what it felt like to not be on the losing team, and it was a joke, but the father was cold to him for weeks. Mom said he was worried he'd failed to give us a proper moral compass, and I was convinced a moral compass was an object and couldn't understand why no one would step up and go buy one and put an end to the silent war between Leonard and the father.

———

The only thing in the news my siblings ever got all up in arms about was the government's talk of banishing homework for schoolkids.

"As if everyone wasn't dumb enough already," Simone said.

"But there's a rise in teenage suicide," my mother said.

"That has nothing to do with the load of homework," Simone said. "Kids want to die because no one likes them, and you can't pass laws against that."

Homework or not, I didn't care either way, but when I tried running away for the fourth time and Simone caught me—my hand on the doorknob, my backpack and helmet on—and asked what the hell I was doing, I told her I'd planned on running away to protest the homework ban. She said I was stupid and told me to go back to bed. I thought that she'd bought it, my poor excuse, but then she didn't bring it up in front of the others for a laugh the next day, or any other day.

———

Simone was lying on our bedroom's carpet and breathing loudly through her nose. She called it yogic breathing, even though she'd never taken a yoga class in her life. Her stomach was tense, and when she'd exhale, it barely deflated. She applied a certain pressure on it with the palm of her hands—she called it kneading the pain. She had the doomed face of her period days.

"You feel like shit?" I asked.

She looked in my direction and made sure I understood the effort it required. She was a good actress, Simone. She could control her ocular tension so that her eyes would be on you without seeing you. She gave you the flabby eyes.

"You want me to get you the hot-water bottle?"

"It's very nice of you, Dory."

"Don't call me Dory."

"You're too nice."

"I know."

"I mean it. You'll never get yourself a girl."

She burped and pretended it was part of yogic breathing.

"Take note of this, for my biography," she said. "Take note that I was always a great big sister who gave you precious advice on how to get a decent girlfriend."

We heard our mother come home, the rustling sound of plastic bags. She walked into our bedroom without knocking.

"Simone, look at what I found at the mall, for Rose . . . you think she'll like it?"

She unwound from its bubble wrap a mug with Brad Pitt's face on it. Simone folded both her forearms on top of her face and screamed.

"Didn't you tell me Rose was a Brad Pitt fan?" my mother

asked, now unsure. "Just look at it, will you? Do you think Rose will like it?"

"Why do you keep saying her name?" Simone said, and it came out muffled from behind her arms.

Rose we didn't know yet. She was Simone's pen pal. Simone's French teacher had come up with a project, at the beginning of the school year, to have her whole class correspond with another class at the other end of the country, to help teach them the basics of epistolary literature. Simone had never met her pen pal, but she despised her already. She also despised her French teacher, for that matter. She said educational projects of this sort were crutches for the incompetent. She said back in the day (Simone often spoke as if she'd lived there before ending up with us), one was taught *Les Liaisons Dangereuses* and that was good enough for the epistolary genre—which she, on top of everything, liked less than any other.

"I don't give a fuck if she likes it or not."

"But, I bought it for her," my mother said, "for her to feel a bit at home when she comes and visits, don't you think it's a good idea?"

The *climax* (that's what the paper Simone had our parents sign called it) of the pen pal project was to have each student meet their pen pal in the spring. Rose was going to come spend a week with us, Simone a week at her house after that. No one in our family was excited about having Rose over, except my mother. She'd already started planning meals and activities for Rose's stay.

Simone unfolded her arms and looked at the mug with disdain.

"It's hideous," she said. "And I don't particularly want that girl to feel at home here. If she feels too good, she'll keep on writing to me even after school is out."

"Would it be so bad?"

"Mom. Please."

"I don't understand why you have to be so negative all the time, Simone. I don't understand why you decided that you and Rose can't get along. You don't even know her."

"I didn't *decide* anything. I just have no desire to meet this person. Our desires are not controllable."

"Of course they are."

My mother was very calm as she declared our desires to be controllable. My mother was always very calm. She'd decided a long time ago that she knew what was best for her children and would never let go. Her life was dedicated to making us happy and sociable, to making us understand the two adjectives were married, and the fact that none of my five siblings were either never discouraged her.

"What do *you* think, Dory?" my mother asked, regarding the mug.

"Meh," I said.

"All right then. I'll return it to the store, if everyone hates it."

"Yeah, do that," Simone said. "And please, *please* don't get her anything else. She doesn't deserve the lousiest gift. Our correspondence didn't teach me anything. Anything at all. She's lucky enough I kept answering. It's the only gift she'll ever get from me."

"I'm sure you have more in common than you think."

"She's illiterate, Mom."

"Don't be silly. She wrote you ten letters at least."

"Oh, her *letters*! Let's talk about them! Her spelling is hopeless. For a whole line it seems like she understands a basic grammar rule, and then in the next sentence, she makes the mistake she just avoided . . . she doesn't even reread herself. She relies on pure chance. Worst kind of human being."

"So because she occasionally spells something wrong, your friendship is doomed?"

"Of course it is!"

Our mother started rewrapping the mug in bubble paper. She sighed.

"Sometimes, I feel like I brought up a batch of little misanthropes," she said. "You're all so intolerant. You only look up from your books to criticize the rest of the world."

She turned to me at that point and said, "Except for you, Dory, honey, of course."

Simone didn't like to be called intolerant. It was her weak spot and her paradox: always teary eyed when the time came to quote the French Revolution (she found opportunities), and always the first to rank her classmates on merit, intelligence, and culture (she was first in all).

"What do you want me to do, Mom? For sure men are born and remain free and equal in rights, but if they decide to grow up and never open a book, nothing says I have to endure their conversation."

"I don't want you to *do* anything, honey. I just wish, in general, you would *be* more open, and I say this for your own good. I wish you would leave your bed and your books sometimes, go out and meet people . . ."

"People?" Simone spat, outraged. "But I know so many already."

My mother didn't let this undermine her. She saw, on the carpet, the pack of NurofenFlash pills Simone took when she had her period.

"I see you're not feeling well," she said. "We will talk about this later."

—

Simone had me look at a couple of Rose's letters and a draft of her response to the first one. She said it was in preparation for the biography I would later write of her, but I believe our mother's calling her intolerant had affected her and she wanted confirmation that Rose was not smart.

Dear Simone Mazal,

I hope you are well.

I am very happy to meet you and that our classes are going to make that correspondance. I don't know the town where your from but my mother went to Ardèche once for holidays and she says it's not far from where you live and it's a beautifull part of the country.

I introduce myself: my name is Rose (like in the movie "Titanic" . . . I'm lucky, because it is my favorite movie!!!). However, I dont like the flower rose, I like sunflowers as favorite flowers. I have a cat Popcorn and two brothers Raphael and Romeo. My favorite actor is Leo of course, do you love him? I have a lot of posters with him.

The teacher Mrs. Duchesne explained to us when we have a pen friend we have to tell her what my life is like, what music I like and food, and also we have to show intrest in our pen friend and ask you questions about your life, so I will now ask you questions. Can you answer them in your next letter?

Thank you so much!
Questions:

1/ what is your favorite color?
2/ do you have brothers and sisters? If yes, how many? are they nice?
3/ do you have a pet?
4/ what is your kind of music you like to listen to?

PS: my best friend is Laetitia, she's pen-pal with Alice in your class. Do you like Alice? My second best friend is Marie, she is penpal with Virginia.

Sincerely,
Rose Metzger

Dear Rose,

It is interesting you mention <u>Titanic</u> since it aired last month on Channel 2 (I assume you watched it again on that occasion). I, for my part, had never seen it before, and it brought about a few questions I'd like to share with you: do you think we are supposed to believe the paintings Kate Winslet has in her suite (Picasso, Monet) are the authentic works? Is James Cameron implying that the MoMA and the Musée d'Orsay only have copies of those paintings? Or is he just abstracting himself from reality in portraying <u>Les Demoiselles d'Avignon</u> as having sunk down into the Atlantic with the ship? I believe all he wanted was to signify that his main female protagonist *had extremely bold taste in art for her time, and that using world-renowned paintings was the only way he could come up with to do so. I find it a tad too easy. It would've been more interesting, in my opinion, if Cameron had taken this opportunity to put in his movie works by more obscure artists who've been unjustly forgotten. That would've been taking a stand. It would've made Kate Winslet all the more interesting, I think. On another note, I found the husband-to-be character to be way too much of a caricature, but that's just a personal opinion. I'm not denigrating your taste in film.*

I personally love Charlie Chaplin's City Lights *and Akira Kurosawa's* Seven Samurai. *I assume you haven't seen those.*

Also, I wanted to tell you that Ardèche is not at all close to where I live. Anything is relative, of course, and depends on what reference point we decide on to distinguish the near from the remote, but let's say we're talking on the scale of the country: Ardèche is, inside of metropolitan France's limits, pretty far from where I live. It still is closer to me than where you *live, but as the crow flies, it is pretty much as far from my city as my city is from yours, for instance. I think it would be helpful to look at a map of our country, so I've attached one to this letter. I circled your town, mine, and Ardèche in red, in order for you to locate all these places in relation to one another. In green, you'll find the main mountain chains; in blue, the most important cities, from an economic viewpoint; purple, our main rivers; yellow, a few of the many places recognized by UNESCO as World Heritage Sites. My choices to circle one place and not another might look arbitrary to you, but I think, seeing as you don't seem to know too much about geography, that this map is* altogether a good way to start and will give you a general idea of how our country works. My advice is you should memorize it once and for all.

Cordially,
Simone

Dear Simone,

I hope you are well.

I dont really know how to anser your letter because you don't really ask any questions. Like, I don't understand what you say about "Titanic"?

Thank you for the map of the country, I pined it over my desk.

My mother is sorry she mistook Ardèche for another place, but now she doesn't remember what place she meant to say.

I never saw "City Lights" or the japanese one (is it a film of violent contents? I dont like violence) but I will ask my father to look for them next time he goes to the videoclub.

Today I am happy because I scored 18 out of 20 on my biology exam, and I am happy because I want to be a doctor later and you need good grades in sciences. My father is a doctor as well, and he was very happy as well.

What do you want to be later?

What do your parents do?

You can also answer the questions from my first letter in your next letter if you want. Its not too late!

Please ask me questions in your next letter.

Cordially,
Rose

At some point Simone decided taking notes for her biography was not good enough and we ought to start doing interviews.

"Observation is a good thing, but there's about thirteen years of my life that will never be covered if we don't artificially revisit them."

"What questions do you want me to ask?" I said.

"What do you think this is? Stalinist Russia?"

I didn't know who Stalin was at the time, though Leonard and Simone referred to him now and then, and so I did what I did when I didn't understand something, which was pretend I hadn't heard it.

"*You* pick the questions," Simone said. "After all, you were around for most of those thirteen years, I'm sure you have a perspective on my life that I couldn't possibly imagine."

"Is that a compliment?"

"It wasn't meant that way," she said. "But sure."

Simone borrowed Jeremie's Dictaphone the next day. It worked with little cassettes. Jeremie supplied two he said could be erased because he'd uploaded the bird sounds he'd recorded on them to his computer. Simone tested the Dictaphone and placed it on the night table we were supposed to share but that had always been all hers.

"I'm ready when you're ready," she said, and on the tape, you can hear me unfold the list of questions I'd prepared.

"Do you remember when you got lice in first grade and Mom was going to cut your hair real short in the bathroom and before she did you wanted to save as many lice as possible and asked me if I would shelter them and rubbed your scalp against mine?"

"What kind of question is that?"

"I was thinking about it. I'm pretty sure it's my first memory of you."

"Well it's not going to be a book about you, is it? Next question."

"Have you always been the smartest person in your class?"

"Absolutely. Even in kindergarten, I drew my houses with perspective—"

"What is your first memory?"

"I don't think we were done with the previous question."

"No?"

"You have to leave me some time to answer, to reminisce."

"Okay."

"So. Yes. I've always been head of the class. In every subject. Even now in German, which I'm not particularly good at, I'm miles and miles and miles ahead. People envy me, but there's a big drawback to being smarter than the rest, and I'll tell you what it is, because I assume it will be in part responsible for the kind of person I'll become: loneliness. You know, I happen to be good at everything I try, but it doesn't mean that I *want* to be the best, and people get the two things confused. The truth is it would be good for me to have competition once in a while, or even someone to look up to that is not just Berenice or Aurore or the boys but someone my own age. But when you're first in everything, you have to know better than to say you want competition. That would sound false or spurious to everyone. You have to be humble, you have to be ashamed of yourself, sort of. I guess it's the same thing when you're very happy. I've never been very happy, but I assume it's the same. You can't be too obvious about it. You have to show some restraint."

"Did you ever think about failing a test on purpose?"

"Why in the world would I ever do that?"

"So people wouldn't think you're a freak? To fit in?"

"I don't see why I should be the one to make the effort and reach down to everyone else. Why doesn't it cross everyone else's mind to reach up to me?"

"Well, it's not easy being smart."

"Of course it is. You just have to shut up nine out of ten times you think you want to speak."

"Do you do that?"

"Well, not right now. Not with you guys."

There's a few seconds of silence there on the tape.

"You say you want competition, but you never had any so far, so how do you know you would be okay with it?"

"That's an interesting question, Dory."

A silence here.

"So what's your answer?"

"I don't know."

Silence again.

"There's a girl, in art class, she's a pretty decent painter. I mean, I'm a better sketcher, by a long shot, that's how I stay head of art class, but she's a better painter, and I have no jealousy whatsoever toward her."

Another silence.

"It's quite the opposite actually."

"Why don't you try to be friends with her?"

"I don't know what to say to her."

"Just say you like her paintings."

"I don't really know how to say nice things. When I have something nice to say, I don't know how to be honest without sounding fake. Or condescending. Are you taking notes? I mean . . . isn't this thing recording?"

"You're the one who set it."

"Plus, I'm sure she thinks I'm pretentious. Everyone does."

"I think you're pretentious sometimes."

"I know. That's because I *do* talk down to you sometimes. On purpose. But at school, I'm always very careful not to do that, and I still get morons saying I'm full of myself, or calling me pretentious, if they actually know the word. You know what really pisses me off, Dory?"

"When people misuse words?"

"Misuse of words. Yes. Sloppy usage. *Pretentious* has come to define someone who talks about a thing that others don't understand. But it's not what it means. *Pretension* is a form of lying, it's looking to impress people with knowledge you haven't really mastered, or giving yourself more importance than you have, but calling me pretentious for *actually* knowing things, well, that's a fucking disgrace, that's a misuse of language. It's more than that: it's language abuse. It's like when people use the word *symbol* left and right. What's up with that? Or *problematic* as a noun, because *problem* doesn't sound edgy enough. If I'm not sure how to use a word, I won't use it 'til I've looked up its meaning. It would be *pretentious* to do otherwise, you follow me? People who call me pretentious, they're the pretentious ones. I mean, should I surrender and start using words inappropriately the way they do, just to fit in? Dory, why are you taking notes? This thing records everything we say."

"I'm taking notes on your body language."

Another silence.

"Even people who talk to you about some idea like it goes without saying that you'd know the idea when they themselves only read about it for the first time that morning . . . even *they* are not pretentious. They're just being polite in assuming you know what they're talking about, and they won't make fun of you for not knowing, they'll explain. Maybe in the process, they're sizing you up, trying to get a sense of where they stand knowledge-wise, sure, but that's a different thing. That's human. You're taking a hell of a lot of notes, Dory. Do you think we should get a video camera?"

"Why are you pretentious with me sometimes?"

"What?"

"You said you were pretentious with me sometimes, on purpose. Why?"

"To impress you. That's the only purpose of pretension."

"Why do you want to impress me?"

"I'm your big sister. You have to look up to me."

"But I do already."

"Well, it should stay like that. For a little while at least."

"Then what?"

"Then at some point you'll stop being impressionable, and my mission with you will be complete."

"Do I have a mission with you?"

"This is not a book about you."

"Off the record?"

She stopped the recording there and you can hear static for a second and a bird chirp. Then the interview resumes.

"What is your first memory?"

"I have many. Define an area of interest."

"Your first memory of a funny thing."

"Grandma's farting fit at Grandpa's funeral."

"I remember that too . . . it can't be your first memory."

"You have a great memory, Dory, no one's ever denied that. And maybe you don't really remember the farting fit but we talked about it so much that you believe you do."

"Your first memory of something sad?"

"I guess it could be the same one. And also when the father rented a magician for my fifth birthday."

"The magician made you sad?"

"The fact that Dad thought I would like it."

"Who do you prefer: Berenice, Aurore, Jeremie, Leonard, or me?"

"Berenice."

"Mom or the father?"

"I don't know."

I'm not sure I was stupid. It's not that I didn't understand anything my teachers talked about, it's that when I did, I doubted I had. I believed there had to be a trick. Maybe I just assumed the world was more complicated than it was. I thought the time-difference thing worked in minutes, for example. The day they explained time zones in school, we were shown a map of Europe: it's an hour earlier in Portugal than it is in Spain, the teacher said, and I looked at the map, and I thought it had to be roughly half an hour earlier in Madrid than in Barcelona.

My habit of seeing tricks everywhere could be traced to the day that I, at four years old, started singing "Au Clair de la Lune" out loud in kindergarten and the teacher pulled me by the ear and asked me to stop because I was bothering everybody. It hurt, and I cried, but I kept singing through the pain anyway, and the teacher pulled harder and harder, until I finished the last verse I knew. I thought the ear pulling was a test to see if I'd understood what the teacher had said earlier about how "what has been started must be finished," but it turned out it really wasn't, and when I proudly—though in tears—finished my song, the teacher explained the phrase "What has been started must be finished" only applied to vegetables and homework and chores. So it should have been "Everything boring that has been started must be finished," I thought, but I knew it didn't sound as good as the real phrase.

⁓

Rose arrived on a Tuesday. The Tuesday activity my mother had planned was going to the pool, and so she dropped us all there (all but Aurore, of course) while she ran some errands. In the car on the way to the pool, Simone refused to talk to Rose. She stared out the window the whole way. Rose kept asking her questions, regarding just about anything, and I kept answering on Simone's behalf.

"Have you ever watched synchronized swimming, Simone?"

"I don't think she ever has."

"Do you like my bracelet? I made it myself."

"Simone doesn't really like jewelry. Or plastic beads."

"I can make one for her with other things, like, shells or something."

"She never wears bracelets or necklaces, really."

Jeremie and Leonard didn't acknowledge Rose's presence either.

Once at the pool, they all headed to the fast swimmers' lane and I stayed with Rose in the chaotic part of the pool with the kids and the old people. Rose wanted to go to the jets just to hang out and have her thighs massaged. She said the jets were her favorite part of any pool. She said we would know where the jets were once we'd spotted a couple of still old ladies with their backs to the wall and their elbows on the lip. We found the old ladies and waited for them to be done with the jets. While we waited, Rose suggested we try to spot who was pissing the pool. I'd never pissed the pool. I kept my eyes on the water. Rose said I had to attend to the faces, that the faces were what would betray the pissers. I didn't know what she meant. Simone had told me that when someone pissed the pool, the water around them turned green, I told Rose.

"Why would the water turn green?" Rose asked.

"Blue plus yellow," I said.

"Your sister is funny," Rose said. "And pretty," she added. "I didn't think she would be."

"Why not?" I said. I didn't have an opinion on the way my sisters looked, but everyone said they were beautiful, so I assumed they were, and I didn't know how it could surprise anybody.

"She sounds so smart in her letters, you know? I thought she had to be kind of, *whatever* looking," Rose said.

A couple of three- or four-year-olds with arms wrapped in water wings passed us with a slowness made remarkable by their manic kicks. They were discussing how many dead kids they thought were at the bottom of the deep end of the pool, given that they'd been told that those who swam in the deep end without parental supervision died. "Five thousand!" one kid said. "Five thousand millions!" the other kid said. They were both acting as if pool water kept coming into their mouths by accident and they had to constantly spit it out, but they were really lapping it up.

"Your brothers don't look too bad either," Rose said. I glanced at the fast swimmers' lane. Leonard was spitting in his goggles.

The old ladies left the jets. I wanted to tell Rose I was good at holding my breath underwater, but I thought it might be showing off. We didn't talk much once at the jets. At some point, Rose just turned to me and smiled.

"Did the water turn green around me?" she said.

On Wednesday we went to the movies. My mother let Rose pick the movie, a comedy about teenagers who go to a party. Aurore came along, to everyone's surprise, after deciding she needed to get some fresh air, and declared as the end credits were rolling that we should never let her out of her room again if it was to see such a terrible piece of shit. Rose liked the movie, and I didn't really, but I understood why she did and so I wasn't as mad as everyone else. On the walk back home, we saw a kid screaming and his mother dragging his body along the sidewalk by the arm, because he refused to get up until she would agree to take him to McDonald's. We walked by them silently and without staring, as we'd been taught to do when passing fighting couples or car wrecks, and then my mother turned to us and proudly said what she always said when a kid threw a tantrum nearby: "None of you ever did that to me."

On Thursday, the school bus that was driving Simone's and Rose's classes to the science museum got into a small accident. Only Rose was injured. The window by which she was sitting shattered as the bus made a turn into too narrow a street. Rose got a couple of light cuts on her right arm and two stitches on her forehead.

"Are you okay?" my mother asked Simone when she picked her and Rose up, and Simone said yes, of course she was okay, she'd been sitting at the other end of the bus when it happened.

So there was no activity on Thursday. We just watched TV and Rose fell asleep next to me on the brown suede couch.

On Friday, after school, Rose and I made cookies for the family. I'm not sure Simone had spoken to her at all yet, but Rose didn't seem to mind too much. At dinnertime, while we waited for everyone to come down to the table, Rose inquired about the blue plate my mother was always eating off of and asked her if she was on a diet, because she sure didn't need to be.

"Oh, how nice of you to say that," my mother said, and then she asked Rose how she knew about blue plates cutting your appetite and Rose said they used blue plates in fat camps, and my mother asked her if she'd ever been in a fat camp and Rose said no, but both her brothers had.

"How interesting," my mother said, and then she asked me to make sure Aurore came down to sit with us tonight because she really wanted to have us all around the table. Once we were all gathered, my mother said, "The father won't be coming home tonight," and this time it was because he was dead. He'd had a heart attack. Simone said she didn't believe it for a second, but it looked like she did. Jeremie and Leonard and Aurore and I said nothing.

"I am so so so so so so so sorry," Rose said, "so very sorry," and she started crying, long before any of us did. She cried loudly, and my mother had to get up to wrap her arms around Rose's shoulders while we, her actual kids, the actual children of the father Rose had never met, stared blankly at the swordfish steaks my mother had placed at the center of the table, swordfish steaks we would later declare to have been our father's favorite dish, though none of us could really be sure about it, the father always having expressed the exact same enthusiasm for everything our mother cooked.

Berenice came home early the following morning. She called me Isidore when she saw me come down the stairs, and in doing so confirmed the seriousness of the situation. She was sitting with my mother in the kitchen, her fingers crossed in front of her on the table, as though she was praying. My name is all she said. I went and wrapped my arms around her neck, and she leaned her head against my shoulder, but her hands stayed on the table.

I asked where Rose was.

"Simone's teacher took her for the rest of the stay," my mother said.

"When did she go?"

My mother looked at me like I was asking for details from years ago. I hoped Rose was all right but knew it wasn't appropriate to say so. I wanted to eat the cookies she and I had made the day before, but that also seemed uncalled for.

The others came down and had cookies and milk and hugged Berenice just as I'd done. No one said a thing for a while, until Aurore asked Berenice how her dissertation was coming along. Berenice said she'd been solicited for an article about her research for the next issue of a philosophy quarterly. She said she'd probably send them her third chapter, which almost made sense on its own. We said congratulations.

———

I was usually the one to take the least amount of time in the bathroom, but the morning of the father's funeral, I looked at my naked self in the mirror for a while, and Leonard knocked on the door to make sure I was all right.

"Well," I told him, "I'm fat."

I heard Leonard laugh a little through the door.

"You're not fat, Dory, you'll grow it away."

The second part of his sentence indicated that I was, indeed, fat. For the next few weeks, I barely ate, and everyone thought it was out of grief.

———

After the father died, we all slept in the same bedroom for days but didn't talk about why. We dragged mattresses into the boys' bedroom, because it was the biggest. We brought in bottles of water, books, bedside lamps, and changes of clothes we kept rolled in bunches at the feet of our beds. I look back upon these nights very fondly. I slept a lot, and better than I ever had before. It was in the days following the father's death that I learned to sleep in late, and realized days didn't have to be as long as they'd always been. We barely left the room. Berenice worked on her article; the others read, or slept, or ate in bed; and I would just look at them all and fall back asleep feeling safe.

I don't want to sound insensitive and give the impression that my father's death didn't affect me. It did, of course, but everyone knows that death is tragic, while there's not much focus on the upsides of losing someone you loved, the main one being, you sleep pretty well. No counting sheep, no too-hot pillows, no bad dreams. No dreams at all, in fact. Just a blank, heavy sleep.

When Berenice went back to grad school, though, the sleep alliance broke. Aurore took her mattress back to her room and Simone figured it was time for her and me to do the same.

Sleeping got more difficult. Nights became a bathroom ballet of sorts. Every half hour, I'd hear a different sibling, or our mother, get out of bed to go take a piss. We all stopped drinking water after dinner, and that solved the problem for my brothers and sisters, but my mother still got up every night. She didn't leave her room, though. I just heard her get up to turn all her lights on and walk back to her bed. After nights and nights of this, I went to see what she was doing. We were usually not allowed in her bedroom at night. All of us, as kids, had heard her tell us that after ten p.m., she wasn't our mother. She needed time to herself, she'd say, to read and recharge her mother batteries during the night, otherwise she wouldn't even be able to be our mother during the day. I'd tried going to her room once after ten with what I believed was a good excuse (Simone wouldn't turn her reading light out), but all my mother had said was, "Can you see the clock, Dory? Can you see what it says?" and I'd had to go. We'd all learned to deal with insomnia on our own, to wait for the morning to describe our bad dreams. We'd all learned to give our mother the post–ten p.m. privacy she requested. We wanted her to remain our mother. But that night, around one in the morning, I knocked on her door and she let me in. The radio on her nightstand was on, at the lowest audible volume.

"I like to be talked to before sleep," she said. I knew she'd called the father from her bedroom phone the nights he wasn't home, but I didn't think they had actual conversations.

"We can talk a little while," I said, and we did. I sat by her in bed. Everyone in the house was asleep, so we whispered. She said, "Tell me something I don't know about you, Dory," and I said I wanted to be a German teacher. We talked about it without reference to the father, which was sort of an achievement, given that he'd been the only person we knew who saw the point of the German language. The closet facing the bed was half-open and I could see his clothes hanging there, the jackets and the shirts. I knew clothes didn't have emotions but they seemed to understand that the father had died and that they would never be worn again. They looked embarrassed not to have disappeared with him, to just be there reminding us of his absence, resigned, prepared to meet their fate and be discarded when my mother was ready. She asked me to tell her about good memories I had, and I talked about our vacation in the south a couple years back, with the lightning bugs. I did most of the talking. Every time I left a space for her to share a memory of her own, or to offer a reaction, she would just say, "Please go on, I'm listening," but her eyes were shut and I don't think she really cared about what I said, and it went on like that until I left a space she didn't fill at all.

The Defenses

AT SCHOOL, DENISE Galet told me she was sorry for my loss, but she looked mostly jealous. I didn't particularly like Denise, but because no one else did either, we often sat together in class. She asked for details about the funeral, like open casket or not, and I told her everything she wanted to know, mainly about what happens to a dead body. I knew Denise was dark. She told you about not liking life or anyone in it every chance she got. Her and suicide, though, it was like me and running away: she kept failing. She'd tried to slit her wrists the previous winter but hadn't cut nearly deep enough. She'd taken twenty of her mother's sleeping pills a few weeks after that, but they were placebos, so no one was sure whether it had been the real thing or a cry for help. She had therapy sessions every day of the week after class. She ate meds in front of a psychiatrist and couldn't take the bottle home. At recess she sat on a bench and fed pigeons in spite of its being forbidden. I'd never thought I could do anything to help her. Denise belonged to a different stratum of humanity, I believed, and there could be no real communication between us.

"I wanted to come to the funeral," she told me, "but my parents wouldn't let me."

"It's nice of you," I said.

"I want to know how it goes, you know? I've never been to one."

"It was my fourth," I said, and Denise looked impressed.

"Grandparents?" she asked.

"And an uncle," I said.

I told her the family had to pick clothes for the dead person, give speeches if they could, dress in dark colors, and that no one should bring inappropriate things to the ceremony, like a newspaper or a snack. Denise said she knew all that already. She wanted to know more about the body.

"Who dresses it?" she asked.

"I don't know," I said.

"Who puts it in the casket?"

"I don't know."

"Are there smells?"

"What do you mean?"

"The body, does it give off smells in the church or whatever?"

"My father's ceremony was at the cemetery," I said. "Open-air."

"And the other funerals you've been to?"

The question of smells seemed to be the most important to Denise. It was the first time I could recall being asked something that really mattered to the person I was talking to.

"There's definitely a smell," I said, after pretending to think about it.

I'm pretty sure Denise held her breath after that. She tightened her lips, which she usually kept ajar (I'd wondered many times if she was capable of really closing her mouth). She didn't try to kill herself again for a couple of years.

———

Rose's letter came one week after the father died. It was addressed to me, not Simone. She hoped I was good, admitted she only said that because she knew no other way to open a letter but was pretty sure I didn't feel good at all, more like miserable. She said she thought about me and my lovely family a lot, to give them all her best. I didn't give anyone her best, because I knew they wouldn't reciprocate, or care.

"Love letter?" Simone asked. When she looked at the back of the envelope with Rose's name and address, she furrowed her brow.

"You can land better than her," Simone said, and though it was the first time I heard the verb *land* in that context, I immediately understood what she meant. Simone, as I said, was only thirteen and already in tenth grade. I knew she had no understanding of how or why people in her class would want to form couples, but she'd mastered the vocabulary. I knew of Simone's lack of interest in couple-forming because we shared the same bedroom and I'd been on the lookout for the first signs of a need for independence and/or privacy on her part since she'd had her first period a year earlier. I paid attention to her body language, sighs, fidgeting, the smallest displays of restlessness. I tried to be in our bedroom a lot so that she could get irritated by my presence. I thought if she asked for her own bedroom it would cause our parents to move to a bigger house, where I would also have my own bedroom to think about girls in the privacy of—I, for my part, understood the urge for couple-forming. Maybe we could get rid of the old stained couch in the process, I thought. But Simone never asked for her own room. As far as I could tell, she enjoyed my company. Sometimes, before bed, she picked her clothes for the next day and asked me what I thought when she made the smallest changes to her regular combinations of blue jeans and plain long-sleeved shirts. When she had a presentation to give in class, she rehearsed it in front of me and had me ask questions about it so that she could be prepared for an interaction with a misinformed audience. I was of use to her. Sometimes, when I despaired that she would ever show any desire to gain her independence, I wondered if she looked for signs of my adolescence, dreading the moment they would appear and we would have to go our separate ways.

"It's not a love letter," I told her, and it was true. Rose, like me, had skipped zero grades, which made her a normal age for grade ten: sixteen. I knew she had no interest in an eleven- (almost twelve-) year-old boy who didn't even have his own bedroom. "It's just a nice letter," I said.

"Whatever you say," Simone conceded, after staring at me for a few seconds. "It's none of my business anyway."

That was so unlike her it reinforced my fear that she was keeping my growing up under close watch.

Rose wrote me a few more letters after that. Simone didn't ask about them again. Nor did she ever write to Rose. When the time came for her class to visit Rose's, she simply didn't pack and didn't go.

———

Every birthday, I updated my will. I'd written the first draft at age eight, after finding out about the existence of wills in American movies. It seemed mandatory to have a will, in American movies. When someone died, a will was uncovered, and complications and tensions could arise from a nonupdated version. That's why I went back to mine at least once a year, to check its accuracy and, if needed, make minor changes. If I broke something, though, I wouldn't wait for my birthday and would just take my will out of its binder and cross out the thing I'd broken without necessarily reassessing the whole document.

When I turned twelve, I removed the father from my inheritors list, obviously, and reallocated what I'd wanted to go to him (desk lamp, pencil cup) to other family members. As I did every year, I added my new possessions (essentially what I'd been gifted that very day) and drew new arrows:

Desk lamp → Berenice
Letter opener → Aurore
Pencil cup → Leonard
Flik Flak Swatch → Jeremie (he might not like it, but I
    didn't know what else to give him)
Etc.

I didn't think I possessed anything really interesting, and most of what I had, I suspected my siblings wouldn't care to inherit anyway, either because it had already been theirs in the first place, or because it would be too childish or small. My biggest paragraph, therefore, was a list of things I wanted to go to charity. "Unless," I specified, "a member of my direct family wishes to keep any particular item for sentimental value."

I, on the other hand, envied my brothers and sisters many things (Leonard's bike, Aurore's leather backpack, Jeremie's sound system), and I'd assumed all these years that they'd been writing and updating their wills, too, and I was curious to know what they'd set aside for me. I didn't want my brothers and sisters to die, of course, but writing one's will was a nice thing to do, I believed. It showed the people you handed something down to that you'd thought about them specifically. When the father died, though, there wasn't a will. I was the only one disappointed, it seemed, and I didn't say anything about it. I came to understand that the others were probably not keeping a will either, and for a while I thought about giving mine up, or at least ceasing to update it. But then my birthday came, and I didn't question the habit. It didn't matter what my siblings did or didn't do, what the father hadn't done. If I died, I still wanted them to know I'd thought of them.

Daphné's next birthday—the first after she became the oldest person in France—was an event in town. The mayor had banners hung from trees and street lamps. "Happy 111th!" they said. The grape-harvest dance was pushed back a week so that a party could be held at the community center. The state secretary for the dependent and elderly was due to make an appearance. People feared Daphné would die before the party, the way they feared it would rain on the Bastille Day parade every year.

Everyone my mother greeted on the street planned on attending, but most didn't care about Daphné, hadn't even known how old she was before her nomination. They wanted to come, my mother said, to stock up on gossip and pretend they didn't like their photo being taken. She wasn't sure the whole family should go. She thought maybe it would all be too phony for my siblings, that maybe just she and I going would be better. Because none of them had friends or dates or places they went to after school (except for Jeremie with symphony practice), my mother wanted my siblings to go out in the world a bit, but she didn't want to impose any outing too easy for them to criticize. The goal was to make them like going outside. She had to pick her fights carefully.

"Aren't the best parties supposed to be phony, though?" Leonard said, to our mother's surprise.

"I believe the best parties are the ones where one enjoys oneself," my mother responded diplomatically.

"Exactly," Leonard said. "By finding a small crowd with which to make fun of the larger crowd."

"Well, as long as you find yourself a crowd, I guess. That's all I want for you," my mother said.

"No need to *find* a crowd," Leonard said. "Jeremie and Simone will do just fine."

And so we went, all of us but Aurore. It was the perfect occasion to run away, as everyone in town was gathered to get drunk in the same place, but I wanted to see the party, so I didn't take advantage. It wasn't often that we had anything going on in town.

The community center was decorated with a timeline that went over all the major world events that had happened during Daphné's lifetime. Pinned over the timeline were pictures of Daphné herself, at different ages, that let you know what she'd looked like when those events had unfolded. Those events she'd *witnessed*, it said, like she'd actually been on the first commercial aircraft or in a concentration camp. Daphné was so old that the timeline started on the wall just right of the stage and went all the way around the room, a room that fit four hundred people (standing), to the other side of the stage. I spotted Sara Catalano right away. Sara still showed no sign of knowing who I was, but it had to be an act. I thought maybe she found me more interesting now that my father was dead but couldn't admit it and that it was my role to reach out to her. She was looking at the part of the timeline where Daphné was already old but Sara and I had just been born.

"Hey, Sara," I said.

"What's the Berlin Wall, exactly?" Sara said, pointing at a picture of it. I thought I should never tell my siblings she'd asked me that, but then I didn't really know what the Berlin Wall had been either.

"It was a wall between the communists and the capitalists," I said, and it seemed to be enough. At least, Sara nodded like I'd cleared the matter up.

"We were in the same class last year," I said, because it was, to my knowledge, the only thing we had in common.

"I know," Sara said. "Your father died."

"He did," I said. I didn't want to sound too cheerful but I was glad she could place me.

"I knew him," Sara said. "He came to the practice a couple

years ago. I used to do my homework in the waiting room. My mother fixed his front teeth."

I'd been trying hard to forget about that time the father had gone around without his front teeth. He'd come back from work one day missing them, and his excuse ("I fell") had seemed so stupid to me I'd thought it had to mean he was a spy and couldn't say in what specific fight for world peace he'd been damaged. I'd been very excited about the father's showing signs of being a spy, but then he'd taken too long to get his teeth fixed. A few days with that gap under his gum, sure, I thought, maybe he had to look goofy for a bit, so people would never suspect he was a spy. But weeks? It couldn't be that his boss was on board with having one of his agents looking homeless (unless his cover was being a homeless guy? But then he could've just painted his teeth black). He'd ended up making an appointment with Sara's mother to get new teeth only because my mother had insisted he should, for their anniversary dinner, at least try to look a little like the man she'd married.

I asked Sara if she'd talked to the father that day.

"He just asked me what kind of homework I had," she said. "He was very sweet. He looked sort of scary, or dumb, maybe, without his teeth, but I mean, at least you knew what he was at the dentist's for. Some people, I think, they just show up to have my mother's fingers in their mouths. Men are really fucked up."

Sara took a step to her right and looked at a picture captioned "Gulf War" and the photograph of Daphné that matched the year. I crossed my fingers she wouldn't ask about the Gulf War. Or even just the gulf.

"I think he thought I was in your sister's grade or something.

He talked about *her* homework, how smart she was and all. Simone? Is that it?"

"Yes," I said.

I wished they'd spoken about me, how great they both thought I was.

The room had filled up and I saw Denise Galet walk in, flanked on either side by her parents. I smiled at her, even though I knew she wouldn't smile back—she never did. I still thought it was worth a try.

I was glad to be talking to Sara, and to be seen with her in a public place, but then I couldn't help wondering what my siblings would think of her. I scanned the room and spotted them, Simone and the boys, looking at me talking to Sara. Leonard gave me the thumbs-up.

"Your father is the first person I actually knew who died," Sara said, and she looked upset, like maybe I should apologize for it.

"Do you want to go somewhere quiet?" I said, having no such place in mind.

"Are you taking advantage of me?"

"What?"

"I start opening up to you and right away it's *let's go somewhere quiet?* What a perv."

"I'm sorry," I said, "I thought we were having a conversation and this place is getting kind of crowded—"

"Well, enjoy the party," Sara said, and she turned away very dramatically, to walk as far from me as she possibly could while still staying in the same building. I didn't want to, but I turned my head to the corner where my brothers and Simone stood, as a reflex. They all avoided my gaze and pretended to have been looking at something else.

The reason I wanted to forget about the father's toothless period was that memories of his face at that time were too easy to summon when crying was required and tears were hard to come by. Not that crying was ever *required* of me, but I'd felt I had to cry at the funeral, and at least a bit every day for a month or so after the father died, in order to honor him, and so I'd started setting time aside to do that—when Simone was in the shower, for instance, and I had the bedroom to myself. I wanted to think about details I'd miss about the father, his voice, about how I'd never have a chance to make him proud, important things like that, but even though it all made me sad, it was never enough for tears to be produced and I had to revert to images of his looking stupid, like when he was missing his front teeth, or when he'd stepped in dog shit and hadn't noticed and I couldn't bring myself to tell him. That worked every time, focusing on these moments when he'd looked weak. And even if I always felt better after crying, like I'd done my duty, I knew it wasn't fair to him. It was the opposite of honoring him. That's why, a few weeks earlier, I'd decided to push back the ready-to-cry images when they popped in my head, and I did it that day, when Sara told me about my dumb-looking father, and I've done it ever since. I've done it so diligently, actually, that when I started writing about my father's teeth earlier, I thought I'd pushed the image back for so long that I'd managed to erase it completely from memory, but it came back within seconds, and with all of its original power, before

I had time to decide whether I should be happy or disappointed about having let it go.

The rest of the night I stuck with my mother. People walked along the timeline that showed Daphné's development parallel to the world's and made comments about what had gone on in their own lives at this or that time. We stayed by Daphné's date of birth, at the end of the nineteenth century. It was the best spot to enjoy some "personal space," my mother said (she was uncomfortable in crowds), because no one had memories or much to say about the end of the nineteenth century, and without an anecdote to share, people tended to go on their way. Some stopped a few seconds to say things like they didn't have phones back then, or hot water, but that was pretty much it. I saw Simone leaning against a wall opposite us, trying to look lost in thought, but I knew she was really eavesdropping on the conversation between her French teacher, Mrs. Fondu, and someone I assumed to be Mr. Fondu. Simone looked bored by their exchange. She couldn't help eavesdropping on people when she had the opportunity, but she was dissatisfied 95 percent of the time. "People have no storytelling skills whatsoever," she'd complain, like it had been their role to entertain her without knowing and they had failed. Simone gave the Fondu couple a few more minutes to say something interesting and gave up. "People have no storytelling skills whatsoever," she told my mother and me as she joined us in our corner.

We stood between one end of the stage and an exit door hidden in the side wall. I stared at the stage until the mayor appeared and said in many different ways what an honor it was to greet the state secretary for the elderly. The state secretary thanked the mayor but didn't mention being honored. He gave a speech about how horrible it was to be old in general but how lucky we were, here in France, that, on average, our old people enjoyed healthier days than in other places, and also had more money in their pocket for buying power, which allowed them to be fuller members of our society. Then someone rolled Daphné onstage—she could still walk then, but probably too slowly for a crowd to bear—and she got up and another person lowered the microphone to her level. Daphné thanked all the classes and professors of Birch Elementary who'd set up the lovely timeline about her life. By that point, the secretary of state had already snuck out through the discreet exit by which we stood. A car was waiting for him in the parking lot, with the engine running.

The person who interviewed Daphné onstage was trying hard to act amazed by the timeline of her life without reminding her that death would be the next big step for her. He made it all about the past. There were questions about how the town had changed over the decades. About her favorite TV shows of all time, and he kept repeating how "of all time" was not an exaggeration since Daphné had been born before TV. He couldn't curate the questions the audience would ask, though, and the first one was pretty straightforward.

"Are you afraid of death?" someone asked, and the interviewer stiffened and squinted and actually put his hand over his eyebrows to try to spot the person who'd dared to ask such a rude question.

"Of course I'm afraid," Daphné said.

Everyone must've been hoping for a different answer because the crowd froze and ceased looking around to see what was being set on the buffet table to focus on Daphné instead.

"Fear of death is the only thing that doesn't abandon you as you age," Daphné insisted, humidifying her lips with her tongue every five seconds or so. "On the contrary, I would say. Death gets scarier every day. I'm so much more diminished now than even last year . . . this physical degradation . . . it's all a preview, you know? And the movie doesn't look good!"

There were a few forced laughs, but the couple closest to us got pissed. "Why is she saying this?" the man asked his wife, as if she'd been the one writing Daphné's answers for her.

"Do you remember your mother?" someone else asked Daphné, and Daphné said it was a valid question, given her mother had been dead almost a hundred years.

"But I'm not senile yet," she added. "Of course I remember my mother. I think about her every day, as all of us should think about our mothers every day, dead or alive." The interviewer thought Daphné was done talking about her long-dead mother and got ready to take another question from the audience, but Daphné went on. "She was a very shy, very modest woman," she said. "To the point that it could be painful for me. How she would always talk about us as little people. She never thought she was worthy of anything—even amidst her worst bouts of delirium, she believed she was persecuted by priests and vicars, and I remember thinking, Poor woman, poor woman. Even completely lost to paranoia, she can't see herself as important enough for bishops or cardinals to bother. It was always lower clergy. Only lower clergy. The only ones who oppressed her were priests and vicars. Vicars and nuns. Only ever lower clergy. The lower clergy plagued her. Why them? Why not the Pope? If not the Pope, why not a bishop? Why not a cardinal? Why always lower clergy?"

I thought Daphné would repeat the words *lower clergy* until the end of time but she suddenly seemed to remember where she was and thanked us all for coming to her birthday party and announced it was time to eat and dance.

———

Denise and I were not in the same class that year, I think because I'd picked German as a second foreign language (the first foreign language was English for everyone) and she'd picked Chinese.

"My parents said it would be more useful to know Chinese," she told me at recess the day school started, "for the future." She said *future* as a joke word, with a little snarky laugh on the F. Denise's nickname—I'm not sure she was aware of it—was "Sunshine."

"They're probably right about that," I said. "I only picked German because I want to be a German teacher."

"You do?"

"But aside from teaching German, I don't know that knowing German is good for anything."

"It's such an unusual ambition."

"What do you want to be?" I asked.

She knew I knew she wanted to be dead when she grew up, so she was free to invent something else.

"I'd like to have my own bookstore in Paris," she said.

"That's it? That would make you happy?"

"Who said anything about being happy?"

"I don't know . . . you're just so smart, I thought you'd want to be a doctor or something."

"Doctors don't know anything."

One of the recess monitors interrupted us there to tell Denise feeding pigeons was not allowed on the school premises. She'd gathered a dozen pigeons at her feet, around her crumbled ten o'clock snack (I'd mixed some of mine in, too).

"I have special authorization," Denise said.

"I don't think we do that," the monitor said.

"It's tacit."

"There's no such thing as a tacit authorization," the monitor said. "*Tacit* is only said about agreements."

"Well then the principal and I have a tacit agreement," Denise said. "And you're wrong about *tacit*. It's a far more malleable word than you think."

The monitor stamped his foot and the pigeons flew away and then he left to forbid other kids from doing other things.

"You'd get along with my sister Simone," I told Denise.

"I don't get along with anyone."

"She doesn't either."

The pigeons came back. A couple sparrows joined the feast and showed more audacity. They went for the crumbs that had fallen closest to our feet.

"Isn't your sister in high school already?"

"But she's only a year and a half older than us," I said.

"That must suck for you."

I looked at my watch, and at the birds again, and around the playground. I'd never understood recess, why it had to exist and be so long. I usually spent it alone in a staircase, pretending to be finishing some homework at the last minute, but that didn't work on the first day of school. That's why I'd gone out to sit with Denise beneath her poplar.

"Look at the new kids," she said.

Denise and I were only starting seventh grade, but it seemed she looked at the new fifth graders with a lifetime's hindsight.

"This one came with porno mags *and* a bag of marbles. He didn't know what kind of playground it would be."

We looked for the versions of our former class's leaders and assholes in the new batch of kids. It was hard to do. The first few days of junior high, kids kept a low profile. We didn't admit it, but I think Denise and I both looked for new versions of ourselves, too. I didn't spot a new Denise. I looked for the main characteristics: tired eyes; awkward posture; one more layer of clothes than necessary; a dry sadness, like all the tears had run out long ago. Denise was the saddest person I knew, but it didn't seem like she could ever cry, whereas any other kid on the first day of school looked like you could shake a pond out of them if you tried for a minute. I guess that's because Denise was actually more hopeless than sad. Those without expectations don't find much to cry about.

For the new version of me, I tried to single out a kid who, were he to suddenly disappear from the playground, would go unnoticed. I realize it might sound a little dramatic to sum things up this way, but I really thought back then, and with no particular bitterness, that nothing would be disrupted if I were to disintegrate. I'd never been part of a group, or willing to join one (try and fail: that's when you got singled out for loserdom), and I was fine with that. If you're part of no group, you're not really worth anyone's while. You can be picked on for a minute, sure, if you encroach on someone else's territory by accident, but if you withdraw right away, no contest, you're all right again. In the end, everyone knows making fun of nobodies is too easy. I didn't find a new version of myself in the new kids, though, because trying to spot an unnoticeable kid is just as hard for another unnoticeable kid as it is for regular people. It's not like we can "see each other" or whatever. And even if we did, we would probably not want to hang out together and double up on our transparency. Only people like Denise would want to get sucked into that.

———

I started reading rather than talking my mother to sleep—I didn't have many stories of my own. I'd never been a big reader before, I only ever went through what school assigned, but to my mother I started reading anything: novels, poetry, biographies. I even read from my schoolbooks and German vocabulary lists the nights before tests. When Berenice's first article got published, I read her that. That I actually read several times, because I wanted to understand it. My mother said she wanted to understand it, too, but night after night she fell asleep halfway through.

"Should we pick up where we left off?" I'd ask, but she always wanted to go back to the introduction to make sure she wouldn't miss a step of Berenice's reasoning.

One of the keywords on top of the article was *humorism*, which I'd assumed to be a kind of humor in the Spanish golden age (Berenice's area of expertise) but wasn't. Humorism was something doctors had believed in in the old days.

"Doctors from the old days thought the human body was composed of four different fluids," I summed up one night, when my mother realized that if we kept going back to the beginning of the article, she'd never hear the end of it. "Blood, black bile, yellow bile, and phlegm. They believed that every single person in the world was born with more or less of each, and that the one fluid they were born with in surplus determined their temperament."

"That sounds familiar," my mother said.

"One Spanish doctor from the golden age, Huarte, even said that the kind of fluid the person had in excess, combined with the one type of intelligence he was born with, determined what the person would be good at in life and what kind of job he should look for."

"What are the types of intelligence again?"

"Reasoning, memory, and imagination," I said. "And you can only be good at one."

"I know which one you're best at, Dory."

A great memory sounded like the most useless of the three skills listed by the Spanish doctor from the golden age.

"I should ask Berenice if she knows what kind of jobs are suitable for people with good memories," I said.

"I'm sure memory's the best for those who want to become German teachers," my mother said encouragingly.

I'd read the beginning of Berenice's article so many times, with the descriptions of each temper associated with each fluid, that I was starting to think I could've been a great doctor in the Spanish golden age. Diagnosing people back then seemed easy. I could tell that Simone, for instance, had a surplus of yellow bile: she was ambitious and short-tempered. Leonard was all blood. It made me sad to admit it, but I was obviously phlegmatic. Phlegm and memory, the most boring of all combinations, I thought. Being black biled and melancholic just sounded better. Certain melancholics had a special type of black bile that the Spanish doctor called "burned," and it made them particularly smart, he said, so smart in fact that they were the only people to be good at two things instead of only one. *"Those whose black bile has been burned,"* Berenice quoted, *"have both a powerful understanding and a vivid imagination. [. . .]Although they lack memory, their imagination itself serves as memory and reminiscence."* I thought this had to be a really nice thing, to have an imagination so strong it could serve as your past.

"But then if imagination replaced your memory, you wouldn't care about us," my mother said. "You would imagine a better family and forget about this one entirely."

I tried to imagine a better family for a minute, or even just another family. I tried to replace Simone with Rose as a sister, see how that would work, but my near-perfect memory of Rose's face kept shifting into Simone's features the second I thought the word *sister.*

"Then I guess it's lucky I have no imagination at all," I said.

The other keywords at the top of Berenice's article were *Juan Huarte, Cervantes, Don Quixote, ingenium, homeopathy, Siglo de Oro,* and *melancholy.*

My first German teacher was Mr. Coffin. We had to call him Herr Coffin. He would only talk to us in German, no exceptions, and that's why I learned the words *Ruhe bitte* and *ʒum Beispiel* first. After that, the first words I remember learning were *Dichtung, Leiden,* and *Briefe,* as we mainly studied poems and poets with Herr Coffin.

The school library only had a handful of books in German, young adult for the most part and a couple Kafkas in bilingual editions, and I borrowed them all to read to my mother at night. At first, I'd bring two books to my mother's bed, the one I was currently reading to her in French and the one I'd borrowed in German to read for myself after she'd fallen asleep, but one night she asked why it was that I never read to her in German and when I said it was because she didn't understand German she said it didn't matter.

Berenice defended her PhD in Paris, on the top floor of her university (a spectacular building, my mother noted), in a room made almost entirely of windows on its east and west sides. Berenice and the five professors in her jury talked about her work for so long that I had time to watch the sun go from one set of windows to the other.

After the defense, we went to Monte Viterbo, an Italian restaurant of Berenice's choosing. As a family, we only ever went to restaurants when we absolutely had to, like when we took road trips or after funerals. My mother was against families eating in restaurants. Restaurants, she said, were for lovers and friends and, if really needed, business lunches. We were staying in Paris that night, though—we'd arrived early morning by the Corail train—and Berenice didn't have much of a kitchen in her attic room, let alone space to have us all for dinner.

Weeks earlier, my mother had started brainstorming with us about what would make Berenice happiest on her big day. "An original edition of something," Aurore had said—but Berenice didn't care much for precious things. "A nice fountain pen"—but Berenice was very public about preferring disposable Paper Mates. She didn't care for clothes or makeup or jewelry. "A round-trip to Madrid?"—but she had no boyfriend or friend to go there with and would only take the opportunity to work some more. Finally, my mother resolved to call Berenice and ask her directly. It seemed all Berenice wanted was for us to be together and "have a good time." My mother encouraged her to recommend the best restaurant she could think of. "Something fancy," I heard her say on the phone, "something extravagant. Don't even think about cost." Berenice called the next day to say we'd go to Monte Viterbo, and my mother got really excited about the name. She started picturing a Roman villa at sunset, elegant waiters carrying sun-gorged vegetables and tender meats and chilled white wine. She took me shopping for a new dress for herself and a button-down for me. When the salesgirl asked her if she needed the dress for a specific occasion, my mother said her daughter was defending her PhD, and I thought this was going to confuse the girl more than anything, but she didn't raise an eyebrow. "What will your daughter be wearing?" she said. She just wanted to make sure my mother and Berenice would look good together. That was her job.

When we walked inside of Monte Viterbo, my mother's heart must've broken a bit. The restaurant was two-thirds empty;

there'd been no need for a reservation. We were all overdressed, the tablecloth was paper, and nothing on the menu cost more than 19.80 euros (the osso buco).

"You heard good things about this place, honey?" my mother asked as we sat down.

"I've seen professors come here on their lunch break," Berenice said.

"So it's like a good neighborhood joint. A family kitchen." My mother seemed reassured at the sound of her own words.

"You lost an awful lot of weight, Dory."

I thought I had, but Berenice was the first to notice.

"I liked your article," I said.

"Oh, did you?"

Berenice looked relieved, like she'd expected me to say something about her article all along.

"But I didn't understand all of your dissertation," I admitted. I'd read the whole of its 490 pages to our mother as well.

"You shouldn't have bothered reading that," she said, "it's all a bunch of malarkey anyway."

She smiled to change the subject and ordered some wine.

"How's your osso buco?" my mother asked the waiter, a sweaty round man in overalls.

I wanted Berenice to ask me what I'd liked about her article, so I could prove to her that I'd understood it (in part), but she wasn't in the mood for more Spanish golden age.

"Get yourself a nice pepperoni pizza, Dory. You shouldn't be losing weight at your age. Focus on growing some inches."

"It's true he dropped a few pounds," Leonard said. "What is it, Dory? You have a girl or something?"

"Leave him alone," Jeremie said.

We ordered. Everyone talked about what they wanted to see in Paris the next day, before the train back home. I had no particular request. I trusted Leonard and Jeremie to come up with a nice little tour. Berenice had lived in the city for six years, but she didn't have any suggestions to make and didn't seem to know where anything was when Leonard suggested places. He stopped asking her for directions.

Whenever she wasn't being spoken to, Berenice looked as worried as she'd been before her defense, but you just had to say her name and she would look at you and glow. That's how she'd always been. I used to think one of the two states of Berenice had to be fake, but I'd stopped wondering which.

"What I really want to see is Berenice's place," Simone said. "I bet it'll be in the future Paris guides."

"It's not much of a place," Berenice said. "It's just a little room in an attic."

"You make a better puttanesca than this, Mom."

"I think the waiter wants to take you on a date, Ber," Aurore said.

"What makes you say that?"

"He keeps calling you *la bella donna,* like the rest of us are turnip crates."

"His accent is terrible by the way. I bet he's never even seen an Italian *movie,*" Simone said.

"Well he's just saying that because Mom must have told him it was a big day for me."

"I told him nothing."

"You never realize someone's hitting on you before they

write their number down in the palm of your hand anyway," Aurore said.

"In indelible Sharpie," Simone added.

We were sitting at a round table. When they all had their hair down like they did that night, my three sisters looked very much alike, as if my mother had only had one mold for girls. I didn't think it was possible to compliment one of them without complimenting the other two. Us boys were all different shapes, different complexions and hair colors. Whenever we were all out together, I imagined we passed for our sisters' dorky boyfriends.

The next day, when we visited Berenice's room, we had to take turns going in, it was so small. We formed a line outside the door, in the creaking hallway. I was last, and saw my mother and all my siblings come in and out of the room at three-minute intervals, like they were coming back ashore. The ceilings were low; Jeremie caught a cobweb in his hair. Simone wanted to pee but said it could wait when she realized the toilet at the end of the hall was shared with the rest of the people who lived on the floor.

I went inside behind Berenice. We could all have stood in the room at once if she hadn't erected a maze of book piles and stacks of paper that left you with only one possible path if you wanted to walk from the entrance to the bed and desk, or from the entrance to the kitchen. (The kitchen was a sink and a hot plate.) Some of the piles of books and papers were used as low tables. There were a few used tea bags in a porcelain plate on top of the pile of books by the bed, red-dotted cotton swabs and a nail polish bottle on top of another pile.

"I tried wearing some for the defense," Berenice said, glancing at the nail polish. "It looked like I'd scratched my way out of a rape attempt."

"You should've gone to a nail salon," I said.

"I can't do that," she said. "You have to have a conversation about your nails with the manicurist."

"I'm sure they're always happy to talk about something else," I said.

"Maybe you're right."

I didn't comment on her studio, as I was sure my mother and the others had asked all the questions and said all the things to say.

"I'll teach full-time soon, make actual money," Berenice said after a minute. "Live in a real place."

"I like this one," I said.

"You don't have to say that."

But I did like her room. I'd never been to Paris before, and I didn't think much of it, but I told myself if I ever tried running away again, I would come here and hide on one of these attic floors. It seemed like you could live there undetected.

When we came out of the room, Simone asked if there was a bus that went straight to Montmartre.

"I couldn't tell you," Berenice said.

———

That Christmas, my mother got a gift for the house. What she called "gifts for the house" were just home appliances or things that would belong to all of us. I think it came from when the father had given her a sewing machine for her birthday and she'd said it wasn't a gift for her but a gift for the house and it didn't count. She'd always gotten books or jewelry on her birthdays after that.

The gift was a computer. We had two computers in the house already, but one was Aurore's and the other was Jeremie's, and Aurore and Jeremie weren't good at sharing. I didn't mind. I wasn't even sure what people used computers for.

"This is the house computer," my mother announced. "It will be in the living room for you to use in the afternoons only. Each of you gets half an hour a day on the Internet for fun or personal edification. If you need more Internet time, you'll make a special request to me. The request has to be well motivated. Then, the computer will be available to type anything you want: school-work, your memoirs, a novel . . . you each get an hour a day. Here's a logbook."

"Can we trade? I'm sure Dory won't want most of his word-processing time," Simone said.

"How would that work?"

"He gets my Internet half hour and I get half of his word-processing hour."

"I'm not really interested in an extra half hour of Internet," I said.

"You can do anything as long as it's fair," my mother said.

My first Internet half hour came. I wrote down my name (actually, I wrote down "Izzie") and the time in the logbook. I didn't know what to search for. I wanted to be sure either it was really impressive and important or that I could make all traces of having searched for it disappear. I wanted to look up something neutral first, in case I didn't find a way to erase it. I stared at the screen, and the small particles I could sometimes see floating inside my own eyes appeared. I typed

little floating particles in the eyes

I clicked on the first result but wasn't too interested in knowing what those particles actually were (people called them "eye floaters," which sounded repulsive to me), so I only read one paragraph about them (pretty much everyone had them and they were innocuous, but the apparent incapacity to focus on them could become a source of obsession and increase anxiety in a depressed subject) and clicked the browser history tab. Simone had looked for different biographies (*deleuze, kierkegaard, kurt cobain*), Leonard for things I knew even less about (*caporetto battle, mad dog theory*). My search for little floating particles in the eyes was there at the top of the list, so all I had to do was check the box on its left and click "clear" to make it vanish. Then I searched:

how does it feel to have a heart attack

Then found a link to:

famous heart attacks (Louis Armstrong, Charles Darwin, William Faulkner, Francis Scott Fitzgerald, Lucky Luciano, Augusto Pinochet, Pope John Paul I, Elvis Presley, Peter Sellers, Orson Welles)

Then I searched:

how many times a week should one shower when one is
   a boy

what age can you start asking for blow jobs when you're
   a boy

isidore mazal (me) (there was no result)

berenice mazal (links to her article, announcements of her
   PhD defense)

jeremie mazal (a couple of pictures from the last
   conservatory concert, Jeremie on cello)

aurore mazal (mentions of her participation on a panel
   titled "Pericles's Funeral Oration: Inferences of
   Thucydides's Underlying Politics")

leonard mazal (someone with the same name who'd been
   arrested for counting cards in a casino on the coast the
   previous March)

simone mazal (mentions of Simone's winning a local
   spelling contest three years in a row)

denise galet (nothing)

humorism

I cleared all searches but the last one.

Simone called for her next interview around the New Year.

"We haven't been very diligent," she said in a way that blamed us both equally. "This biography isn't gonna write itself."

She said I should really start carrying a notebook around at all times. She said one could never know when revealing moments would take place, and that such moments weren't even necessarily revealing right away but would only show their relevance after the fact, in the grand scheme of her lifetime.

"It sounds like I should take note of every little thing you do or say, then," I said.

Simone thought about it.

"Definitely err on the side of taking too many notes, yes."

Because I hadn't prepared any new questions that day, she said I could just listen to her think out loud and ask questions as they came.

"The New Year is my least favorite holiday," she began. "There's never anything good on TV."

"You hate TV."

"I hate it when all it shows for entertainment is people with negative IQs counting down from ten. Otherwise, I find it pretty enlightening."

"You don't find it enlightening. You always know what's going to happen, in all the shows and all the movies we watch, before it happens."

"Doesn't mean I don't enjoy watching them. It's good to know in advance, sometimes, what's gonna happen. The surprise element is overrated, if you want to know what I think. Which I guess is the point of these recordings. Knowing what I think. As you grow up, you come to enjoy repetition. In certain things at least."

"You're only eighteen months older than me."

"It's a skill I like to practice, stating in advance, and in the right order, what will happen in shows and movies. It's reassuring. It's like a rehearsal."

"Of what?"

"Of the rules of fiction."

"Aristotle's?"

"Who else's?"

"Why do you need to rehearse them?"

"'Cause they're also the rules actual people live by. Not only Aristotle's, but all the Hollywood subrules. People live life as a fiction. I'm sure I do, in a way, and you, for sure. You'd never have thought about running away from home if you hadn't seen a bunch of movies about runaways, for instance."

"I never thought about running away from home."

"Right, Dory. *Come on*. I read your note. All I'm saying is that it's normal. You feel like you have to do something prohibited in order for people to notice you, because you think, for some reason, that they don't. Your behavior makes perfect sense."

"Does it?"

"You're a very coherent character."

"Is that a good thing?"

"I can't tell for sure that it's a good thing in real life, but because you seem to be interested in things beyond your own life, yes, character coherence is a very good thing. It is the first step to predicting a movie plot."

"How so?"

"Well, the tensions, the twists . . . they're all there for the audience to get to know the characters, how they react in such and such a situation, almost like chemical elements, you know? You get to know the characters through the things they're faced with and what their responses to these things are. And with that knowledge, you can pretty much infer what they'll do. The coherence of a character is itself part of the plot, so nailing it down is the first step to plot predictability."

"But sometimes you know how a whole movie will unwind within the first few minutes. You don't even need time to find out about the characters."

"That's Hollywood movies. Hollywood scripts use telegraphed moves. What I call the big ropes. The big ropes, I don't really know how to explain to you. They just start appearing to you, very obviously, once you've read enough or heard enough stories. Big ropes are culture. Because you don't have much culture, though, you can't see the big ropes yet, you're still very detail oriented. That's why you have problems predicting plots. No shame in that."

Silence. Then I resumed.

"What do you do at recess?"

"Why are you asking me this?"

"You said to ask questions as they came."

"I read, usually."

"On the playground?"

"No, I stay in the classroom. I mean, if there's no classroom change after recess. Otherwise I go read by the next classroom's door."

"And no one makes fun of you?"

"Of course people make fun of me."

"But you do it anyway."

"What else am I gonna do? Go down to the playground and make friends? By taking a side or another in a mindless conflict? Find out about their personalities?"

"Do *I* have a personality?"

"What are you talking about?"

"Sometimes I think I don't. That other people do and I don't. That they're more real than me, or something."

"Are you depressed, Dory? What do *you* do at recess?"

"This is not a book about me."

"Dory, I think you're depressed and it concerns me."

"Why is Berenice your favorite of us all?"

"It's all the more worrying that testosterone is supposed to be a natural antidepressant. Your testosterone levels should be sky-rocketing these days. Or soon. You shouldn't have brain space left for sadness. Maybe you have a deficiency? Do you have arm-pit hair yet? I don't even know."

"I'm twelve."

"You're right, you're right. Maybe the testosterone hasn't kicked in yet. We shouldn't worry."

"I don't worry."

"And also: personality is overrated. I can only ever use the word as a joke. It's a good thing to believe you don't have a personality and a mistake to try to build one, I think. That's how people become fake. That's why I feel the opposite of you, see? That I'm real and everyone else on the playground is fake."

"But you have tons of personality."

"Don't be mean."

"You pay no mind to what people say about you, you stick to your guns—"

"That's not personality. That's admitting to a personal preference. Enjoying books more than recess and acting on it."

"Why do you prefer Berenice to any of us?"

"Do I?"

"You said last time."

"Hmm."

"You changed your mind?"

"No, I didn't. I like her more because she's brilliant."

"You guys all are."

"Yes, but she came first. Sometimes I wonder if we're not just following her lead, if any of us would've skipped grades if she hadn't skipped four, things like that. She set a strong example for all of us."

"I never skipped any grades."

"Well, you've always been slow. I mean, a slow learner. You know, all of us, we talked very early, but you, Mom was worried, you didn't say a word until you were *three* years old, can you imagine that? But then it was all complete sentences. Right away, *'Be careful on the ladder, Daddy,'* or something like that, you said. It was a relief for everybody."

"So you're saying by the time I start college I'll be as smart as you all were out of high school, except the normal age?"

"I'm saying you're not stupid."

"I didn't think I was."

"Of course you think you are. I feel guilty about it sometimes. Like I'm neglecting you, or sending the wrong signals . . . we're only a year and a half apart and I'm closer to college than you are to high school."

"I don't take it personally, you know?"

"I'm pretty sure I was an accidental baby," Simone said there, with no particular emotion but after a longer silence. "Mom won't admit it because she thinks it would hurt me or something, but I figured it out. I mean, I'm seven years younger than Jeremie. They're all a year or two apart, and then here I come, seven years after the last one? It can't have been part of the plan. And what happened with you I think is that Mom decided to have another baby right after me, so I would have company. The other ones were so much older, Mom must have thought we wouldn't get along . . . I mean, for a while I thought *Berenice* was my mother, for Christ's sake. And her and Aurore, you know, I feel like you and I are their niece and nephew sometimes. More than their siblings."

"I know what you mean."

"And my whole life I've been aiming at closing the gap between them and me instead of building something with you. I turn to the girls and Leonard and Jeremie for validation, I try to impress them, but you, I'm not even nice to you, I never ask what's on your mind. I take it for granted that you're gonna love me no matter what. I don't do anything for it."

"Is that why you gave me your biography to write?"

"I don't know. It's a way to hang out, I guess."

"We already share a bedroom. I think we hang out enough."

"But we're not close. I'm not close to the others, either, but at least I know what's on their minds a bit. What they read. What they think about. But I don't know what goes on in *your* head. What's interesting to you, Dory?"

"Well, what do you want to know?"

"I don't want to know anything right this minute. I mean, it's not that I'm not interested, but I was just talking about how I was less close to you than the others, you know, for the record."

"Oh, of course."

"I think, in a way, if this is stated early on, it will make readers consider your book as objective as it can be, you know, but still coming from a family member. From someone who saw me grow."

"What will you be famous for again?"

"It's hard to tell yet. This, what we're doing, will be a precious document on my formative years. It will make it all look like everything was written and led to the Simone I'll have become, but for now, we have to abide some mystery."

Simone paused there and you can hear her crack her knuckles one by one on the tape.

"I think several types of fame will add up, though," she said.

"Do you think we'll be closer then?"

"I hope so."

I feel bad admitting this but sometimes, when I transcribed Simone's interviews on the computer, I hoped that the father had had other kids, elsewhere, who would come and find me. I guess maybe that was all part of my character coherence.

The rest of winter break, we watched the Martial Arts Channel, at first only because it had no commercials, but then because my siblings agreed they liked Viet Vo Dao, the Vietnamese martial art. It was impossible to know when they'd show Viet Vo Dao, though, on the Martial Arts Channel. I don't believe they had a schedule. I don't believe we were supposed to pick up the Martial

Arts Channel either—we'd never had premium cable. It was an oversight by the cable company, we thought, and there was an unspoken fear, every afternoon, when Leonard turned the TV on, that they would have realized their mistake and taken the Martial Arts Channel away from us.

"We have to enjoy it while it lasts," Leonard would say.

I personally didn't understand the rules of Viet Vo Dao, or any other martial art we watched while waiting for Viet Vo Dao to show, and watching sports, in general, made me sad. Not because I wasn't good at sports, but because it seemed so useless to be good at sports that watching people devote their whole lives to them felt wasteful. I thought they, the sportsmen, would regret having sacrificed everything to sports, later in life, and that in the meantime, we, the audience, were just taking advantage of their not having figured this out, using their wasted years for our own entertainment.

I don't think my siblings really understood the rules of Viet Vo Dao either, because they never made comments on anything but the contestants' faces or what were assumed to be their life stories. They tried, like they did with fictional shows, to invent dialogue and a backstory for them, but I never found it too convincing.

"I want to come on your face," Leonard said whenever a fighter wrapped his legs around an opponent's neck ("the scissors," apparently a classic Viet Vo Dao move), but I didn't think it was funny at all. The fighters always changed and Simone and Jeremie tried to connect them to one another in different storylines, but it was far-fetched and there was no real follow-up.

My siblings always cheered for the dorkiest-looking contestant. Sometimes, it was hard to tell which one it was.

I missed the spy show. I wanted to try predicting the plot now that Simone had given me an angle of approach. They'd stopped airing it.

———

On the first anniversary of the father's death, no one mentioned it. Only Rose, whose letter arrived on the exact day.

Dear Isidor

I hope you are well. I think about you today as the first aniversary of your father's death aproches near. I will remember my hole life sitting there at dinner with you guys and finding out about your father being dead. I have never met him, but I wish I had, because he and your mom made a really nice little family, all of you, and so I imagine he was a very good man. I hope I will see you again one day. I'm sending these dried roses petals for your father's grave. Please go disperse them on it with my respects.

Rose

I waited for it to be the weekend so I could visit the father's grave. I didn't tell anyone I was going, because it felt like they'd all forgotten about it and I didn't want to be the one to bring back bad memories. When I arrived though, the stone was covered with things I could link back to each one of my siblings (small evergreen = Leonard, bunch of wildflowers = Simone, a candle = Aurore, white pebbles from our driveway = Jeremie; the orchid had to be from our mother). I assumed they'd all come there in secret and each on their own.

On my fifth attempt to run away, I was on a train to Paris before the school day had even started. I'd looked for train schedules on the Internet, erased my search, made up a lie about having to go to school early to help Herr Coffin set up a presentation on his computer (how my mother managed to believe I could be of technical help to anyone, or what she thought a German teacher would want to present on a screen, I don't know), and packed a few clothes instead of schoolbooks. It was the first time I tried running away in the morning. I'd never even considered running away as a possible morning activity before a gang of birds had settled in our cherry tree a couple weeks before and made the days a little longer. Their arrival hadn't been progressive: one morning, there was silence, the next, Simone and I were woken up at five a.m. by hundreds and hundreds of peeps and chirps overlapping, like the politicians speaking in Parliament on TV. Simone found it cute at first, but a few days into it, waking up at five got to her.

"What do birds have to say in the morning that is so fucking important anyway?" she asked one day at the breakfast table, where no one usually spoke.

"They're just welcoming the new dawn," our mother said.

Our mother liked the bird development. She'd started believing one was supposed to get up this early.

"You're way too cheerful about this," Simone said.

"I'm cheerful because instead of falling back asleep after the birds wake me, I do exactly as they do and get started with my day. By the time you guys emerge, I've showered, read yesterday's paper, done laundry, cooked the night's meal . . ." She pointed at a pot on the stove, beef stew, from the smell of it. "All I have to do tonight is reheat some food I just made. I could even read *today's* paper if I wanted!"

"It smells of dinner at the breakfast table now," Simone said. "That's not right."

"Poor little thing."

"The birds made you too positive, Mom."

"It's a godsend, these extra hours. It's a full little day inside of a day."

"What are you even talking about?" Aurore asked.

Aurore and the boys were not bothered by the birds. Their bedrooms were on the other side of the house, the street side. Simone, my mother, and I, we overlooked the yard, and the tree was right there outside our windows (in the summer, you just had to open the window to grab a pair of cherries).

"We're talking about what birds have to talk about that can't wait beyond five a.m. but loses its urgency after a few minutes."

"Is this a riddle?" Aurore asked.

"Maybe they're just making sure everyone survived the night," I said, "taking attendance."

"Sweetheart, that's very interesting," our mother said. No one else thought it was.

"Not everything in the world is modeled on a school day, Dory," Simone said.

The next morning, I got up with the birds. Unlike our mother, though, I had nothing to do. I got so bored I took two showers. I watched TV, which is something I'd only ever done in the morning when sick. I brushed the stain on the couch. I watched the six a.m. news for the first time in my life. The anchor took regular sips from his coffee cup and looked so unconcerned about the news of the day, it almost seemed like he thought I was the only one watching. I had the lights off in the living room, so the blue square of our TV was reflected in the bay window behind the couch, and it was still so dark out I could've watched the reflection instead of the TV and not missed much. Around seven fifteen, light started to wrap the room. The others got up and didn't say a word at the breakfast table, which I could see and hear from the couch. I watched a cartoon where all the objects in a family's house came to life at night, while the family was asleep. I was seeing no positive effect in getting up as early as I had.

The main difference between that morning and any other revealed itself when I got out of the house: for once, I was fully awake on my way to school. I saw everything with more detail, like sometimes happens for a minute on winter mornings. I think the cold does that. The lines around things were crisper, the lines around people, between people and things; the colors were sure of themselves. I understood the morning hours could be of use when I reached the school's gate and felt like running away right then, like I had the energy for it—the desire to run away was usually stronger at recess or at night. I didn't have a plan, though, so I just went to school. But that night, I stole all of Simone's pocket money. She had a lot, because she never spent any of her allowance. All she ever wanted was books, and books, no matter how many, had always, as a rule, been my parents' treat. I'd always thought of the rule as not only unfair—I personally never wanted more books than what school prescribed and didn't get more money for it—but also senseless, since my mother always complained that my siblings studied too much while she kept feeding them new material to parse. Anyway, Simone never used her money. She just piled it someplace. I know it seems like I'm trying to get myself off the hook here and make what I did sound okay, but she'd told me herself where she kept her dough, in case she died, she'd said (the fact she needed to say it confirmed she hadn't written a proper will), because she wanted me to have it. I know she hadn't died, but I was planning on disappearing and so in a way we would soon be dead to one another. I guess it was a stretch. But the next morning, I bought a ticket to Paris with Simone's money and made it to Berenice's old building before it was time for recess back home.

Berenice was supposed to have moved out of her attic room to a real apartment close to the university where she now taught. When we'd visited, she'd said that most of her floor was uninhabited, so I'd figured it would be a nice little spot for me to start an escape, figure out my next moves. And if someone asked, I just had to say my sister was letting me stay in her studio. By the time they'd check, I'd be somewhere else. Except Berenice hadn't moved out and when I pushed open the door to what I thought was her former room, she was there on her bed, interlocked with an old guy. The old guy looked like any one of the old guys who had sat on Berenice's dissertation defense jury. That day, I'd only been able to tell one professor from another by their clothes, but this one was naked, so I couldn't associate him with a name. I'd never seen a naked man. Women, only in pictures. I don't know if they'd had sex already or were just thinking about it. Berenice took a sheet to cover herself and told the old guy to go home, that she would call him. She didn't look surprised to see me. The old guy got up and was taller than I'd imagined, though I wasn't even aware I'd imagined things about his height. You don't see old men over six feet that often. I think maybe tall people don't live that long. He was close to six foot three, I'd say; he had to crouch down quite a lot to avoid banging the ceiling with his head. It was embarrassing to see him put his pants on, so I waited in the hallway. As far as I know—the walls were thin—Berenice and the old guy exchanged no words. He came out a minute later and acted as if I hadn't just been in there.

"Oh, hello there," he said. He said I had to be Berenice's brother, with these cheekbones.

"And you must be her PhD adviser," I said. I thought it would be polite to at least try to place him, but he stiffened.

"Berenice is not a student anymore," he said.

Berenice was all dressed when I came back in, and she'd made the bed, opened the skylight. The water was running undisturbed on a pile of dirty dishes in the sink, like it could take care of dried sauce and tea stains without Berenice's intervention. She was stacking books back on shelves at the other end of the room.

"I'm sorry you had to see that," she said. I'm sure she had a specific detail in mind.

"It's okay," I said. "I've heard of sex before."

"You shouldn't have."

"I'm twelve and a half," I said, but she didn't seem to think that made it okay. She blew a cloud of dust off a bottle of perfume and sprayed some in the room.

"Do you want some coffee?" she said. She kept not asking what I was doing in her apartment.

"Sure," I said.

"Let's get out of here then." She went over to the sink and turned the water off. "Dishes are not done yet."

We walked to the closest café and sat at a table outside, on a narrow sidewalk.

"Don't tell Mom I didn't move out," she said, after she ordered her coffee a certain way and I asked for the same thing without knowing what it meant—I'd never had coffee before anyway. "She thinks I have this nice little apartment in the Fifth."

"Do you not have a job either?" I asked.

"Not as good of a job as I told her, no. Not at the moment."

The coffees got to our table and Berenice sipped hers in silence, the saucer held near her heart, the cup moving from there to the lips, her eyes looking nowhere in particular.

"I don't like teaching," she said after a while. "I don't like people. Young people especially."

"You don't have to like them to teach them," I said. "I don't think any of my teachers like me."

"I sort of insulted one of my students," Berenice interrupted me. "I've been suspended."

I said nothing.

"It will be fine though," she said. "It was nothing too bad. I'm just not sure teaching is for me at all."

Her phone rang. She stared at it until it was done ringing and put it back in her pocket.

"I don't like to pretend I'm interested in their future, you know?" Berenice went on. "I'm barely interested in my own already." Her eyes swelled with tears, but nothing came out. I didn't know whether to acknowledge this or not. I'd been hoping that I could somehow go on with my escape after coffee, but I understood then that I would have to take care of Berenice and go home.

"Are you working on new articles?" I asked. "I really liked the one you wrote about humorism, you know?"

"You're the sweetest," Berenice said, and her eyes deflated a bit.

"It made me want to live in the sixteenth century," I said.

"How so?"

"Well, this doctor you write about, who thought he could examine you and determine what you should do in life . . . I don't know. It sounded easier back then."

"Not having a choice, you mean?"

Her phone rang a second time. She didn't look at it but let it be done before she spoke again.

"You might be right," she said. "I would definitely want to hear what he had to say about me."

Maybe Berenice believed I'd come all this way to check on her.

Around twelve thirty, the waiter set the tables for lunch and told us the café was reserved for diners for the next couple of hours. If we didn't plan to eat there, we had to leave and make room for them, even though no one had yet arrived.

"Let's just walk," Berenice said, not even asking if I was hungry.

She had no destination in mind but walked so fast it was hard to have a conversation. No one on the street looked too happy. We passed a few arguments, stood beside withdrawn women at intersections.

"Why did you insult your student?" I asked. We'd had to stop for the green light.

"She was being difficult," Berenice said. "She wanted me to agree with her that Don Quixote was impotent, and that that was really why he was so melancholy and saw windmills—which she claimed were evocative of erect penises—as monsters. I just couldn't get behind that."

"What did you call her?"

"I told her just because no one could get it up for her didn't mean the great classics needed a new reading. Something like that. Maybe I said a new *interpretation*."

"I guess the main problem was not with that part anyway."

"I thought it was funny."

"It is," I said.

"But no one laughed. And then I realized that I was in class. And that I was teaching that class."

"I'm sure Simone and the boys will find it funny."

The lights changed, but Berenice didn't start walking. She turned to me and made me promise not to tell anyone she'd been suspended, and promise again not to say anything about the apartment.

"I know Mom can't stand the thought of me living in that room, but I like it. It's so small . . . it's almost like living with someone. You hear the neighbors get up and use the bathroom on the landing at night, the shower early in the morning . . . it's like at home, you know?"

We walked some more, maybe for an hour, until Berenice stopped to look at a map on a board by a subway station. She had no idea where we were, and I could tell that looking at the map didn't help.

"Let me see," I said. I was good with maps. We'd walked

through five different arrondissements. As I was figuring out the quickest way to get my sister home, I noticed someone had written "STOP loneliness!" in silver marker on the side of the frame. The writer had run out of room on the right so the latter half of the "loneliness!" was crowded, its letters progressively slimming. Just beneath the message was a phone number.

"Another isolated initiative," Berenice said.

She was exhausted when we got back to her place. I did the dishes and cooked elbow pasta with butter for her while she lay down in bed. When I brought her the bowl of pasta, she was half-asleep and mumbling about how I shouldn't do the dishes and cook elbows with butter for her.

"Berenice," I said. "It's too late now, food is ready."

I wanted to ask her for money, to replace Simone's. I still had some for the train home, but that would've left me with only five or six bills to put back in Simone's hiding place where there'd previously been fifteen.

"I'd like to go home with you, Dory," Berenice said faintly. "I miss home. When we all slept in the same room, remember?"

"Well, you'll come visit for Aurore's PhD defense, right?" I asked.

"Of course I will."

We were both whispering. The pasta was getting cold on the nightstand. It didn't look worth keeping Berenice awake anymore. I waited 'til her breathing steadied to pull the blanket up to her chin. The old guy from earlier had dropped his wallet at the foot of the bed. At first, I only wanted to take exactly the amount of money that I needed, but then I remembered he hadn't been too nice to me and took the whole thing.

"Where were you on Friday?" Denise asked. "I didn't see you outside at recess, and you weren't here either."

"Here" was the narrow staircase at the end of the hallway, past the restrooms, where I spent recess most of the time. The staircase led nowhere, and no one ever hung out there but me, and Denise sometimes, when it was too cold or too hot outside. I'd sit at the top of the stairs, she at the bottom. We usually wouldn't talk.

"I was in Paris," I said.

I knew she wouldn't repeat that. She had no one to repeat things to but me.

"To see your sister?"

"Among other things."

Denise went up the first couple of steps to where she liked to sit, but she remained standing.

"Did you check the door yet?"

The staircase that led nowhere didn't actually lead nowhere. I guess there isn't anywhere that really leads nowhere. What it led to was a single door (no landing) that was locked at all times—I checked every recess.

"I did," I said. "It's locked."

"What do you think is behind there anyway?"

"I don't know," I said. "I want it to be the principal's secret apartment. Or like, an apartment where the principal tells kids who have problems at home to stay for a while, you know, time to straighten things out. Or an apartment where he hides the illegal ones. And it has to be kept secret because otherwise all the kids would pretend to have problems at home or to be illegal just to stay there in the hidden apartment, because it has a big TV and a queen-size bed and a mini-fridge, and no one ever bothers them."

"Well, they would still have to go to school, which is the biggest bummer," Denise said.

"Maybe they wouldn't, though. Maybe they would just stay in and hear us all scream at recess from their beds and think about how lucky they were to have problems at home."

I pictured myself in the hidden apartment at the center of the school. I checked the door again.

"Well I think it's the broom closet," Denise said. "For the cleaning guy."

"Did you see him come out of there or something?"

"Why? Have you seen illegal kids go in? I'm just guessing is all."

"Maybe it's *his* apartment. The cleaning guy's."

"Why do you want it to be an apartment so bad? It would be a lousy one anyway. Think about it: no windows. We can't see windows from the courtyard that match that spot in the building."

"But maybe the door opens on more stairs, and these stairs go up to the last floor of the school, where no one knows what's there either. The last floor has windows. Could be a top-floor apartment."

Denise thought about it.

"I guess it could," she said.

"Plus," I said, "I don't think it's very practical to have a broom closet at the top of a flight of stairs. It doesn't make much sense."

"I've never been inside an apartment," Denise said. "Everyone has houses around here. So boring."

"Whose house have you been to?" I asked.

"Why would I go to anyone's house?" she said.

"I don't know, you just said that . . ."

"No one ever invites me to their houses. I'm not complaining, by the way, just saying."

"No one ever invites me either," I said.

"Sara Catalano said you came to her house once."

"Sara talks about me?"

"She said you came to her house once. That you were in love with her or something."

"Did she say anything more about it?"

"No."

Denise was lying about that. No girl just talked about how a guy was in love with her and didn't elaborate on how it made her feel.

"Well, that was over a year ago," I said. "I don't love Sara anymore."

"Oh no?" Denise didn't believe me. "I thought you were the one who dropped anonymous flowers and gifts at her house over the weekend. She talked about it all morning between classes. How she got Chanel No. 5 on her front porch, and a Hermès scarf, and a bunch of wildflowers from the park. From an anonymous admirer."

"Anonymous could be anyone," I said.

I'd spent half the money in Berenice's lover's wallet on those gifts.

"Plus, I don't have that kind of money," I added. "You know how much Chanel and Hermès cost?"

"I bet you know *exactly* how much," Denise said.

"I have many sisters," I said. "There are women's magazines at home. I know the prices."

There had never been a women's magazine at home, but I had seen a few at the town's library—a homeless guy who hung out there always had a pile of them on his table and had once lectured me about them. They told you what women really wanted (Hermès and Chanel) while letting you know about what women thought they wanted (to have opinions about culture, to be outraged by the condition of women worldwide). "See," he'd told me, "women want to be beautiful. Those who are not like to do everything they can to feel that they are. And those for whom the situation is hopeless like to see pictures of beautiful women so that they can criticize society's objectification of women. These magazines win them all over." Also, he'd told me that the main perk of women's magazines was the perfume samples hidden underneath the glossy perfume ads: he could pamper himself for free before a date.

"Well if the gifts didn't come from you," Denise said, "you won't be too sad to know that Sara thought they were old-women stuff and gave them to her mother."

"She can give them to her dog, for all I care," I lied.

"Her dog died," Denise said.

"How?"

"Don't change the subject."

"She loved her dog."

"Honestly, I don't think the dog died. I think her parents abandoned the dog on the side of the road before Christmas because they couldn't find anyone to take care of him while they were away skiing and Sara is too ashamed to admit it."

"That's horrible," I said.

"It's something people do. It's something people do to their dogs that dogs should do to people."

"But people would find their way back home," I said. "It wouldn't work."

"You always take things very literally, don't you?" Denise said.

"I do? I try not to."

"Or maybe I always speak too metaphorically . . ." Denise said. "I don't even *like* dogs."

The end-of-recess bell rang and Denise didn't move from the bottom of the stairs right away as she usually did. She waited for me to come down. She eyed the door at the top of the stairs again and said, "Don't you think, if this was really an apartment for troubled kids, that they would've offered to let me stay there by now?"

I looked at the door, as if someone were projecting my answer on it.

"Maybe they did, but it's a secret apartment and you're not allowed to tell anyone," I said.

"But I would tell *you*," Denise said.

My mother eventually heard from the principal's office and was waiting for me on the couch. She was only pretending to be upset, I thought—she'd been waiting for years to give one of us the line about school's being important—"What about your future?" etc. It had been a part of parenting she felt my siblings had taken from her. She'd once admitted having been jealous of other parents in the past, when we were in middle school and she came to pick us up. Other mothers complained about their kids' spending too much time with their friends in the park, always trying to buy a few minutes on the curfew, not studying enough, and my mother was the only person she knew to have the opposite problem. She didn't want us to be uncivil or dumb, but she'd've been happy, she'd said, to hear from the principal once, only once, about one of us picking a fight, maybe, or having insulted another kid (who deserved it, she'd specified), just to make sure we were capable of disobedience.

"Why did you miss school last week?" she asked me, incapable of concealing her excitement.

"Heartbreak," I said, thinking at once that no one would ever reply "heartbreak" right away if it were true. My mother bought it and frowned. I was depriving her of her well-rehearsed speech again.

"Heartbreak?" she said. "Who's the little snot?"

"I don't want to talk about it," I said.

This concerned her. She got up to face me and I started looking at my shoes. If she wasn't able to make eye contact, I wouldn't be trapped into making up details.

"But you're better now?" she half asserted/half asked after a minute. I nodded.

"I'm sorry I skipped school," I said. "It won't happen again."

"You know you can talk to me about heartache anytime, right?"

"I know I can talk to you," I said, but I knew I'd never want to. "Good."

"And you know you can talk to me too, right?"

My mother's offer to be my confidant having slightly repulsed me, I had no idea why I reciprocated it.

"Why would I want to discuss heartache with you, Dory?" my mother asked. "What heartache, anyway?"

"Dad?" I tried.

Because we never talked about the father—the fact that he was dead, the fact that he'd once been alive—saying the word *dad* itself felt out of place, or like I might've used it wrong.

"That's not heartache, honey, that's grief," my mother said.

She sounded as uncomfortable with *grief* as I'd been with *dad*. We were only testing out the words for now, each making sure the other one was okay with *dad* and *grief* before we went any farther. *Dad* and *grief* only being code words at that point, we could still change the subject entirely and retreat without too much damage or consequence.

"Will you want a new boyfriend, one day?" I asked. I didn't want to have that conversation but I wanted to have had it.

My mother raised her eyes to the ceiling. I'd said something stupid.

"I'm too old, Dory. Boyfriends are for young women."

I didn't know how old my mother was exactly, so I didn't argue.

"What about a husband, then?"

"What's the difference? A husband needs to meet his wife when she's young, too. That's how a marriage lasts. The man has to be able, years into it, to cling to memories of a prettier, more fun woman. Weigh them against the daily annoyances and pregnancy stretch marks."

"You're still pretty," I said, though about that, I didn't exactly know either.

"It's your memories with the person that become your love for the person, you know? And building memories takes time. A lot of time, actually. I don't think I can do it again. I don't believe I have enough time left to do it again." It sounded like she might have had a rehearsed speech about love as well. "When people talk about love, Dory, they call it love because it is a festive word, like *champagne*. You hear the cork pop just saying *champagne*. But what they're really talking about when they say *love* is *attachment, ties,* which are, admittedly, less glamorous words. And when they say you only love once," she went on, "they don't mean it in a cheesy romantic way or anything, you know? It's very practical, in fact: there is no time in life to get to really know and . . . tie yourself to more than one person."

"That's a lot of pressure," I said.

"What is?"

"That you only have time in life to love one person. What if you set your mind on the wrong one and waste years on her?"

"Well, then you're fucked," my mother said.

I sat on the couch and started brushing the stain, which I'd refrained from doing in front of anyone for months.

"Don't worry, my Dory," my mother said, sitting on the armrest beside me. "You have plenty of time ahead. You will learn to recognize the girl for you."

I wasn't worried about girls. I didn't want to be the last one to live here with my mother was all. Aurore was about done with her dissertation. Who knew where she would teach next year? Leonard maybe had a year left on his, Jeremie was about to be done with his master's, and Simone only had a few months of high school left. Soon they'd all be gone, and I'd be stuck here, unable to ever move out and leave my mother alone.

"You're not even gonna try to fall in love again?" I asked. "Maybe it doesn't have to be love exactly but . . . companionship?"

"Companionship?" my mother said. She repeated the word twice more, putting the stress on *pan* the first time and then on *ship* the second. "Where the hell does a child learn the word *companionship* nowadays? Is this the moment where you tell me I should post an ad on the Internet and seek recently widowed men?"

I hadn't thought about it.

"What would be wrong with that?" I said.

"Well, I would have to hear everything about the dead first wife, for starters—and the romanticized version, of course, how *she* was when she was young and pretty—"

"But then you could talk about the father as well."

"No man wants to hear about his woman's exes."

"Do women want to?"

"Of course not. But they can manage, so it's different."

"What about the butcher?" The butcher had gotten divorced a few months before. "You've known him awhile, you have a few memories together already . . . it wouldn't be starting from scratch."

It took a little bit out of me to suggest the butcher. He'd behaved with dignity since the father had died, true, he'd put the dirty jokes on hold some, but still: I didn't think he was a good match for our family. My mother's only reaction to the butcher idea anyway was to shake her head no until I said something else. She wasn't going to help me help her be less lonely, I thought. The father's having died had provided her with an irrefutable excuse to give up on men.

"Maybe you're aiming too high," I said. "Maybe you should start with just building a couple of good memories with new people, you know, in a nonromantic way. See what each day brings."

"The memories you make as you get older," my mother said, "they're not as bright, you know? They're more like memos. They have a certain flatness. And a veil."

"A veil of what?" I asked.

"I don't know . . . a veil," she said, and she slid a flat hand through the air in front of her face to emphasize *veil*. "You'll see."

For a while, we remained silent on the couch, me brushing the stain now and then, but without conviction. I didn't know whether the conversation was over or not. I knew if we let too much time pass without reviving the important words we'd used so far, they would lose their charge and not come up again for a very long time. I looked for things to say about the father before the time to talk about him was up, but all I could think of was that I missed him, and it seemed too obvious and useless a statement—one there was nothing to reply to.

Before my sixth attempt, I pulled a map of Rose's neighborhood from the Internet and drew it on a piece of paper. There was no direct train to where she lived, so I took the same morning train to Paris I'd taken before, and from there hopped another to Rose's town. There had been bombings and bombing attempts in several European cities over the past few months, and I noticed they'd replaced all the opaque garbage cans in and around the train stations with metallic structures—a bar bolted to the ground, and a circle attached on top like a basketball hoop—from which only translucent plastic bags were hung, so that if someone dropped a bomb in the garbage now, people could see it and warn the authorities. Prerecorded voices enjoined us to be "watchful together." I looked through all the garbage bags I saw hanging, but I wasn't sure what bombs looked like exactly. In the spy show, it had looked like they came in all sizes.

By noon, I was waiting across the street from Rose's house for her to come home. She didn't look surprised when she saw me, even though I hadn't warned her I was coming or answered any of her letters.

"You been here long?" was all she said.

"A little while," I said.

"Did you run away from home?"

I said I had. She opened her door and let me in before her. The house smelled strongly of fruit candy.

"So what's your plan?" she asked as she got rid of her coat and boots and backpack, tossing them on different parts of the living room floor. No one was home. "How many nights do you need to stay here?"

"I don't know." I hadn't even thought I would spend the night at her place. "I didn't really plan anything."

"Well, how long have you been gone?"

"Just a few hours," I said. "This is my first stop."

The living room looked like a waiting area. There were multiple coffee tables with magazines on them. A glass cup with individually wrapped caramels. We never had magazines at home. I think that's why we didn't have coffee tables. We didn't have family photos on the walls, either, the way Rose's parents did. My mother's stance on family pictures was that they were only sadness left behind after someone died.

"You want to see my bedroom?" Rose asked.

We went up the stairs to a door that said "Rose" in black wooden letters. She offered to sleep with me right away.

"Maybe later?" I said.

I knew people didn't have to be in love to sleep together, but that's how I wanted it to be for me. At least for my first time. Rose didn't seem to take it personally. She told me to have a seat on her bed and that she would sit by me and that I shouldn't freak out.

"I'm not gonna rape you," she said.

"I know," I said.

She lit some incense and apologized for it.

"My boyfriend is a smoker," she said. "Whenever he comes over here, I light incense to cover the cigarette smell, 'cause my parents would lose it if they even believed for a second that I smoked. Which I would never do, by the way. But then it makes it suspicious when Kevin's not around, if I don't light incense. So I basically have to light incense all the time now. It's a real bummer. That stuff stinks."

"It's pretty strong," I said.

She shook the stick of incense in the air to get the tip burning steady. The door to her room moved almost imperceptibly and a cat walked in without paying us any attention. I watched it jump on the windowsill, wrap around itself, and fall asleep right away. The ease with which it did all this made me super body-conscious.

"Did you ever run away from home?" I asked, trying to ease into the bed.

"Yes," Rose said, "but I was with a boy, so it doesn't really count I guess. He took care of everything."

"Where did you go?"

"He took me to his grandma's in the suburbs. It was nice."

"How is it running away if you're going to stay with a relative?"

"He wasn't the one running away," Rose said, slightly annoyed. "*I* was. His grandma wasn't any relative of *mine*."

"Why did you do it?"

"My parents had grounded me. I just wanted to teach them a lesson."

"What lesson?"

"That where I go and what I do is entirely up to me?"

I didn't say anything more about it. I thought Rose's attempt didn't really count, but the way she talked about teaching her parents a lesson and the fact that she was allowed to have boys over, it seemed like she'd gotten what she wanted out of it.

"Why are *you* doing it?" she asked me. "Your family is so chill, I don't see why you would want to leave. I mean, I bet you've never even been grounded. Am I wrong?"

"They're not particularly chill," I said. "They're just busy with other things."

"Well that's the best kind of family. Maybe they won't even notice you're gone."

"I think they will," I said, and I looked at my watch. They would actually notice it in about four hours. Even if I turned around right this minute, assuming all train tables aligned to get me home as fast as possible, I wouldn't be able to make it back for dinner. It was the first time I'd ever gotten as far in terms of the three phases of running away as I understood them (start running away/don't go home before anyone notices you ran away/keep running away). I felt no pride or sense of accomplishment. Instead, I felt like something in my chest had deflated and disappeared, and I couldn't tell whether it was pleasant or frightening.

Rose's parents came home together. We hadn't had time to plan or agree on a lie about my presence in their house, but Rose took me by the arm and led me down the stairs to introduce me.

"I totally forgot to tell you guys: Tom here is my pen pal this year, he's going to stay here for a few days."

Rose's parents both sized me up from over their magazines and then looked at each other as if to agree on believing their daughter.

"Well I didn't know they were eager to reiterate the pen pal fiasco this year," Rose's father said, getting up from the couch to shake my hand. "Wasn't that crazy girl they set you up with last time enough? They decided to pair you up with a boy now, see if it works better? Jesus, these people."

"Simone wasn't crazy," Rose said. "She lost her father in the middle of the pen pal experience. The reason she didn't come here is because she was *mourning*."

"Honey, that girl was crazy before her father dropped dead. That movie we rented because of her? Because she said it was good? The ugly kid with the drums? And the yelling? Jesus, what a piece of shit. What a waste of a movie night. That girl was disturbed."

Rose's father was still shaking my hand as he spoke ill of Simone. I put some more strength into the shake to remind him his hand was there. It caused him to turn to me, but he still didn't let go. "What about you, pal?" he asked me. "What kind of movies do *you* like?"

"*Star Wars?*" I said. "*Goodfellas?*"

He let my hand go and tapped my shoulder.

"Well that's better," Rose's father said. "That's much better."

Simone had made me watch these movies.

"Isn't he a little short for the twelfth grade?" Rose's mother asked. "They must pick on you quite a lot, dear," she said to me directly, after no one echoed her first remark.

I just smiled at her.

"Where do you live, Tom?"

"In Paris?" I lied.

"Fancy," she said. She could barely hide her disdain. "Well, you make yourself right at home, young man. This is not Paris, we serve real portions of food. We're gonna cook something that will make you grow overnight."

"Thank you, Mrs. Metzger," I said. "Maybe I should call my mother before dinner though? Let her know I made it here all right?"

I took the phone to Rose's bedroom and Rose followed me.

"Are you really calling your mother right now?" she said. "Are you gonna tell her you've been kidnapped or something? Try to make a little money out of it?"

"Can you please pretend you're one of my classmates' mother?" I said.

"Why?"

"I just don't want her to worry. I'll tell her I'm staying at a friend's for the night, and if she asks to talk to his mother, I'll hand you the phone. Can you do an adult voice?"

"Sure, but then what?" Rose asked. "You'll go back? Or you'll just call your mommy every night for the rest of your life to say you won't be home for dinner?"

"I don't know," I said.

Rose sighed and looked at her cat.

"You sure you don't want to fuck?" she said.

"Can we call my mother first?"

"Sure," Rose said. "Whatever you want."

I dialed our number.

"What do I say if your mother asks where I and my son live?" Rose whispered as the phone was ringing home.

I wrote Denise's address on a piece of paper and handed it to Rose. I knew my mother didn't know Denise's parents.

"It's me, Izzie," I said when she picked up. I hadn't given up on people calling me Izzie. "Can I stay at my friend Dennis's tonight? We have a ton of work for school tomorrow. He offered to help me out with physics."

"Who's Dennis?" my mother said.

"I told you about Dennis."

"I don't think you have, Dory. In fact, when I ask you about it, you always say you have no friends at all."

"Oh, you know me," I said. "Always dramatizing."

"Actually, I wouldn't say that about you." My mother paused there. "But maybe it's puberty. Maybe you're gonna become a whole different person now."

"I wouldn't mind that," I said.

"Oh, stop with the nonsense," my mother said. "You're perfect just as you are."

Rose was pacing, looking down at the paper I'd written

Denise's address on and up at the ceiling, then down at the paper and up again, rehearsing a number and a street name as if they were a complex monologue.

"What's this Dennis's parents' phone number anyway?"

"Why do you need it?"

"I don't know, just in case."

"Let me ask his mother," I said.

"Better yet, put her on the phone for me, Dory, I want to make sure she's not a psychopath."

"Of course, Mom. Thank you. I'll see you tomorrow."

I blocked the receiver and whispered to Rose to write down her phone number, which she did. I changed her area code to mine and gave her a thumbs-up with my free hand and she understood she'd have to give that number to my mother herself if asked. I handed her the phone. Rose cleared her throat.

"Well, hello dear!" she said to my mother. She sounded like the horrible women on daytime TV shows who did nothing all day but drink and ask their lovers to leave their wives.

"Oh, nonsense! It is such a delight and an honor to have Isidore over," Rose said. I couldn't hear my mother's part.

"Uh-huh."

". . ."

"Oh yes, yes, very much. My Dennis is so excited."

". . ."

"Ha ha."

". . ."

"Ha ha ha."

". . ."

"Of course, dear," and then she gave my mother the address and phone number without a hint of hesitation.

After she hung up, Rose started taking her clothes off and went to lock her bedroom door. The sound of the key turning in the keyhole raised the cat's attention after the whole phone conversation hadn't disturbed her at all.

"Your mother sounds good," Rose said. "Really happy for you that you have a good friend. Does she have a new husband?"

"She doesn't," I said. "And she's not gonna."

I thought Rose would find this sad, but she said that my mother probably knew best what was good for her or not.

"What about your brothers?" she said. "How are they? Still good-looking?"

"They look about the same to me. But I never really talk to them," I said. "Do your brothers ever talk to you?"

"If I want them to, yes," Rose said, and then she asked if I was going to keep my clothes on. She was down to only underwear and socks.

"I don't know," I said. I couldn't believe her breasts were right there. "Are you sure you want to do this?"

Rose looked at me right in the eyes, which isn't something that happened to me a lot. My siblings mostly looked around me when we talked, and I think I did the same.

"You're a virgin, right?" Rose said.

I said I was.

"Then what's your problem?"

"I don't have a problem," I said. "I just wonder why you would want to have sex with me. I mean, I could be your little brother."

"My brothers are disgusting human beings," she said.

"Are you a virgin too?" I thought maybe she wanted to practice on me before she started having sex with her boyfriend Kevin.

"Of course not," she said. "I just thought I could help you out with this. Get the being-a-virgin thing out of your way, so you can start thinking about things more important than sex all the time."

"I don't think about sex all the time," I said, and it was true. I did think about sex a lot, I won't lie, but I also thought about death a fair amount, and about how impossible it was to know if everyone else thought about sex and death as much as I did. That last part may have been what I thought about the most, actually.

Rose's mother knocked on the door and said dinner was ready. "It's not even eight yet," Rose shouted through the door. "I know," her mother said, "but your brothers are hungry."

Rose's brothers were shaped like the brass weights on old counterweight scales. They were less fat than Rose had led me to believe, but their heads were so small it didn't matter. They would always look overweight. We ate dinner watching the news. A jogger had been stabbed and her body found in some woods in the area.

"Oh my," said Rose's mother. "What days we live in that an innocent woman cannot go out and exercise safely."

"Because you think it was better before?" Rose's father said. His aggressiveness didn't match the setting, the bamboo trays each of us had set like bridges over our thighs, the balanced meal, the wicker bread basket on the coffee table. "You think you didn't go out for a run and get stabbed in the old days?"

"It's a way of speaking," Rose's mother said.

"Well you did get stabbed before," Rose's father said, pointing his fork in his wife's direction. "And quartered, and burned, and for way less than that. Sometimes even for no reason at all.

People have to stop crying about how things were better before. I'd like to see them try living in the Middle Ages, hear what they have to say about that."

"I'm just saying, it's hard to feel safe in this world."

"You don't even jog, honey," Rose's father said. "If you jogged, it would be a different conversation."

Rose didn't seem to care about her parents' arguing. She kept staring at the TV like she could hear the next news bit about how Christmas was coming, but with her parents yelling like that, there was no way she could. I looked at her and tried to fall in love. People said it was details that made you fall in love, and so I looked for details in Rose's face, but all I could see was a nose, two eyes, a mouth, and a chin. I looked at her earlobes carefully, her eyebrows. Nothing stood out.

One of her brothers, out of nowhere, said that he thought Jewish people should be allowed to go to heaven if they wanted. "I think if you led a good and generous life," he said, "it shouldn't matter if you were baptized or not."

"We don't believe in heaven and so on in this house," Rose's mother whispered to me apologetically. "But the boys have questions, so we sent them to Bible study. They should get over it soon."

"I mean, it's unfair that Schindler cannot go to heaven," the same brother went on, "after all he did to save those children. And it's unfair that the Jewish children he couldn't save from the camps couldn't go either."

"Schindler probably went to heaven, honey. He wasn't Jewish."

"He wasn't?"

"Of course not. He worked for the Nazis, remember?"

The brother was puzzled by that piece of information. He looked at his potatoes awhile and brought his tray closer to the coffee table to help himself to more.

"I think it is possible you didn't understand the movie, sweetie," Rose's mother said.

"Still," the brother said, chewing his potato. "It's not fair."

After that, we watched the movie that followed the news, something about a couple that seemed happy at first but realized they weren't and then were for real, and no one made comments about it either during or after. In my head, I was able to predict most of the plot.

Rose had one of these trundle beds I'd seen advertised on TV: you pulled open the drawer under the bed and the drawer contained another bed. When she came back from the bathroom, I was standing in my underwear between the drawer where I would sleep and her desk. She had the map of France Simone had sent her pinned on the wall.

"Did my sister send you this map?" I said, just for conversation.

"It's really useful," Rose said. "I add things to it sometimes."

All she'd added were colored round stickers where Disneyland was, and the Futuroscope.

"I think we should sleep together but I'm afraid it won't be great for you," I said. "Because I'm not in love with you yet."

Rose started undressing.

"I'm not in love with you either, you know?" she said, and then she slid her right arm out of the right arm hole of her T-shirt. "And I know you're probably thinking that I offer to sleep with boys and cheat on my boyfriend all the time, but I don't. I'm in love with him, even if he smokes and all." She was still mostly inside her T-shirt but the right arm and shoulder were there naked, and the right tit in its bra cup. "I know it sounds weird, but sometimes, I see people who look like all they need is to be hugged and fucked once in a while, you know, someone to love them, and usually they're old and fat and kind of ugly but I'm never disgusted by them the way other people are. I just feel for them that they're virgins. And it makes me sad that I can't do anything for them. Because I'm not Mother Teresa or anything. I do want a good-looking boyfriend and cute kids and money, I don't want to be with an ugly fat guy who seems very sweet just to be nice, but I'm very aware of their pain."

"So you're saying I'm one of these sweet sad-looking fat dudes and you want to do me a favor?" I said.

"No, I think you're very cute," she said. "But there's a chance you might turn into one of the lonely fat guys, so I'm thinking maybe I can help you *now*, prevent it from happening."

She took the rest of her T-shirt off, and then her bra before the pants. I'd always thought that before sex, the bra had to be taken off last. She said if I lay on my back and she was on top of me it would be easier because she could help me get in, so we had sex like that. It felt really nice as it was happening, the short time it lasted, but the effects faded fast. It was like the first night I'd managed to wait for midnight. I'd been thrilled to see the numbers go from 23:59 to 0:00, I'd held my breath for the great change-of-day show to happen, but then it had gone to 0:01 and nothing had been altered.

"Did you like it?" Rose asked, and I said very much. She had a mole on the side of her left tit, but it didn't work as a detail to fall in love over.

"You should stay in my bed for the night," she said as I was putting my shirt back on. "Snuggling is not part of sex, but it is still important to do it I think."

"Okay," I said, and she wrapped my arms around her the way she wanted them. After a minute, we heard the cat scream from the hallway and Rose got up to open the door for her before she'd wake her parents up. The cat stormed into the room like she was being chased and needed a place to hide, except the thing that was chasing her seemed to be attached to the bottom of her tail.

"What's wrong with the cat?" I said, and Rose started laughing as silently as she could.

"This happens sometimes," she said, "she swallowed one of my hairs!"

I looked at Rose's hair—very long, straight, brown—and then at the cat's ass.

"When she takes a shit, it just comes out wrapped around the hair, I don't know why! All her little balls of shit just come out one after the other along the hair, and the hair is usually longer than the cat has to shit, and so she drags it around, the garland of shit! She's being followed by her own shit!"

The cat was freaking out. I didn't know cats shat so dry. The line of little brown balls looked like the clay beads on the necklaces you make in art class for Mother's Day.

"Are you gonna help her?" I asked.

"Why? No! I'm not going near that. It's so gross. Not to mention funny."

"So she's just going to drag the garland of shit behind her all night?

Rose couldn't stop laughing. "I love when this happens!" she said. "I'm so glad you got to see it."

I wasn't as excited about the garland of shit as Rose was, but she looked truly happy, and that wasn't something I got to see much. I don't mean to say that my family was unhappy, but I suspected that their moments of happiness were not sharable, or at least that they didn't want to share them, that they considered happiness a private emotion, one to go through alone. Watching the cat failing to run away from her own shit and listening to Rose explaining how much she liked it, I thought that we might've been reaching a level of intimacy that was greater than what we'd just experienced having sex. I thought maybe I could fall in love with her. But then she decided we were too excited to go to sleep right away and that we should tell each other jokes. She wanted to keep laughing, she said. I told her the 69 joke I'd heard the butcher tell Daphné and she liked it. "I have to tell it to Kevin tomorrow," she said. "He'll love it."

"Your turn," I said, and I was starting to be as excited as her, because I didn't actually know that many jokes.

"Okay," she said. "Do you know why France replaced all of the garbage cans with see-through plastic garbage bags?"

I knew the real reason was homeland security but since it wasn't funny, I didn't think it would be the answer to her joke.

"I give up," I said.

"It's so the Arabs can go window-shopping!" Rose said, and she laughed even harder than she had at my 69 joke.

I didn't get the joke. I thought maybe it worked for homeless people, but I couldn't see the connection with the Arabs. I thought maybe it was because I still didn't know enough about Arab culture.

"Why is it funny?" I said, even though I knew there wouldn't be a satisfying answer and I was just ruining the moment.

Not even a week after I lost my virginity, I was told I needed braces. Of the six of us, only Aurore had had to wear braces, so I'd hoped I'd avoid the whole thing. The metal kept spearing through the inside of my lips and cheeks. I woke up every morning with the taste of blood in my mouth.

"I don't think they fit quite right," I told the orthodontist on my first visit back. He said that nothing ever really did. He made it sound like he was speaking of things beyond dental gear, maybe, as if it were part of his job to make remarks that vaguely sounded like life lessons, since he mostly dealt with teenagers, and teenagers had to be taught life lessons, like for instance that nothing in life ever fit quite right. I'd noticed, lately, that boys my age couldn't really say anything to adults anymore without having it turned into something more than what they'd meant. A boy in class asking our teacher, "Is this going to be on the test?" had been sent off to meditate on the inherent uncertainty of all things ("I don't know, Jules, is a giant asteroid going to hit Earth and wipe us all off the map like it did dinosaurs?"); another inquiring about the relevance of mathematical functions to everyday life had been offered parallels with other useless things people engaged in without too much questioning (marriage, soccer). I was okay with this bluntness—my siblings had never really spared me their brutal observations—but I could tell some kids had a hard time adjusting to it. They didn't dare speak up as much, aware that any group of words they'd say would only incite the nearest adult to speak an aphorism he'd be forced to listen to. I didn't know what it was that made grown-ups think teenagers were ready for a reality check all of a sudden, ready to find out that everything that happened or would ever happen to them was or would be either random or exactly normal, their experience no more nor less uncommon than anyone else's, after having been told the opposite and cautiously spared the truth for the previous thirteen, fourteen, fifteen years. I didn't know what it was that made adults think, *They're ready to take it all in now.* But then I got metal glued all over my teeth and I understood how maybe there was no better time to have a person find out about something horrible than right in the aftermath of another horrible thing's having happened to them, like having been disfigured by braces, which usually happened around our age. When a child starts looking like a monster and notices it is when you can start unloading the pile of ugly truths on him, and then it's done. He can become an adult. That's how it seemed, at least.

"Nothing ever fits quite right," the orthodontist said, and he gave me some transparent wax to stick between the braces and the parts of my mouth that kept being caught in the wires.

"You have to roll the wax between your fingers for a little while before you cover the brace with it," he explained. "To soften it."

"Okay," I said.

"And then you stick it up right on the guilty brace."

"Okay," I repeated.

"Nothing ever fits perfectly, son, but we have mastered work-around techniques for nearly everything."

I stuck little balls of wax in every night before bed. Looking at myself do this in the mirror one day, I thought if I ran away while I had braces, I would have to wear them forever because I could never pay for another orthodontist to remove them. I wondered if anyone had kept their braces on forever. What happened to your teeth if you did. If they just kept retreating back into your mouth until they fell out.

———

"The setup was much nicer in Paris," my mother said when we walked into the room where Aurore was about to defend her PhD. She was disappointed, I think, mostly because people from the neighborhood had come to listen to Aurore and she would have preferred them to see the ancient Parisian lecture hall we'd all gone to for Berenice, with the strips of dust-enhancing sunlight.

"If your only concern is for people to be impressed—people who, by the way, no one gives a shit about—" Leonard said, "just wait 'til Aurore starts talking."

"See, that is exactly why environment matters," my mother said. "People have to be able to look around, to look at *something*, when they're bored."

"Maybe the bare surroundings will invite them to reassess and reflect on their lives," Jeremie offered. "As they probably should."

We all sat in a middle row, like Aurore had requested. The chairs were plastic and uncomfortable. My mother waved politely at women who entered the room and immediately pointed out different seating options at their disposal so that they wouldn't come talk to us. My mother wasn't really friends with any of these women, but they still invited her to weddings and parties, and although she never went anymore, she'd felt an obligation to reciprocate.

"They'll never come," my mother had predicted a week earlier, when she'd made the calls. "Who wants to hear about Thucydides?"

It so happened that all the women invited came, some with the grown sons they'd always wanted to marry Berenice or Aurore (the reason why they'd started inviting my mother everywhere in the first place, twenty-something years before, the reason why my mother had stopped going), some with younger daughters who were encouraged to be more like my sisters. One of them came with a boy she'd forced, I assumed, to wear a bow tie. The boy was too young to have been a former classmate of either Berenice or Aurore. His mother probably wanted him first in line for Simone's attention.

I spotted Martin, Sanchez, and Ohri in the first row. I was only a kid when they'd started showing up at our door in turns, whenever Berenice had missed school, to offer the notes they'd taken in lit class, or chocolates, or feel-better mix tapes, but they'd kept on ringing our bell now and then, years after she'd left for grad school, and I'd gotten to know them a bit. They'd come to "see how the family was doing," bring my mother flowers, ask the father's advice on how to invest their money—even though the father had been the last person to ask about things like that. They'd leave saying, "My best to Berenice," very matter-of-factly, like they'd just remembered Berenice happened to be these lovely people's daughter. My parents were always nice to the suitors, as they called them, but the minute Martin, Sanchez, or Ohri was out the door, my siblings would launch into what they'd themselves dubbed a "condescension fest," quoting the audible spelling mistakes one or the other suitor had made, commenting on their laughable ambitions, the lack of self-esteem (or as Martin would say, "self-of-steam") one had to be plagued with to keep on trying to get the daughter by way of charming the parents, even after the daughter was long gone. After a while, we'd realized the suitors had given up on Berenice and were going for Aurore. Aurore had then declared she wouldn't be the next best thing and stopped leaving her bedroom to say hello when one of the boys visited. They'd all ceased coming shortly after that. Ohri had been the last to let go. I liked Ohri the best.

The three of them were either engaged or married now, but they still tried to catch a glimpse of Berenice whenever they could. Simone said some people needed to dwell on the past and be reminded constantly of what they'd missed in order to have some sort of inner life. I wanted to believe that it was the opposite, that Martin, Sanchez, and Ohri were trying to have Berenice realize what *she'd* missed, but I'd seen their faces fold when Berenice had failed to recognize them at the father's funeral ("They were out of context," Berenice had later said in her defense), and had to admit that Simone was probably right.

I smiled at Ohri when our eyes met. He smiled back but turned away immediately. He had to know my siblings made fun of him, and he probably believed I did the same. It saddened me that he would think that of me, but then I'd never defended him during condescension fests either, and I knew by then that silence meant consent.

I'd actually enjoyed all our condescension fests, not because I felt superior to those my siblings condescended to, but because the fests seemed to unite my family around something, to bring us all closer. I'd learned a lot about us thanks to guys like Ohri— what we didn't like, what we had respect for, what was funny, and what was better left unsaid.

When Aurore started her presentation, my mother looked at me and squeezed my hand like we were about to skydive. "We can do it!" her eyes said. She'd taken energy boosters to not fall asleep. We'd agreed to go listen to the defense before I would read her Aurore's dissertation. "Maybe if we hear about it first, we'll understand her writing better," my mother had said, but Aurore started talking and we were immediately lost. I must've glanced at my mother two thousand times—I'd promised I wouldn't let her nod off. Berenice took notes the whole time. She'd arrived from Paris that morning and we'd both acted like we hadn't seen each other there a few months before, and I'd thought she'd be impressed by my having kept her secret and would comment on it later, when it would just be her and me, but then it had only been her and me in the kitchen and she hadn't said anything.

After the jury announced that Aurore had passed the test with the highest distinction, they acknowledged the presence of an audience for the first time in five hours and invited us to the next room for a friendly get-together.

"I like how they always specify 'friendly,'" my mother said.

"That's because all academics hate each other," Berenice explained.

Everyone attending seemed to have fought a violent fight against sleep, and to not be quite certain they'd won it yet, and they looked at each other in disbelief, making sure it was okay to go eat and drink. They went to the buffet in small steps, cut their cake and poured their wine cautiously, as if they had to relearn the simple gestures of civil life. Some stretched their limbs. The professors in Aurore's jury, though older than everyone else, were in much better shape. They ate vigorously, laughed heartily, as if nothing had happened. Maybe that's what made academics academics, after all: a higher resistance to boredom. Or maybe they *needed* more boredom than regular people in order to enjoy the small pleasures of life to the fullest, the way you need to travel once in a while to fully appreciate the comfort of your own bed.

"You must be so proud," a woman said.

My mother responded by apologizing for the food and decor, as if it were Aurore's wedding and the groom's family had planned the whole thing without consulting her.

"As long as there's wine!" another woman said, and then there were laughs and polite conversation.

My brothers were talking to some girls. Simone was inquiring about Aurore's dissertation adviser's own current work. Behind her, the woman who'd brought the kid in a bow tie was waiting to introduce them, and I suspected Simone was not so much interested in Aurore's professor's career as she was in avoiding an encounter with someone her age.

I had no one to talk to, but that kind of thing didn't make me uncomfortable at the time—I still wasn't sure that people could see me. Ohri desperately needed to put up a front, though, so I went over to him.

"Where are Sanchez and Martin?" I asked.

"We're not exactly friends, you know?" Ohri said. He seemed insulted anyone would think they were.

"Sorry," I said. "It's just that I see you together a lot."

"Ever thought they might be following me everywhere?"

I'd assumed Ohri would be relieved to have found someone to talk to, but he kept looking over his shoulder for better conversation opportunities.

"How's married life?" I asked. I didn't really care about married life but I knew adults asked about it.

"I'm not the one who got married," Ohri said. "That was Martin."

"Oh, sorry. I thought my mother told me you had. But you're engaged, right? Isn't it roughly the same?"

"I don't know," Ohri said. "I sure hope not."

"Is she giving you a hard time?"

"She's pretty jealous. She says it's insecurity, you know, bad self-image, stuff like that, but I don't know. Maybe marriage will give her confidence."

"Why didn't you bring her along?"

"Well, that's the thing: she's so insecure she says she doesn't want to embarrass me in social circumstances, but then when I tell her she won't embarrass me, she doesn't believe me and it turns into this fight because, according to her, I didn't really mean it, and she knows she's not as pretty or as smart as my ex-girlfriends, and then it becomes this whole thing where *I'm* the asshole and she wouldn't want to stand in the way of my catching up with old 'friends,' and she air-quotes *friends*, too, like . . . she doesn't believe in male-female friendship, for instance. She doesn't understand that your sister and I are just friends now."

"As opposed to when?"

"Excuse me?"

"You said you and Berenice were just friends *now*."

"So?"

"Well, you were never anything else."

And it was already nice of me to let *friends* fly.

"Oh, give me a break, dude," Ohri said, and he looked over his shoulder again. It was still not a good time to go congratulate my mother on Aurore's success, so he turned back to me. "You know what I mean," he said.

"You mean wanting to be someone's boyfriend and actually being someone's boyfriend are pretty much the same thing, right?"

Ohri told me to go fuck myself and I said that he shouldn't talk to me that way. "I always say hello to my sisters for you when you ask me to," I said. "Not everyone does that."

I went outside where I knew I'd find Aurore and Berenice. They'd taken their drinks to a bench in the university's courtyard and were smoking pink cigarettes.

"Someone left a pack half-full of that shit," Aurore said. "Guess what flavor it is."

They both blew their smoke my way. It smelled of burned caramel.

"Strawberry?" I tried.

"Chocolate," Berenice said, and she handed hers to me. "You smoke it, I need a real one."

I let the cigarette smoke itself between my fingers and tossed it. I didn't know how to smoke. I thought smoking would be like when my mother had tried to clean my nose with a neti pot. Like drowning.

"Is everyone in there talking about how impressive I was and how all these years of hard work were completely worth it?" Aurore asked.

I said everyone was.

"Your sister is depressed," Berenice said. "Tell her she did real good, Dory. You're the only person whose opinion matters to any of us anyway."

That was a lie, of course, but not the mean kind, just the kind you tell small children to make them believe their existence isn't entirely meaningless.

"You were great," I said to Aurore. "I'm very proud of you."

"I was depressed after my own defense too," Berenice said, and she gave Aurore a real cigarette. "It was the best day of my life. It's only natural everything should look dreary after that."

Aurore lit the regular cigarette while she was still smoking the pink one. She looked like a walrus who'd just broken a tusk.

"Ohri and Martin and Sanchez can't stomach each other," I said, to change the subject.

Aurore dragged on her two cigarettes at once.

"It'll suck for them when they figure out they really are the same person," she said.

"But nothing says you can't start *another* PhD," Berenice said.

"Why in the world would I want to do that?" Aurore said.

"'Cause being a student is the best?"

"Ohri goes around telling people you used to date," I told Berenice.

"Which one is Ohri again?"

"The Japanese one."

"Oh. Of course. That's pretty funny," Berenice said, but she didn't seem too interested, or actually amused. She turned back to Aurore and resumed her talk about multiple PhD getting. I interrupted her right away.

"But you don't mind him lying to everybody?"

"Who, Ohri? Why?"

"I don't know, your reputation?"

"If telling everyone he used to date me helps him bear himself, what do I care? It's not like I'll ever have to talk to anyone who listens to his crap anyway."

"Well *I* just listened to his crap," I said. "*I* live here. And I don't like people lying about you like that."

Berenice looked at my face, but not directly into my eyes, and pushed smoke through her nostrils very slowly.

"Did he tell you why we broke up? In his story?"

She was only pretending to care, but that wasn't as different from actually caring as people liked to claim, so I didn't pick up on it.

"He only said his fiancée was very jealous of his exes, and you were an example."

"What a prick," Berenice said. "I hope she leaves him for one of the other two."

"Who's his fiancée?" Aurore asked.

"You think I should go talk to him?" Berenice said.

"Talking to him would only add verisimilitude to his bullshit," Aurore said.

"Maybe Dory should just steal his girlfriend."

"Maybe *you* should steal his girlfriend," Aurore told Berenice, and they both laughed and said *eww*.

"It probably wouldn't be that hard. Beneath every jealous woman is a lesbian who has yet to realize she's a lesbian," Aurore said.

"Is that so?" I asked. I'd heard someone say Sara Catalano was very jealous.

"No, Dory, don't listen to me," Aurore said. "I don't know

shit about anything that doesn't directly relate to what I talked about today."

She gulped the last of her plastic cup and started crying. I went inside to get her more wine.

———

I never read Aurore's dissertation to my mother. The night of the defense, she decided it was time I stopped sneaking into her bedroom to read her to sleep. She said I was getting too old for this, but I thought she was just tired of trying to understand what her children were working on. Or maybe it was my braces and the gooey stuff I had to put on them. Maybe my reading voice was too wet or something. Maybe she didn't want to tell me that's what it was because she didn't want to hurt my feelings.

———

Berenice went back to Paris a couple of days after Aurore's defense, pretending she had a good job to get back to. Aurore stayed in bed for a month but insisted she wasn't depressed. She just needed time to think. When I'd go in her room to see how her thinking was going (we all visited her in turns), she'd be lying completely dressed atop her blankets and staring at the ceiling, or through the window, her hands perfectly still on her stomach, feet crossed at the ankles. I knew that when she went to Aurore's bed, Simone told stories of her own making, and that Leonard brought her the latest news from the world of Thucydides studies. I didn't know what Jeremie talked to her about. No sound ever came from Aurore's bedroom during Jeremie's shift. I didn't tell her much either. I mostly just stared in whatever direction she was already staring and if something appeared in our field of vision (a spider, rain), I would make a comment on it. One day, I passed by Aurore's door while my mother was in and I heard my mother say, "You worry too much, honey. Everything is going to be fine. You've always worried and it's always been fine."

"Exactly," Aurore replied. "That's exactly why I need to keep worrying."

I didn't understand how they could agree that everything had always been fine.

Sometime around the end of her second week of thinking in bed, Aurore asked me for a strawberry-pistachio sponge cake from Moiroud's and I thought she was cured. It was her favorite thing in the world, this cake, but even though Moiroud's was just a couple blocks away, she only allowed herself to have it on special occasions. When I came back with it, she didn't even sit up, just put the box with the cake on her chest, cut through the cake with a fork, and brought the piece to her mouth without lifting her head.

"It's no good to eat lying down," I said.

Aurore didn't budge and brought another forkful to her mouth. Her swallowing seemed to trigger the vespers bells, which started ringing in the distance. We didn't hear them every day. The wind had to be blowing sounds a certain way. It always made me weirdly happy and nostalgic to hear the vespers bells, like I was in a movie, but I tried not to let on, because Simone had caught me listening to them at our window once and started singing horrible historical facts about the Catholic Church along with the joyful melodies. The lyrics had stuck in my head for a long time.

"You don't think it's weird that I've never had a boyfriend?" Aurore asked me.

"Well . . . you've been pretty busy," I said. "With the PhD and all."

"No, but don't you think it's weird that I don't really want one now?"

"I don't know," I said. "Simone doesn't want a boyfriend either."

"Simone is a child," Aurore said.

"She's got her period already," I said.

Aurore sat up and put the box with the rest of the cake in it on her nightstand. She lit a cigarette and seemed to listen to the bells for a second. I thought maybe she was trying to tell me something important and I wanted to make it as easy as possible for her.

"Is it because you want a girlfriend, maybe?" I asked.

"No," Aurore said, and it wasn't a disgusted or dismissive no, but one that implied she'd given some thought to that, too. "I don't know what's wrong with me," she said. "It's not that I'm not interested in sex. I think I am. I do have erotic dreams and all, and it feels nice, but then when I'm awake, I never want to try the actual thing. It barely ever crosses my mind."

The bells sounded like a mix of "Frère Jacques" and "Auld Lang Syne."

"And the erotic dreams I have, they're always about guys I don't want to have erotic dreams about," Aurore said.

"I always dream about the wrong people too," I said. I knew

exactly what she meant. "I have dreams about Denise Galet all the time when I'm really in love with Sara Catalano."

Aurore ashed in the box, careful to avoid what was left of the cake.

"I don't know about that Denise chick," she said, "but Sara Catalano is a dumb bitch, Dory. The last one in a long line of dumb bitches."

"I didn't know you had an opinion on her," I said.

"I have an opinion on everyone who seems to have a good time being a teenager."

"Well, maybe you'd like Denise then," I said. "She's suicidal."

Aurore smiled and said I was funny, which wasn't something I heard much. People usually told me I was sweet, but it seemed to worry them, or at least make them a little sad for me. Funny, though, was always a compliment 100 percent.

"I'm not joking," I said. "She really is suicidal."

"It doesn't matter," Aurore said. "Funny is not just for jokes. It's the way you said she was suicidal that was funny. The timing."

The bells stopped. I asked Aurore if she wanted advice on sex.

"What would *you* know about it? Would I get a description of your erotic dreams with the suicidal girl? Thank you, sweetheart, but I think I'll pass."

"I had sex last month," I said.

Aurore took the cake box back from her nightstand and put it on her knees. She was still smoking and she started alternating puffs and cake bites slowly. The box had uncovered an ugly flyer on her nightstand advertising a conference titled "Aristophanes/ Plautus: Confrontations."

"Are you gonna go?" I asked, grabbing the flyer.

"What are you talking about? How old are you?"

"Thirteen," I said.

"How can you have had sex already?"

"A girl offered. So that I could be done overthinking it," I said.

"Were you overthinking it?"

"I don't think so," I said. "But I sure was thinking about it some."

"Leonard and Jeremie were planning on talking to you about all that stuff soon. Sex. I guess they're way behind on their appraisal of your puberty."

"They were planning to talk to me? Leonard and Jeremie never talk to me."

"I'm sure they will want to now," Aurore said.

"Yeah?" I asked.

She wouldn't confirm.

"When did it start snowing?" she said. "I stare out this window all day long. I look away for one second and it starts snowing. What's wrong with me?"

"Because you missed the beginning of a snowfall something's wrong with you?"

"It never snows," she said.

I was under the impression Aurore was okay with missing out on stuff, having barely left the house the past few years.

"I'm sorry I made you miss it," I said.

She didn't say anything for a while and I looked at the flyer about Aristophanes and Plautus. It listed the talks people would give on the matter over the course of a three-day symposium. It all sounded pretty abstract except for the last part, which was titled "How to End a Comedy."

"Do you want me to leave you alone?" I said.

"Has it been an hour? You usually stay with me for an hour."

"It's been an hour if you count me going out to get the cake at Moiroud's. Otherwise, it's only been forty minutes or so. But I can stay for as long as you want."

"Then stay," Aurore said, and she lay back down in the position she was usually in during my visits, her gaze back on the window.

"What does Jeremie talk to you about when he comes in?" I asked.

"He mostly just hums," Aurore said.

"And you like it?"

"What are you gonna do? He hums. It's his thing."

"He's been composing new things? I don't hear him play piano or his cello much lately."

"He's been trying to compose without instruments."

"Why?"

"I don't know why, Dory. People are strange."

You could tell the snow wouldn't stick. By the time the flakes reached the bottom of the window frame, they'd turned to water.

"Did you wear a condom? When you fucked that girl?"

"No," I said. "You think I could've given her a disease?"

I thought it was always the men who gave the diseases.

"Of course not, dummy, you were a virgin. Maybe *she* gave you something though. You should really wear rubbers next time."

"I don't know that there'll be a next time."

"You don't have to say that just because you feel sorry for me," Aurore said.

"I was just saying, now that I have braces, I doubt anyone will want to be my girlfriend."

"Braces are the worst. I have nightmares I still have them on *at least* once a week," Aurore said, and then she sighed and pronounced her next sentence within the sigh. "Maybe I should just embrace it and come out as France's oldest virgin or something. Get together with Daphné Marlotte and form the saddest duet. We'll do a double act, throw a joint party each year, about her still being alive and me still having not yet fucked anyone."

"You're not the oldest virgin in France," I said.

"I'm twenty-four. That's pretty old."

"Do you need sex advice?" I offered again.

"No offense, Dory, but I suspect you didn't perform too well that one time."

Aurore had the sweetest face in the family, and even when she tried to be harsh, it didn't work as well as with the others. The efforts she had to make to have her features twist in a vaguely mean expression, it looked painful—you ended up feeling sorrier for her than for yourself.

"At this stage, I should probably seek advice from a professional anyway," Aurore said.

"Like, a prostitute?"

"No, more like a sex counselor. But I guess you actually need to have had sex before you go see a sex counselor. Aren't they just for couples?"

"I don't know," I said. "In the movies they are. Maybe you can just go in with a friend and pretend you're a couple."

"What friend?" Aurore said.

"Good point," I said.

Aurore closed her eyes.

"I only went into this because I wanted to know everything," she said, "to be able to answer every question on the spot, you know? Like these old people on *Questions pour un Champion?* But now . . . not only do I know about a very limited field, but even there, there doesn't seem to be a simple answer to anything anymore. I believe I got smarter, but also slower, somehow. Any question now, I need days and days to think about it. I don't understand what happened." This seemed to be the most confusing thing Aurore had ever been faced with. "There should be a postdoctoral program to teach you how to resume a normal life," she went on. "Or a whole PhD program. 'Life Experience Studies,' or something. The student would have to gather a bibliography on the kind of life he'd like to pursue, and his professors would orient him toward potential life partners—both friends and lovers—according to his research interests. Maybe the first forty wouldn't work out, but then the student would get to talk with his adviser about what went wrong, and the adviser would help him back on the right track, so as not to spend too much time trying to fix something that won't work. I mean, people say that to acquire life experience you have to actually live and have experiences, but there must be another way, right? It can't be that any experience is valuable."

"There are dating websites," I said.

"But I need guidance. The Internet assumes you know exactly what you're looking for. I don't know what I'm looking for, even less where to look for it. I need to be educated in recognizing what my life should be like now. Why do we stop having professors after a PhD?"

"I think it's because at some point you have to become your own professor," I said.

I knew Aurore would hate me for saying something like that,

but she spent her life hiding from self-help statements and sup-port systems and feel-good movies: someone had to give her the cheese-ball motivational lines by surprise.

"The only way to get educated is to talk to people who are smarter than you. Period. One can't be one's own professor of something one has no idea how to think about," she said. "There's a contradiction in terms here."

"Not more than in a doctoral program that would teach you how to live outside of academia," I said.

"I guess you've got a point," Aurore conceded, and she didn't make it sound like it was a big deal, but it was the first point she'd ever granted me.

The Funnel

ON THE FIRST day after winter break, at recess, Denise met me in the staircase. We still didn't know what was behind the door at the top of the stairs, but by that point I'd given up on even checking the lock. I didn't even go all the way up anymore and had taken to sitting at the bottom of the stairs, to be closer to where Denise would be.

I asked her how her Christmas went, what gifts she'd gotten, but she said she didn't want to talk about it, as if something horrible had happened, except I was pretty sure nothing horrible had happened to Denise over Christmas break other than being at home with her parents—whom she thought were stupid, who maybe were (she complained they often wore matching T-shirts stating their star signs)—and being forced to eat more than she wanted.

"Isn't there one thing you like about Christmas?" I asked her. "One food?"

"As far as meals go, I only tolerate breakfast," Denise said, which would've been understandable if she'd been talking about a real breakfast with lots of bread and butter, but I knew she meant fruit and eggs. I knew that was all Denise ate, and that she would only eat it in the mornings, sometimes for lunch if she really had to, but she didn't understand dinner. Dinner was for her the most useless thing because she said we didn't need energy before bed. I didn't know how anyone could elect not to have dinner. I sometimes thought dinner had in fact only been invented to give people a reason to go through the day.

"I don't know what I would do with myself at night if dinner didn't exist," I said.

"That's because you've been raised with dinner as a convention. And you're a conformist. All children are."

I took this as an insult but then I realized taking the word *conformist* as an insult was the most conformist reaction and so I let it slide.

"Did you watch the New Year's TV movie this year? On Channel One?" Denise asked.

I said we never watched French TV movies in my family. "My brothers and sisters are strongly anti—"

"Right," Denise said. "I forgot you came from people of taste." She wasn't being sarcastic. She didn't know anyone in my family but for some reason assumed we formed a perfect inverted model of hers, of which she was the only child and the only intelligent member (I wondered if that made me, to her mind, the only dumb member of mine).

"We watch stupid American shows all the time," I said, to make my family sound more normal.

"Anyway, my parents obviously make me watch the Christmas special every year, and it was really bad once again, but guess what?"

I couldn't possibly have guessed what Denise would say next.

"Do you remember those videos they showed us in fourth grade?" she asked, knowing I would. "With the kids who'd never seen the ocean?"

"Of course I remember," I said, a little too enthusiastically. "I didn't think anyone had paid attention to those videos but me."

"You did put a lot of money in Miss Faux's jar back then," Denise noted.

"You saw me?"

"Everyone saw you. You must've dropped like thirty coins in there. Slid them in the slot one at a time, all solemn, like you were saying a little prayer after each coin drop."

"I wasn't," I said.

"You really wanted those kids to see the ocean, I guess."

Denise was making fun of me. Her mood that day indicated school had just started again. She was always slightly less depressed after school breaks, because she felt she'd broken free from the "parental yoke" and experienced a rare sense of lightness, "like when you bike downhill after a tremendous effort going up," she'd once explained. The feeling usually subsided by the third or fourth day back.

"Well guess what?" Denise repeated, serious again. "One of the actresses in the Christmas special, the star of it, actually, I swear to God, she was in that video. She was one of the 'poor kids' seeing the sea for the first time."

"Which one?" I asked. "Juliette?"

"Juliette," Denise confirmed.

She didn't look surprised that I would remember not only the faces but the names of the kids in the charity video, but I still felt I had to justify it.

"Juliette is actually the only one I remember," I said. "I had a little crush on her."

"Me too," Denise said, and it caught me so off guard that I pretended both our confessions had overlapped and I hadn't heard hers.

"So she's famous?" I said. "That's nice. I bet she's able to see the ocean whenever she wants to now."

"You're not following me," Denise said. "I think Juliette was never a poor kid who hadn't seen the ocean. I mean, I guess at some point early on in life, she was, unless she was born on the beach like those turtles or something, but anyway, my point is: I think those videos were entirely scripted. I think the kids in the videos were all fake. All actors."

"I don't buy it," I said.

"You should look her up online. Juliette Corso. You'll see."

I went up the stairs to check the door. It was locked.

"It says she was already an actress four years ago?" I asked, and Denise said yes, that she'd spent a while doing research on Juliette these past few days.

"Maybe both things are true," I said, coming back down the stairs. "Maybe she was a child actor *and* had never seen the sea, and the charity helped her and her little brother."

"I guess it's possible," Denise said.

I'd often wondered what had happened to the kids in the Let Them Sea video. Despite my donation, I was ambivalent about their work, the work of one-time charities in general, as opposed to the charities that helped people, the same people, over and over, for as long as they needed it. Of course, the one-time charities left you with a memory to cherish, you got to have something for a little while, but then you had to pass it on for the next guy to enjoy, and I couldn't tell whether it was easier to live without something you'd never experienced or experience it once and go back to living without it. I hoped for the kids in the videos that they'd gotten to see the sea again and again, not just that one time. I realized I hadn't seen the sea myself since the father had died. It made sense that the father's being dead meant we would never take a road trip again. My mother hated driving.

"So you like girls?" I asked, because I wanted to think about something else.

"I don't like anybody," Denise said.

I decided it was time to focus on school and getting smarter. My German had reached a plateau that year. Herr Coffin was less encouraging than he'd been, even though I was still among his best students. One day after class I decided to speak to him directly, ask him if he thought I had what it took to be a German teacher. I'd never talked to any of my teachers one-on-one before, the way my siblings had done since kindergarten. I believed only great students were allowed to stay in the classroom after the bell to chat with teachers while they packed their satchels. I believed details about the day's lesson were discussed, points of view exchanged, extra reading suggested. But then in junior high I'd started seeing kids even dumber than me linger around after French or math hours. Did they think they were smarter than they were? Why did teachers allow their five-minute break between classes to be wasted on mediocre students? What did they have to say anyway? I'd asked Simone what she thought about this and she'd said that "regular kids" were only interested in talking about themselves, so she assumed the only reason they went to a teacher after hours was to seek advice about their future in a way they believed to be humble but was in fact a conspicuous play for attention, a way to verify they'd been noticed in spite of their lack of academic promise. "Even worse than that," Simone had said, "they talk to a teacher in the hope that the teacher's detected something unique about them. They know they suck, but they've been told everyone has a purpose in life, so they want to find out what theirs is. They think teachers have the means to decode the *particular* ways in which a student sucks and make them correspond to a career path the student should engage in. They think their sucking at something automatically indicates they'll be good at another thing."

I didn't think I fell into the category of students Simone had described. I didn't suck at German, and I was planning to go to Herr Coffin with a reasonable question, not for a pat on the back. I wanted his honest opinion. As I walked toward his desk, though, after everyone else had left the classroom, I became nervous about what Herr Coffin would say. What if I didn't have what it took to be a German teacher? What else was I remotely good at?

"Herr Coffin," I started, and I stopped awkwardly right there because I didn't know if I should address him in German. He spoke French and allowed it in class now sometimes, when we did translation from German texts into our native language, but still. I would make a better impression, given the question I wanted to ask him, if I put it in German. Or would it just sound like I was trying too hard? As far as I knew, no one had ever stayed beyond the bell to talk to him. There was no precedent for me to refer to. I tried German.

"Herr Coffin," I started again. *"Denken Sie, dass ich einen guten Deutschlehrer werden könnte?"*

Herr Coffin looked over his glasses at me.

"Is that what you aspire to?" he replied, not in German. He seemed to be trying to make sure I wasn't pranking him. "Are there any other lines of work you're considering?"

"Just German so far," I said.

Herr Coffin looked down at his satchel like I'd just delivered very sad news.

"When did you know you wanted to be a German teacher?" I asked him.

"Me?" Herr Coffin said after realizing there wasn't a third person in the room, genuinely surprised, it seemed, to be asked a personal question. "I never wanted to teach," he said. "The vocation of teaching is a rare and precious thing. In thirty-seven years of teaching, I have only met a handful of passionate professors." He paused there, as if to pay them a silent tribute. "The majority of my colleagues, though, are only passionate about the German *language,* the way I was. The way I am," he said, correcting himself immediately.

"So, what is it you wanted to do?" I asked.

"I love German. I wanted to know everything about German, every subtlety, every possible double entendre. I wanted to read Schlegel all day," he said, assuming I knew what he was talking about, "his own writings as well as his translations of Cervantes, and Shakespeare, and understand why he translated a certain thing a certain way and not another, figure out when it was that the sounds a German sentence made became more important than a word-for-word translation—"

"So you wanted to be a translator?" I said.

"No, not exactly. I just wanted to study, to keep studying. But it is a mistake to think that teaching a discipline is another way to keep learning about it."

Talking to Herr Coffin was starting to feel like talking to a sister.

"I'm not a good teacher," he added.

"I think you're great," I said.

The silence that sat between us at that point was made even more awkward when we heard one of my classmates, out in the hallway, distinctly call another a "fissured anus." Herr Coffin played deaf and went back to his satchel.

"I don't think I am really passionate about German," I admitted.

"Good," Herr Coffin said. "Then maybe you'll like teaching it."

The only practical advice I got out of Herr Coffin as I inquired about ways to improve my German was that I should look for "conversation partners," people who were fluent and would help me catch the rhythms of daily German and bask in its melodies.

"School makes you believe one needs years and years of classes to learn a language when what it really takes is a few months' immersion," Herr Coffin had said. "Immersion will forge an internal compass inside your brain," he'd added, moving his index finger left and right in the air to illustrate *compass* in a way that looked a lot more like *metronome*. "When the time comes for you to craft a sentence in German, the compass will tell you immediately if you're heading in the right direction." Herr Coffin hadn't offered to be my conversation partner, though, and now that the father was dead I didn't know anyone who spoke German, so I decided to place an ad on the Internet.

It seemed, however, that all websites that put you in touch with other people were dating platforms. Even those that advertised their goal as "building a stronger community" had pictures of romantic sunsets or older couples holding hands. Some were very specialized, targeted at businessmen and young women who never wanted to work, for instance, or at widows and widowers. At Calvinists, even. I thought maybe the proportion of Calvinists who spoke German would be greater than that of the general population, but the Calvinist website was for dating only, and I didn't want to date a Calvinist. Not that I had anything against Calvinists, but I'd been told they were serious people, and I didn't want anything serious. I wanted to focus on my studies.

I picked the website with the sunset. I had to create a profile first if I wanted to see anyone else's. While I was at it, I thought it would be a good idea to look for "conversation partners" for Aurore as well (she still couldn't drag herself out of the house). And for my mother too, maybe. By "conversation partners," I meant boyfriends of course. I set up a profile vague enough that it could work for all of us.

GENDER: n/a

SEEKS: men/women, friendship/casual/lifetime partner/
love/conversation

AGE: undisclosed

FIELD OF WORK: other

CARE TO SPECIFY?: humanities

HOBBIES: indoor activities

SMOKING: occasional

DRINKING: occasional

SAY A FEW WORDS ABOUT YOURSELF [200 MAX.]: Hello!
Guten Tag! Looking for bilingual friends (German,
French) for conversations, and a boyfriend between
ages 25 and 60. I would like to meet you if you like
talking about life and books, if you speak German, or
if you just want to have a good time. I have a yard and
a big house. I have no pets but they are welcome if you
have them. Looking forward to hearing from you!

Once our profile was set, I started browsing through the people listed in our zip code. Only one person had mentioned speaking German in his profile, and it was Herr Coffin. Herr Coffin
was seeking a life partner to have glasses of wine and take strolls
with along the river on the weekends. I tried to picture him as a
stepfather. I broadened the search to include the five zip codes ad-
jacent to ours—there was a button just for that. While I reviewed
the profile of a potential candidate for Aurore, I got my first alert.
A red heart-shaped icon with a white envelope drawn inside it
started beating in the right corner of the screen. I clicked on it. It
was from Alex79#69, the first person I'd added to my favorites

(you had to click a thunderbolt icon under the description some-one had written of him- or herself if you liked it). "Hi," the mes-sage said. That was it. I said hi back and Alex79#69 responded, "are you a boy or a girl? yr prfile is confusing."

"Girl," I said, with Aurore in mind—Alex was a twenty-eight-year-old man, too young for my mother. "24 years old. PhD in history."

"Wow," Alex79#69 said, and then he didn't say anything more.

OscarOscar showed more interest when I told him about Au-rore's academic achievements in first person, but then out of no-where sent this: "would kill mother 4bj rite now."

"do you speak german?" I asked OscarOscar, just to make sure I wasn't letting an opportunity go, though I guessed if he'd been of German descent, he would've called himself OskarOskar.

"if u blow me good, i speak all language u want," he re-sponded.

I decided to call it a day on the conversation partner hunt and looked up pictures of Juliette Corso, the destitute/child actor girl from the charity video, instead. Juliette had her own website but the Let Them Sea campaign was not listed among her "works." It was a pretty short list, actually, a couple TV movies, one com-mercial for a soda I had never heard of (the commercial had only aired in Belgium), and the movie Denise had seen her in over Christmas break. Her bio said she was from Clermont-Ferrand but had moved to Paris the year before to pursue her acting ca-reer. There was mention of her having a dog but nothing about a little brother.

Simone watched me struggle over math homework one evening and reminisced out loud about how easy life had been when she was in my grade.

"I thought every grade was easy for you," I said.

"I'm not talking about the work," Simone said, "but about the decisions that had to be made behind the work."

"What decisions?" I asked.

"Exactly," Simone said. "My point exactly. You're in eighth grade: you have no decision to make. You can just do the homework and not question whether you like it or not."

"I know I don't like it," I said.

I thought our conversation would end right there but Simone had an image she wanted to share with me.

"We're all in this funnel, see?" she said, and she grabbed my notebook and drew a funnel on a new page. "Here you are," she said, drawing an *X* at the top of the funnel and naming it Dory.

"Here I am." She drew another *X* a little lower down the funnel.

"What does the funnel represent?" I asked. "School?"

"The funnel represents our lives," Simone said. "The possibilities, the choices." She put her pen to where I was on the drawing. "When you're born, you virtually have an infinity of options, you get to swim at the top of the funnel and check them all out, you don't think about the future, or not in terms of a tightening noose, at least." She pointed at the bottom of the funnel. Then back at the top again, at the *X* that represented me. "You think, if anything, that the future will be even more of *that*, get you more freedom, more choices, because you see your parents pushing your bedtime farther and farther and you think, Well that's swell, you think it means being an adult will just be super, but then little by little, you get sucked to the bottom. You don't realize it at first. It starts with the optional classes you elect in high school. More literature or more physics? Should you start learning a third foreign language or get serious about music? And then choices you could've made for the future get ruled out without you knowing it, and you sink down to the bottom faster and faster, in a whirlwind of hasty decisions, until you write a PhD on something so specific you are one of twenty-five people who will ever understand or care about it."

"PhDs are not the only option," I said.

"But they're the slowest possible way down the drain," Simone said. "They buy you time, they allow you to believe for a while that the amount of specialization of your thesis verges on some kind of universality—and for the best academics, it does, or at least I want to think so—but then in the end it doesn't matter how brilliant you are, or that you think you can apply that brilliance to other areas of research: academia has already confined you to the one field you picked years before. That's why Aurore is all depressed. Aurore is reluctant to go there." Simone pointed at the neck of the funnel and made an *X* for Aurore right at the threshold.

"Isn't everybody?" I said.

"Don't be so sure, Dory. Some people enjoy being trapped. Some people need it."

The sound of her own words, or the thought of what she was about to say next, made Simone declare we were on to something and she requested that I start recording our exchange for her biography.

"I was working," I said.

"Let me repeat myself: what you do in eighth grade is of zero consequence."

"That's not what you used to say when you were in eighth grade."

"Well, I know better now. Trust me. That's the whole point of having a big sister."

I took the Dictaphone out of my desk drawer and pressed the REC button without even checking whether I wasn't erasing a previous interview. I didn't think I would really write Simone's biography, and the little part of me that thought I actually might also suspected that when the time came, my memory would be of more help than Simone's half-true recollections and funnel theories anyway. She cleared her throat.

"I think my biography should start with me gazing through the car window on our way back from summer vacation," she said.

"When you were practicing melancholy?"

"Right."

"I never really understood what you meant by that."

"Practicing melancholy meant looking at everything lying in front of me as if it were already belonging to a distant past."

"Okay."

"And making up stories in my head of highly unlikely futures. Trying to remove myself from the present at all costs. It's like the opposite of meditation, in a way."

"Why did you do that?"

"I still do it."

"Why?"

"As an exercise. To boost my imagination."

"You can't work on your imagination if you're in the present?"

"Well, to some extent, sure, you can. But you don't have that much control over the present—say, the weather, or what other people around you will do. You mostly go through the motions, you know? The possibilities are limited. There's too little room for analysis and most important, too little room for improvement, which is the key to all art."

"Do you have to imagine sad things to work on your melancholy?"

"Not necessarily."

"Why do you call it practicing melancholy then?"

"Because what goes on in your head when you step out of the present is always richer and more satisfying than what you come back to when you're done. That's the sad part. That's what's at the core of melancholy, not the things you actually imagine. The present is disappointing in a way that you can't act upon while it's happening. But once you've made a memory of something, you can throw away the meaningless parts and write better versions of it."

"Like Don Quixote?"

"Well I don't have *that* kind of imagination," Simone said sadly. "But sure. Yes. Don Quixote doesn't imagine sad stuff most of the time. When he thinks he's being knighted by the innkeeper, for example, that's not sad."

"I haven't actually read it," I said.

"Anyway. Most people find it sad that someone would think the present so mediocre that they'd be eager to retreat to a life that is only a figment of their imagination, which is what melancholics do. That's why they, like you, equate melancholy with sadness, but they're wrong. Practicing melancholy and being sad are two very different things." She paused there, before adding: "Also, being in the present sucks because there's always something sort of annoying going on in your body, whereas if you think in another time dimension, the body becomes less of a problem."

"What goes on in your body that annoys you?"

"Don't get me started."

"What does all of this have to do with the funnel?"

"Everything has to do with the funnel, Dory. We all have to go through the funnel and abandon things on the way down, and I want to be careful about what I leave behind. Lately I noticed I don't devote quite as much time to my imaginary conversations as I used to. It made me realize I'd gone farther down the funnel than I thought."

"Is that what you were crafting in your head on the car trips back home? Imaginary conversations?"

"No. The car trips were for imagining implausible futures. Or whole life stories for the people in the other cars. I had the imaginary conversations to fall asleep. I used to have a dozen of them going, and every night, depending on my mood, I'd pick one, rehearse it, polish it . . . that was the best way to fall asleep. I miss that."

"Why don't you do it as much as you used to?"

"I don't even know. That's my whole point. The funnel takes things away from you before you know it."

"Who were your imaginary conversations with?"

"That's a pretty private question."

"Don't you think the readers of your biography will want to know?"

"Well. There were quite a few different types of people. Real people, I mean, people that I knew, famous people, people I made up entirely . . . Some conversations were aspirational and some pure fantasy. Some I just worked on for a few days—they had to do with world events, you know, like, when they planned new reforms on the education system a couple years ago? I imagined a whole debate with the president on this. I knew the chances I would meet the president on my way to school the next day were pretty slim, but still, I imagined I would, and wrote a whole argument in my head, to be prepared when I did. A pretty powerful argument, as I recall. Some conversations were more plausible, like, when I had a frustrating teacher? A teacher I was smarter than but who pretended not to notice? Well, I imagined a whole conversation where I crushed him in front of the whole class. It was very satisfying. In my head, I had a conversation with Mr. Mohrt every single night of ninth grade, or close to it. I spent so much time on that one I'll probably remember it on my deathbed. Just talking about it now I have whole portions rushing back to my head."

"What about the people you made up? Were they like imaginary friends?"

"No, of course not. That would be sad."

"Who were they then?"

"Interviewers, mostly."

"Many?"

"Just two different ones. I mean, I didn't invent much about them to be honest, they were basically faceless, we didn't have conversations per se, they were just there to interview me. I'd pick one or the other, again, depending on my mood. One of them was just there to make me look good, ask the questions for which I had cool and smart answers. And the other one was more of an opponent, you know? I could just lash out at him and verbalize everything I thought was wrong about the world. They were both a great way to work some of my thoughts out."

"What kind of interviewer am I?"

"You don't challenge me much."

"So I'm the first kind. I'm here to make you look good."

"Both my fake interviewers made me look good. Those are imaginary conversations I'm talking about. I'm always going to have better arguments than the other guy."

"Always?"

"Yes, I don't think there really is a way around that. I tried not to make it too obvious for a while, to leave the other one a chance to say something as smart as me, but it's hard to be a hundred percent fair in an imaginary conversation, you know? It's like when you play both parts in a chess game because you can't find a partner."

"I know exactly what you mean," I joked. Simone didn't get it was a joke.

"Right? You'd think because it's your brain playing both sides, it's going to be hard picking which side you'd rather see winning, but then as the game goes on, you develop a fondness for the way you've been playing on one side of the board rather than the other. And I mean, of course you're always going to win the argument or have the best lines in your imaginary conversations. What would be the point otherwise? You're creating them for yourself, for your own personal use, so they should empower you a little. That's why people have them."

"You think everyone has them?"

"They have to. With their bosses, wives, everyone. Fictional characters."

"Dead people?" I asked.

"I don't know about that," Simone said. "I tried once. I think there's not as much satisfaction in it if there is no hope at all that you'll get to actually have the conversation with the person at some point."

"What dead people did you try with?"

I thought she would say the father but she said, "Romain Gary."

———

The only imaginary conversations I'd had had been reenactments of real ones gone bad, like the one I'd had with Sara Catalano at Daphné Marlotte's 111th birthday party when she'd called me a perv. I never invented from scratch. What I did sometimes to fall asleep, instead of inventing conversations with actual people, was to make up extra dialogues in the movies I loved. I often imagined having a part in them. But it was hard to write myself in and keep the movies good, so I tried to have a secondary role, minor but efficient, to not alter too much of the plot. I would only be there to change a small little thing that would make the main characters happier. Like, in *Return of the Jedi*, for example, I was a rebel who'd been made prisoner on the Death Star, and I'd managed to escape from my cell during the panic ensuing from the first rebel-fighter hits on the station. On my way out, I saw Luke dragging dying Vader to safety, and I helped him out with that. Instead of leaving Luke and his estranged father to have a rushed last exchange on the deck of the imperial shuttle, I managed to hurry them on board and save Vader while Luke flew us away from the Death Star. After we landed on Endor, I let them both have the space and time they needed to really make peace—they had a lot to talk about, and it seemed that the few seconds Luke and Vader had been given in the real version of *Return of the Jedi* didn't nearly cover everything. While they caught up, I just rested and lay on the grass and looked at the stars, and then when they were done, Luke took Vader and me to the Ewok party, and introduced me to Han and Leia, and then since Leia needed her own time to process the Vader situation, I meanwhile tried to make friends with Han. Han sort of sized me up; he felt a bit threatened (I looked good in the movie), but then I made a few jokes, told him my story, and proved myself to be a nice guy who was just happy to chill after everything he'd been through, and who, if Han wanted, could become a lifelong friend and would never put any moves on his lady. THE END. I say "THE END," but it was in fact never the end. I got caught up in my dialogue with Han Solo sometimes, and started to write a whole backstory for my character, added him to scenes in the previous two episodes, making room for him to potentially appear in the next ones if there ever were any. Maybe it was as Simone said when she talked about her imaginary conversations and how it was impossible not to keep the best lines for yourself: I guess it was hard, even with my intention to not ruin the shape of the movie, to be such a minor character. But what if my presence in the movies I rewrote in my head made the movies bad? Of course I'd be the only one to know, yet I still felt guilty reshaping perfectly good movies by joining the cast, so I started imagining that the movies could all exist as they were, with all the twists and action the audience needed, while I ran a parallel world where little things could always be adjusted and the characters I loved would come for a while and rest, away from the drama and the tears. It had always seemed unfair to me, the amount of complications and bad luck that writers stuck my favorite characters with. And I understood it had to do with Aristotle's rules of fiction etc., but still. If I'd cheered and felt sad for a character, he automatically had a place in my parallel world of movies where nothing traumatic ever happened.

That winter, Denise finally lost someone. She couldn't wait to tell me. Because it was her grandmother who'd died and not someone young, she said it was not such a big deal and fell "within the natural order of things," but still, she'd been fond of the old lady and was going to put all she had into her eulogy.

"You should come," she told me. "The funeral is Thursday."

"I can't skip school," I said.

"You skip it all the time to run away to Paris or whatever," she said, and she was right. I just happened to not be as interested in attending funerals as she was.

"I'll see what I can do."

We were at the school cafeteria. Denise had taken up the habit of joining me there, even though she never ate anything. She said she only ate in the mornings, but I think some days she skipped breakfast too.

"You should eat a little before gym class," I said. I knew her schedule. "Have a bite of my rice."

"Why would I do that?" Denise said. "I'm fat enough as is."

"You're the skinniest person I have ever met."

"Well, I know I'm not fat *relative* to the others," she said. "But I'm still fatter than I'm comfortable with."

"Don't you want to have tits and stuff?"

"Am I your girlfriend now? What do *you* care if I have tits?"

"I'll come to your grandmother's funeral if you eat some of my rice," I said.

"My parents tried blackmail," Denise said. "Doesn't work."

I knew I wasn't putting enough heart into convincing her. My mind was elsewhere. It seems to me sometimes, when I look back on it, that all I wanted to do in eighth grade, whenever I sat anywhere, was to readjust my boxer shorts, and I couldn't bring myself to do it casually, the way other boys did, reaching down there unapologetically for quick positional fixes and scratches. Since my conversation with Aurore, I'd been constantly checking my penis for bumps and depressions, but it didn't seem like Rose had given me any of the sex diseases I'd read about on the Internet. I didn't really know when I could stop looking for signs and consider myself out of the woods, though. It had been four months.

"Tits . . . ," Denise said. "What would I do with tits anyway? I get why some girls want them. I mean, Sara and Stephanie, they carry theirs well, you know? It's not disgusting or anything. But me? What am I supposed to do with tits? Lean against the lockers and wait for a boy to notice them? I don't think so. No. Doesn't suit my personality. Tits are not for everybody."

"My sister says personality is a myth," I said.

"Which one?"

"All of them," I said. "All fake."

"No, I meant, which sister?"

"Oh. Simone," I said.

Denise only knew my sisters from a distance, of course, like most people, but unlike most people, she had no trouble keeping track of which sister thought or had said what, while even teachers who'd had them all in their classes one after the other talked about them like a three-headed entity, sometimes asking me in a hallway to congratulate Aurore for an article Berenice had written, or telling my whole class how my sister Aurore Mazal had once shared with her own grade incredible mnemonics for the Napoleonic wars (mnemonics that encompassed chronology, outcomes, and even some coalition details all at once) while I knew it was Simone who'd come up with them.

"Did Simone start applying to schools yet?" Denise asked.

I said she had, but only to the best preparatory courses in Paris. Simone still couldn't tell what she would be famous for, so she'd decided the best thing to do while she figured it out should be the most impressive. The school that impressed her most was the École Normale Supérieure in Paris, but to even try to get in there, you had to go for two years in what was called a preparatory class, whose workload ranked as one of the highest in the world (or at least that's what the Wikipedia page said). Then you could give the admission exam a shot (it was one of the most competitive exams in the academic world as well). All that to study some more. Simone kept talking about how it was the most prestigious school in the world for humanities, but when people (the butcher, neighbors) asked me what was new with my family and I told them about Simone's latest ambition, they never seemed to know what the École Normale Supérieure was, and it made me sad that Simone was so delusional about the school's fame. When I'd told her about the École Normale Supérieure, Denise had said she knew exactly what it was, but I'm pretty sure she'd lied, because she hadn't expanded any on the subject until recess the next day, when she'd proceeded to list for me all the famous intellectuals who'd studied there, then told me that the workload in the preparatory classes was one of the highest in all the world—these weren't the kinds of things you'd say unless you'd read them the night before on Wikipedia.

"I'm sure she'll get in wherever she wants," Denise said. I said I didn't think Simone doubted that either.

Denise didn't eat any of my rice, but that night at dinner, I still asked my mother if I could skip school and go to a funeral on Thursday.

"Who died?" she asked.

"A friend's grandmother," I said.

"That Dennis friend?"

"Actually, it's Denise."

"Oh, I see," my mother said. "And did you know Denise's grandmother at all?"

I lied and said I'd seen her around school a couple of times, a nice old lady.

"And you want to go to that funeral so you can pay your respects to the nice old lady or for moral support of the younger lady?"

I thought maybe Aurore had told my brothers that I'd gone to bed with a girl—they'd been looking at me differently the last few weeks, and now they looked almost interested when my mother said "the younger lady."

"I don't know." I shrugged. "Does it matter?"

"I don't think funerals are such great activities for teens, that's all," my mother said. "I'm just making sure you'd go for the right reasons."

"And which of the two is the better reason to go?" I asked. "The dead person or the living person?"

It was a smarter argument than I'd thought. In fact, I hadn't even thought about it as an argument, I'd just said it mechanically, earnestly, believing there would be a correct answer to my question and that someone around the table would give it to me. But no one said anything, and I realized I'd been deep by accident. I shouldn't boast, though. I guess pretty much everything one said in a conversation about death came out with extra meaning.

"Maybe if one of your sisters came with you," my mother ended up saying. "To make sure you're okay . . . Aurore?"

Aurore looked up from her plate, surprised, it seemed, to be visible.

"Why would I go to Dory's friend's grandmother's funeral?" she asked.

"Come on," my mother said. "He went to your PhD defense."

"I'm not saying I wouldn't go to *Dory's* funeral," Aurore said.

"I'll go with him," Simone offered.

"But the ceremony is going to be in a church," I told her.

"Of course it's going to be in a church. Everyone's bloody Catholic around here. So what?"

"Nothing. I thought you'd mind. You hate churches."

"I hate *the* Church, it's different," Simone said. "People can

go to church though, obviously, as long as they don't try to sell
it to me." She paused there and added, matter-of-factly, "Mom
goes to church sometimes. Who cares?"

My mother didn't say anything. I didn't know when her
churchgoing had stopped being a secret. Maybe it had never
really been one.

We were still eating when Berenice called to say she'd been
accepted into a PhD program in Chicago. My mother picked up
the phone in the kitchen all cheerful but her face turned to worry
right away. "But you already have a PhD," we heard her say into
the phone, in the same tone actors used in movies when their
character couldn't make sense of someone's death and said, *"But
he was so young!"*

I don't know what Berenice's response to that was exactly, we
couldn't hear her part, but the way the phone call was summed
up to us when my mother sat back at the table was that Berenice
had said American PhDs were much more competitive and prestigious than French ones. Aurore didn't pick up on that. Leonard
didn't either, even though he was in the middle of writing his
own dissertation. There was a moment of silence. We all looked
down at our noodles.

"Climbing back up the funnel," Simone said. She said it to
me, specifically, but loud enough that everyone around the table
could hear, yet no one asked what funnel Simone was referring
to. Maybe they were all familiar with the funnel image and were
just picturing themselves in it, how close they were to the noose.

"Why am I still eating this?" Aurore said after a while, under
her breath. "I'm not hungry anymore."

"What time's that funeral at?" Simone asked me.

"I don't know," I said. "Sometime in the morning."

Simone noted it would be the first time she'd skip school for a reason other than being sick. "I guess it's about time," she said.

She only had two months of high school left.

———

The funerals I'd been to before hadn't lasted more than half an hour, but Denise's grandmother's was near PhD defense in length. Everyone had something to say about her, and then there were prayers and songs. I tried to pay attention when Denise went up onstage for her eulogy, but her voice was so frail, and Simone and I had sat so far back, almost by the church's door, that it was hard to follow. She talked about how her grandmother would never know the end of a soap opera she'd been watching every day for more than twenty years, and how painful that was to think about. About how no matter how old you were when you died, you always left unfinished tasks behind. I glanced at Simone while Denise spoke, to see whether she was repressing laughter or rolling her eyes. Simone's physical reactions to speeches usually helped me know what I should think of them. Simone was actually involved in Denise's words. When Denise said that her grandmother, knowing she didn't have much time left, had stopped reading new books because she couldn't stand the idea of dying in the middle of one without ever finding out how it ended, and that she'd spent her last weeks rereading the books she'd loved, Simone even nodded.

When we gathered around the hole for Denise's grandmother, the grave diggers were on their cigarette break, ten or so graves away, waiting for us to leave to finish the morning job. I wondered if they were ever told about the people they dug holes for—how old they'd been and how they'd died—and if that determined the distance at which they thought it was okay to take their cigarette breaks. They hadn't stood that close to us at the father's funeral.

"What should I tell Denise?" I whispered in Simone's ear as the undertakers lowered the casket with ropes. "Condolences or congratulations on her eulogy?"

"That guy is not doing it right," Simone said, looking at one of the four pallbearers. "He's standing parallel to the grave. He should be diagonal. He's going to throw his back something nasty."

"How can you tell?"

"Or throw himself down in the hole with the coffin."

She seemed disappointed when nothing dramatic happened to the pallbearer. She clicked her tongue behind her teeth and glanced at her watch. She could still make it to philosophy class, she said.

"You're supposed to stay with me and make sure I'm okay," I said.

"Are you okay?" she asked. I said I was.

After Simone left, I went up to Denise and told her how much I'd loved her eulogy.

"Won't bring Grandma back," Denise said. She was in worse shape than when she'd just found out about her grandma's being dead.

"It didn't smell like anything," she said, and at first, I didn't understand what she meant. "You said there were dead-body smells that came out of the coffin, but it just smelled like church and incense."

I'd never seen Denise cry and, like I said before, wouldn't have bet on its being possible. She wasn't shy about crying though, didn't wipe her cheeks or hide her eyes—she kept them open and fixed on me. I put a hand on her arm. I could've closed my hand around it and touched index finger to thumb it was so thin. She didn't like the contact and shook it off.

"I thought I saw your sister," she said.

"She couldn't stay. She told me to give you her condolences."

"How sweet of her."

People started leaving the cemetery but Denise wanted to stay and watch the grave diggers fill the hole. I sat with her on the next gravestone, that of a man who, according to the engraving, had died on a cruise. As the four men shoveled soil into the hole, I noticed Denise's lips were moving, and when they stopped moving I asked what kind of prayer she'd just said.

"What do you mean what *kind*?" she said.

"I mean, what was it? What did you ask for?"

"It's not like that," Denise said. "You don't *ask* for things."

"I see," I said, although her answer confused me. I'd always thought the point of believing in God was that you got to ask him things and see if you'd done good by him, if he loved you back and if your faith was real depending on whether he gave you the things you'd asked for or not. I took a little box of dental wax out of my pocket and started to roll some between my fingers. The inside of my lower lip felt ripped, rough and salty; the braces kept getting caught in the flesh.

"Did everyone tell you to be strong, after your father died?" Denise asked.

"No one really told me anything," I said. Images of the father's toothless period started rushing through my head. I pushed them away as I stuck the wax to my lower braces.

"It's such bullshit," Denise said. "They say 'don't be sad,' and 'it's the way of life' and all, that I should be strong, and that 'it's so easy to let yourself go' while it takes courage and strength to choose to be happy and hold on to the small pleasures of the present . . . as if suffering was something weak people did, you know? I don't get that."

"They worry about you," I said.

"Courage my ass. It doesn't take courage to be in the moment. What really takes guts is to live each day as if you were going to hang around for the next ten years at least. Account for something. Live up to something. Now, *that* is hard. *That* requires a little more pondering and reflection, a little more strength."

The wax provided immediate relief. Not only did it protect my lower lip from more brace spearing, but it numbed the preexisting pain right away. The box said it was the cold-mint flavor of the wax that did that. Very few things in life provided immediate relief, I thought.

"Simone—she also thinks the present is dumb," I said. I refrained from telling Denise about the funnel theory.

"Of course it's dumb. What's there to enjoy?"

"Well I guess you don't like eating much, so that takes a lot out of it," I said.

The grave diggers were working at the hole cautiously, like there might be a chance Denise's grandmother would wake up and complain about the noise.

"You could run away with me next time, if you want," I said. I didn't mean it. "We could go to Paris or something."

"Really? We would stay at your sister's?"

I tried to drown the offer I'd just made under a lot of words, to divert Denise's attention.

"Berenice is moving to America next year," I said. "She's going to get a second PhD."

"But if we go to Paris before summer break," Denise said, "she would still be living there, right?"

"Her apartment is very small. A bedroom, really. She doesn't have money for more. She lied about having a good job. I mean, she got fired from her good job a long time ago."

It was the first time I told anyone a secret I'd promised to keep, but I didn't feel bad about it. My family's secrets were not really interesting.

"Well, we'll find somewhere else to stay then," Denise said. "When are you going next?"

I mumbled something about Easter. It seemed far enough away. I didn't think Denise would forget my invitation by then but I was pretty sure she would chicken out, realize she needed her therapist and her meds, and in the meantime, there was no harm letting her dream of a Paris trip a little.

"I'm sorry I lied about the smells," I said.

———

Most of the replies I got to my Internet ad were from older men who thought the ad was for a whole family to adopt. One of them couldn't have children, he explained. He'd been left by the love of his life twenty years before because he "couldn't conceive." I wondered if that meant he was impotent. It felt insensitive to ask.

His name was Daniel, which I thought was boring, but in a good way, like he would be fine doing the crosswords while my mother read the rest of the newspaper. He wanted to see a picture of her and I described her the best I could—there was a picture of her on the Internet now, because she'd been featured in an article on the city hall website about what people randomly picked on the street thought about the new bike lanes in the center of town, but the picture didn't do my mother justice, I thought, and I preferred not to send Daniel the link. I told him she was ready to date again but didn't know it yet, and that he should wait for her outside her office one day (I gave him the address) and pretend he and I had never corresponded. I told him my mother liked orchids, any movie by Jacques Tati, and the color black. The ball was in his court.

Later that week, my mother came home from work with him. I immediately understood that she'd figured I'd dug him out of the Internet and brought him back to teach me a lesson, but Daniel thought she'd invited him over out of genuine interest. He couldn't believe how well his moves were working.

"Dory, this is my friend Daniel," my mother said. "Daniel, this is my youngest son I was telling you all about."

"Very nice to meet you, young man," Daniel said, and he actually winked at me.

"I invited Daniel for dinner, I hope you don't mind."

Daniel looked older than he'd said he was. I guess my mother, to him, was young.

My mother called all my siblings to join us in the living room and welcome our guest.

"Daniel, why don't you tell my kids all about the book you mentioned working on while I go fix us some drinks?" she said. She disappeared into the kitchen and left us alone with Daniel. Daniel did as he was told and talked about his passion for photography and his ongoing project, a whole book made of pictures he'd taken and compiled over the years of clouds assuming all sorts of poetic shapes.

"What the hell is a poetic shape?" Simone asked, but Daniel only offered her a little laugh for an answer, as if Simone were being cute, too young to possibly understand the term *poetic*.

"I suppose you must be a great Ansel Adams fan," Jeremie said.

"Well ain't that funny!" Daniel marveled. "That is exactly what your mother said! I'd better check that fellow's work . . . You gotta keep an eye out for the competition."

Daniel retrieved a piece of paper from a pocket and seemed happy to take note of the name, unaware that Jeremie's spelling A-N-S-E-L for him was the last time he would ever hear his voice.

"So when you say you have a passion for photography, you mean you're passionate about using a camera, the technology of it, but you're not that interested in the history of the medium," Leonard said.

As far as I could tell, Leonard wasn't trying to be mean, but his remark made Daniel uneasy. He glanced at me for support. I had nothing.

"Well I do enjoy the work of certain contemporary photographers," he said, "like uh, from *National Geographic* and such."

"Would you say your approach to photography is more autobiographical or metaphorical?" Simone asked.

"I'm not sure I understand what you mean," Daniel admitted.

"Well it's obviously not documentary oriented. What gets you to take a picture of one cloud and not another?"

Daniel seemed to pull himself back together a bit, like he'd heard that question before and had worked out an answer over time.

"I find myself more attracted to cumulonimbuses," he explained. "They draw the most dramatic shapes, whole scenes even, sometimes, if you look closely and keep an open mind."

"So it's some sort of an imaginary approach," Simone said, more like a note to herself than anything else. Daniel looked satisfied to have a new word to talk about his artistic process and agreed with her.

"And have publishers shown any interest in your work yet? Galleries?" Aurore asked.

My mother came back before Daniel could answer, carrying a bowl of Provençal olives and a couple of golden drinks. Daniel seemed relieved to see her and moved to his right on the couch as she handed him his drink, to make some room for her, but she didn't notice and went back to the kitchen to grab two extra chairs, one to serve as a table for the drinks and olives, the other for her to sit on.

Daniel went at the olives like they could provide him with clever answers to my siblings' questions. Every time he was asked something, he took an olive from the bowl and ate it before he would give a response. He tried to shift the conversation at some point and asked us all if we had boyfriends or girlfriends. He seemed delighted to find out none of us did. It gave him the opportunity to slide in a fact he thought we'd find witty and amusing.

"Aha!" he said. "All smart and good-looking, and yet all single! I guess the great misunderstanding between the sexes hasn't skipped a generation! Did you know that in some Indian tribes, men and women *actually* spoke different languages? I'm not kidding you guys." No one had accused him of such a thing. "They couldn't even agree on grammar!"

There was hope, I thought. Daniel knew something, and it was something that I'd personally never heard before. Different languages for men and women, within the same society? That sounded quite promising. Maybe we could last all dinner on that topic and have a good time.

"Yes," Leonard said. "Some tribes do have different languages for men and women. Except they understand each other and the men address the women in the women's language, which also happens, most of the time, to be the *maternal* language. The presence of two different languages doesn't necessarily mean incomprehension between people, or inability to communicate. Think about those regions where everyone speaks two languages, like Catalunya, for instance. Kids are just raised bilingual. If anything, it is a tremendous advantage for them on a cognitive level. And you could actually argue that men and women learning all about the subtleties of the other sex's language helps them reach a better understanding of each other."

Daniel grabbed another olive and thought about Catalunya.

"I guess I'd never looked at it that way," he said.

"Where did you go to school?" Simone asked.

With that, my brothers and sisters regained control of the conversation and Daniel swallowed another olive. The olive situation was reaching a critical point. A few years before, Berenice, who was then already fluent in Spanish, had introduced us to a saying Spanish people had about the last slice of pie in the dish, the last piece of bread on the table, the last olive in the bowl: they called it the slice, or the piece, or the olive, of shame. Shame is what you were supposed to feel if you grabbed and ate the last piece of something, and the only way to make it less shameful was to acknowledge that you were conscious of grabbing the shameful item, or to publicly state your intention to do so in order to allow a chance for someone who wanted it more than you to make him- or herself known, which was something that never happened because most of the time people were happy to let another person deal with the shame. My parents had loved the idea. "Shame is a good thing," the father had declared, "people should feel more of it more often," and we'd adopted the Spanish saying without reservation. Something we had only considered vaguely impolite became shameful through the magic of a foreign proverb. One that Daniel was obviously not familiar with. Everyone was looking to see if he would eat the olive of shame without mentioning it. If he asked whether one of us wanted the olive, he would get a pass, I thought, but I wanted him to make a joke about it (the father, for instance, would've sliced the olive in two to let someone else get the half olive of shame), because a joke would surprise my siblings and possibly raise my mother's interest. When he took the last olive in the bowl, he only looked disappointed there weren't more. Simone shook her head judgmentally, and there were some unspoken *I knew it*s around the living room. All Daniel saw was that the end of the olives meant it was time for dinner.

I didn't say a word at the table, remaining a silent witness to my siblings' catastrophic evaluation of Daniel. They inquired about his politics, his taste in books, his hobbies. I wanted Daniel to shine, to have anecdotes about once meeting a famous writer, invent one if needed, but he seemed incapable of sharing anything of interest. I wondered if one could really reach Daniel's age and not have a single compelling story to tell.

After he left, thanking us for a lovely evening, Simone noted it had been a while since we'd had a condescension fest. I felt I'd been at the center of that particular one.

"Dory really is to thank for tonight's entertainment," my mother said.

"How did you meet that guy?" Aurore asked.

"My guess is through the magic of the Internet." My mother was staring at me. "Am I right, Dory?"

"He looked smarter in his profile picture," I said in my defense.

"I believe you were fooled by the white hair," Simone said.

"By the way," my mother asked me, "how old do you think I am exactly?"

"I'm sorry," I said.

"That guy was like seventy years old."

"He looked like Alfred Stieglitz," Aurore noted.

"You should've told him that."

"And spelled the name out for him."

I apologized again.

"It's all right, honey. At least your brothers and sisters had fun."

That night, my Internet privileges were revoked indefinitely.

———

On Sundays, I got bored. Not the way Simone used to get bored as a child (because there was no school on Sundays) but because Sundays made it even more obvious that everyone in our house was capable of finding ways to entertain themselves but me. Years earlier, our mother had tried to get us interested in gardening. She'd failed instantly with my siblings, whereas I'd planted tomatoes to make her happy. "Tomatoes are easy," she'd said, but nothing had ever come out of the ground. I'd never attempted planting anything again, but I'd maintained the habit of checking the yard on Sunday mornings. I picked up dead leaves, mowed the lawn. I didn't mow the lawn much, actually. It was hard work, and no one noticed or cared whether I did it or not, but I looked at how much the lawn had grown over the course of a week. Because our yard was the barest one in the neighborhood, save for the cherry tree, which could sustain itself without human help, my weekly inspection was not much more exciting than the indoors boredom I was fleeing. It was equally boring, in fact, but the silence of the yard was less heavy than the one in our house. There was hope it could be broken.

Our yard looked out on a paved alley and then across it onto another yard, in which all sorts of vegetables and flowers grew. The reason I only hung out in our yard on Sunday mornings and not in the afternoons was that I knew the owner of that perfect yard tended to it on Sunday afternoons, and I didn't want him to see me and be sad for me for having a yard that sucked. I didn't care that it sucked, and there's nothing worse than people pitying you for things you don't even yourself consider upsetting.

There wasn't a lot of traffic in the alley but to some people it was a shortcut to somewhere, or a way to pay your boy- or girl-friend a backyard visit without the whole town's knowing about it. The ones who used the alley as a shortcut said hello, and the other ones pretended I wasn't standing in my backyard and kept on running to their secret destinations, convincing themselves I hadn't seen them. That Sunday, Porfi approached our fence, waving. Porfi wanted to be called by his last name, Porfi, but his first name was Charles. "Can I come in?" he said.

I walked to the gate, unsure I even knew how to open it. It was locked and there was no key in the keyhole.

"What do you want?" I asked through the bars of the gate. I'd known Porfi all my life, but our only interaction so far had occurred in grammar school, when I'd asked him if he was myopic and he'd gone running in tears to our teacher. "He called me myopic! He called me myopic!" he'd cried. "Well, are you myopic, Charles?" our teacher had asked him, and Porfi'd admitted he didn't know. "You do wear glasses," the teacher had observed. "You might very well be. And *myopic* is not an insult. Not last time I checked it wasn't." Porfi had replied that what made an insult an insult was the way it made you feel when you heard it, and the teacher had said, "I really don't think you're right about that," and that had caused Porfi to resent her as much as he resented me. I'd always assumed Porfi hated me because I'd called him myopic that day. He'd always picked a seat as far away from me as possible, within the limited number of seats he and I were allowed to choose from, given we were both myopic and asked by our teachers to sit in the front row with the rest of the vision-impaired.

"Are you and Denise Galet a couple?" Porfi asked me that Sunday without further introduction. There was a combination of fear and immediate relief in his voice as the words freed themselves. He'd done his part expressing his interest in Denise. The next step was for me to handle. That he was in love with Denise came as quite a shock to me. I'd always assumed no one even liked Denise—she openly despised most of those who'd tried to come into contact with her over the years—or even noticed our existences anymore, but I tried not to look too surprised. I didn't want to risk insulting Porfi's feelings.

"We're not a couple," I said as quickly as possible, in case hesitation on my part could change his mind about loving Denise. I'd gotten to like Denise somewhat, but the idea that someone else wanted to share recess with her, try to make her happier, was a load off my shoulders. Denise could be quite a downer sometimes.

Porfi carried with him a spiral notebook in which he'd glued pictures he assured me were pictures of Denise, but he'd taken them from such a distance, and with such shitty cameras (those disposable ones you could buy for a few bucks at the supermarket, he admitted), that you really had to believe it to see it.

"I took that picture of her just outside school last week," he said, pointing at a dark shadow the size of my pinky nail that he assured me was Denise leaning on one of the bike racks outside the school's main gate. "She's always very early," he explained. "Even when her first class is at eight a.m., she gets there before the gate is even opened. The janitors never open the gate before seven fifty."

"Is that so?" I said.

Porfi nodded, a serious nod. He'd learned that fact the hard way. On the next page of his notebook, he'd taped a copy of Denise's weekly schedule.

Pages of the notebook had titles like "Books Denise Has Read," with pictures of dust jackets Porfi had likely cut out from catalogs. The "Known Relationships" page only bore Denise's parents' names and mine.

"How long have you been in love with Denise?" I asked.

"Almost since I started junior high," Porfi said. "I spotted her feeding the birds, you know, with you, and I thought it was a very cute thing to do. But I could never talk to her. She's always running right out of class when the bell rings, to meet you in that staircase, and then she gets back at the last minute. I thought about maybe passing a note to her in class, starting a conversation that way, but I don't know. It seems corny. And other people could intercept it, and I don't think Denise would like that one bit."

"What do you like about her?" I said. "Aside from her feeding the birds and stuff."

"Well I don't know. She's smart, I guess. She reads so many books."

"I didn't know you liked reading," I said.

"Well I don't. But I like that she likes it. And I'm not as smart as her, but I have other skills."

"Like what?"

"Like mechanics, electricity. I'm good at repairing things. Do you know if there's something Denise needs to have repaired? Like a lamp or something? I'm good with lamps. That could be a good way that you could put us in contact," Porfi said. I admired him for being so open about his feelings.

"She never said anything about a lamp," I said. "But I'll ask."

"Don't be too obvious about it, though. I don't want to become a joke between you guys."

"Why would you?"

"I don't know. People are cruel. I'm sure you can be too."

I wondered if he was referring to the day I'd called him myopic. I thought about saying, like I'd said at the time, that I had meant no harm asking about his eyesight but had merely been seeking information since I'd been told myself that I would soon need glasses, but then this guy Victor came out of nowhere on his bicycle and nearly ran Porfi down. The notebook where Porfi had compiled all of his Denise knowledge slipped from his hands and fell to the ground, open.

"What are you guys doing, talking between bars?" Victor yelled at us, although he'd turned around and stopped his bike a mere yard from where we stood. Porfi had managed to pick up his precious notebook without Victor's seeing what it contained, and he seemed grateful to all gods that the notebook had made it back safe to his arms, as though it could've broken in the fall.

"Are you like a couple now?" Victor went on. "Are the bars a metaphor for the prison of gayness you always felt creeping up around you, depriving you of a chance to ever fit in?"

"Get lost, Victor," Porfi said, and his confidence impressed me, considering the fact he was holding something against his chest, first of all, in a very girly manner, something that, second, could've caused Victor to make fun of him for eternity if he ever discovered what exactly it was. Victor was in my German class, because his parents thought he was smart and German was the choice of smart kids, but Victor wasn't smart.

"Chill out, ladies," Victor said, "go get yourselves a sense of humor," and he went on his way.

"Well," I told Porfi after Victor had disappeared at the end of the alley. "That was brave of you. Not quite sure it convinced him we weren't flirting, though."

"It's fine. I prefer Victor believing I'm gay to knowing I'm in love with Denise. People don't like Denise very much."

I wanted to say I would've preferred Victor to know the truth than believe I liked boys, but then why hadn't I said anything in my own defense?

"I guess she's too ... unconventional for people," Porfi went on.

"She's unconventional all right," I said.

"Hold that thought!" Porfi said, licking his index finger to flip through his notebook 'til he landed on a blank page. He took a pencil out of the chest pocket of his overalls; pressed the lead to the top left corner of the page, ready for dictation; and raised his black eyes back to me. There was a minute of silence.

"What do you want me to say?" I ended up asking. "It seems like you know more about Denise than I do."

"Don't be so modest. I don't even know what you guys talk about all the time. Like, what are the topics of conversation that she likes? You have to help me out here."

I thought about all my conversations with Denise, tried to see a pattern. Porfi mistook the time I spent coming up with one for reluctance to share my knowledge.

"What do you want in exchange?" he said.

"In exchange for what?"

"Tips. To make Denise like me."

"I don't want anything in exchange," I said, and it was the truth. I just didn't know what to tell Porfi that could help his courtship. There were a certain number of things I knew about Denise—the medication and dosages she took for her depression and anxiety, that she'd had a crush on a girl named Juliette in a video a few years before, that her favorite movie was *Au Revoir les Enfants*—but it seemed like they would all be turnoffs to Porfi. I was looking for a way to be fair to Denise, and it kept eluding me.

"Come on," Porfi said. "We all want something. I have a skateboard I don't use that I could give you. Dirty magazines."

I pretended to be interested in those because you had to, if you were a boy, but when Porfi listed the titles I lied and said I had them all already.

It wasn't only that I didn't want anything in exchange for my tips, I realized. I just wasn't sure I wanted anything at all, and the thought made me dizzy, the way I felt before a test I hadn't studied enough for. I looked behind me at the yard as if it could help me figure out what I wanted from life. It didn't.

"Do you speak German?" I ended up asking Porfi. I was sorry for myself for being unable to think of anything more exciting, so I tried to be mysterious about it. The way I said it, you could have believed I was assembling a team of spies for a secret mission in Germany.

"Of course I don't speak German," Porfi said. "I have a little Spanish though. My grandfather was from Argentina."

"That won't work," I said, still looking at the bare rectangle of dirt where I'd once tried to grow tomatoes.

"Does Denise want a German-speaking boyfriend?"

"No," I said. "I was asking for myself."

"What do you need a Kraut for?"

I turned my face back to Porfi.

"Would you be interested in skipping school with Denise and me to go to Paris around Easter?" I asked.

Porfi said that anything that could get him closer to Denise, he was ready to try.

"I'll tell her you want to come with us then," I said. "I will leave the whole thing about how you love her out of the conversation at first, see how she reacts."

"Test the waters," Porfi said.

"Right. I'll tell you what she thinks."

"Thanks, man," Porfi said, and then he extended his hand through the bars of the gate for me to shake.

"Of course," I said.

"And you know what?" he said as he was getting ready to leave. "That old lady there, Daphné Marlotte. She speaks German, I think. Her husband was a Nazi or something, back in the day. Or she was. If that helps you any."

"Well obviously, he was kidding," Denise said after I told her all about Porfi's visit.

"He looked pretty smitten to me," I said.

"Don't use that word. It's disgusting."

"Fine. He looked *honest*. And he had all these pictures of you."

"That's so creepy. Tell him I don't want him to take any more without my permission."

"So you would agree to having one taken *with* your permission? I'm sure he would love that."

"Don't be silly," Denise said.

I might've only wanted to see things that weren't there, but it seemed to me Denise was trying to hide being flattered that a boy was interested in her behind her feigned disbelief and her real disappointment that the boy in question was only Porfi.

"What else should I tell him?" I said. "Would you agree to him going to Paris with us?"

"That part's up to you, really," she said. "You're the brain behind the whole Paris operation."

The rest of recess we talked about Denise's impression that she had two different heads.

"I often feel like I have a smaller head inside of this one," she said, "that people don't see. It is smaller but it has more things in it than the other one and so it keeps trying to repel the outer head and take its place."

"You're sure it's not just a headache?" I asked, because it sounded mostly painful.

"You really can be quite dumb," Denise said.

"That's exactly why you should start seeing other people," I said, and then she told me I had a piece of breakfast stuck in my braces, which I'm not sure was true (Denise used that line any time I said something she didn't want to respond to). She asked me what I thought happened to kids who died with their braces on.

"Do you think they get buried with them? That seems wrong for some reason, but I doubt they have special orthodontists for the dead," she said.

I said I didn't care because I didn't plan on dying too soon.

"Well I don't plan on wearing braces," she said.

"You always manage to keep the mood so light," I said.

"I was kidding," she said. "See? You can never tell if someone is kidding you or not."

"I'm sorry I can't always tell when you're seriously suicidal or just trying to entertain me," I said.

I wasn't really apologizing, but Denise took it to heart and said it was okay, that she knew she was the one who should be sorry. "I know I'm a nightmare," she said. She was good at turning a thing you said into yet another example of how complicated she was, but I knew that she didn't get pleasure in doing that either. I also knew the next thing she would say would be a peace offering, something she didn't really mean but believed I would be happy to discuss.

"Does Porfi really keep track of everything I read?"

—

Denise didn't meet me at recess for days in a row and I thought Porfi had to be doing something right. Either he had built up the nerve to go up to her on her way down to our staircase or Denise, now aware of being watched lovingly, had lingered a little longer than usual in the classroom to make it easier for him and he'd taken his chance. I didn't want to feel lonely, I just wanted to be happy for them, but it's not that easy controlling your feelings and I'd gotten used to having someone to talk to, even if only about how little there was to look forward to in life. I wondered if there was a chance I was in love with Denise, but even in the privacy of my own thoughts, the idea seemed ludicrous and I couldn't consider it seriously for more than a few seconds.

On the third day without Denise, I missed talking to someone so much that I went up to Simone after school to see if she wanted to have an interview. She was working at her desk and dismissed my request. "I appreciate that you're taking the biography seriously," she said, "but when I'm busy, you can just do some research. Go interview other people about me. See what they have to say."

Aurore and my mother were out and my brothers' door was closed as usual. I stood in front of it and tried to come up with a way to disturb them without their seeing it as a disturbance. My brothers scared me a little. I felt I had to have something important to say if I was to request their attention. From a very early age, my sisters had made me understand that I wasn't as smart as them but that it didn't matter, that I had other qualities, whereas I feared the reason my brothers never talked to me was because they didn't think I was interesting enough. I'm not sure my sisters and I were close, but I knew my brothers and I definitely weren't, and I couldn't tell whether we never talked because we had nothing in common, or if it was because we never talked that we never found out if we had something in common. Their school grades seemed to suggest they were as smart as the girls, but they never mentioned their work or shared what they were learning. We didn't even know what Leonard's PhD dissertation was about, for instance. He just said he was working in a micro-sociological perspective. Jeremie studied music composition and whenever my mother asked how it was going he would just avoid answering by saying that music was an abstraction and couldn't be talked about. Most of what they said was said in reaction to something one of my sisters had said, or had been said on TV. I'm not sure they needed attention at all, or that they could understand people who did, and that's why I had no idea how to get theirs. I decided I would never find a way to sound interesting and found myself knocking on their door without a speech prepared. I couldn't believe I was doing it. Jeremie sighed a weary "Come in" that suggested people knocked on their door all the time, which was not a thing I could say for sure had ever happened. Leonard and Jeremie were both at their desks, their backs turned to each other.

"Hi, guys," I said.

They didn't invite me to have a seat or anything, but I didn't want to stay on the threshold, so I closed the door behind me and made my way to the center of the room to stand between the two of them.

"What do you want?" Leonard said. He'd rotated his desk chair to face in my direction.

"Well I'm working on Simone's biography," I said, "and I was wondering if you had anecdotes or stories about her that you would want to share with me. Or anything. I mean, we can talk about anything you want."

Leonard squinted as if I'd said something complicated.

"I heard you got laid," Jeremie said. He was still looking at his computer, and sound waves of different colors, but he'd taken one of his earphones out.

"I did!" I said, and regretted sounding the exclamation mark right away. I was excited that Jeremie was showing interest in something I'd done, but he must've thought I was just boasting.

"It wasn't with a pretty girl, though," I said in an attempt to undo the exclamation mark.

"Those who lose their virginity to good-looking girls are very rare," Jeremie said. I thought he would expand on that, but he resumed adjusting sound waves on his screen, and for a while the clicking of his mouse was all there was to be heard.

"What exactly do you want to know about Simone?" Leonard asked me as I was about to sneak out and apologize for having interrupted their work.

"I don't have specific questions," I said, "but I think she'd like it if you had funny memories about her to share, how it was to see her grow, things like that."

"She believed in Santa Claus 'til she was eight years old or something," Jeremie said. "It must be a kind of record."

I knew about the Santa Claus thing because the reason my mother had ended up having to tell Simone that Santa was really her and the father staying up late to put the presents beneath the tree was that I'd figured it out before Simone had and my parents didn't think it was right to let me keep that knowledge from an older sibling. I actually remembered my mother telling Simone the truth about Santa—I'd listened to their conversation through our bedroom door. I'd heard her ask Simone if she was mad that she'd been lied to, and then Simone's voice come out like a thread you pull from a sweater, like something was being irreparably wrecked in its wake. "My throat is closing," she'd whispered, "my heart is beating faster. I wish you'd never told me." I remember it because it was the first time I'd heard Simone express regrets about knowing something. When I'd let her break the news to me later that day (our mother hadn't told her I already knew; she'd thought letting Simone tell me about it would be a good way for her to get over the lie), I'd responded the way she had, stealing the line "I wish you'd never told me" from her. Simone had shown no empathy and asserted that I was being a pussy and that knowledge was power, which I'd thought sounded good but also puzzled me, given how often she complained about always being looked down upon for being a kid by grown-ups who knew less than her about literature and geography.

I didn't want to discourage Jeremie from telling me more stories about Simone, so I pretended his Santa Claus bit was helpful, but when I asked if he could think of anything else, I just heard more mouse clicks. He didn't put his second earphone back in his ear, though, so I assumed he was still considering himself involved in the conversation and just needed a little time to think about my request. I turned to Leonard's side of the room to see what he had to say, but before my eyes landed on him, they stopped on a black and white picture that was lying on his desk. I didn't want to be nosy, but even though I couldn't really see what the picture represented from where I stood, it triggered some sense of familiarity and I understood that it concerned me.

"What's that picture?" I asked Leonard.

He turned on his chair and handed it to me.

"It's for my work," he said.

The picture was a picture of us all, minus Leonard, asleep on different mattresses laid out on the floor, the same floor I was standing on now. I was in the upper left corner, curled up in a ball. Berenice had fallen asleep with a bundle of papers on her stomach, Jeremie with his mouth open to the ceiling, Simone and Aurore top to tail with arms sticking out of the mattress. It looked like we'd all died in awkward positions, like these illegal workers I'd seen on TV who'd been living in a sweatshop and had been poisoned in their sleep by a portable heater. My siblings and I had only all slept in the same room on one occasion: after the father had died. As I was trying to make sense of how that picture could relate to Leonard's PhD dissertation, I saw him, from the corner of my eye, grab a notebook and write something down, something that I could tell by his eye movement was linked to my reaction to the photograph.

"What exactly are you working on?" I said.

Leonard took the time he needed to complete the thought he was writing down before he answered.

"I'm studying the variety of processes and strategies through which a family unit reorganizes itself after the disappearance of one of its members—in my case, the main household provider and paternal figure."

"The father," I said.

"In other words, yes: the father," Leonard said.

I still wasn't sure whether he was talking about the father or the concept of a father.

"*Our* father," I said.

"That sounds interesting," Jeremie said, apparently finding out about the topic of Leonard's research just as I was.

"Wait," I told Jeremie, "you didn't know his dissertation was about us?"

"It's not about us," Leonard objected, "it's about the redefinition of the group members' positions within the group after a death, about structural and behavioral changes, about how the ordinariness of a situation becomes salient once it has been disrupted . . . it's not about you or me as individuals."

"But that's a picture of us," I said.

"I'm not gonna use it as an illustration in my dissertation or anything. It's just a visual reminder. Like a field note, if you wish." Leonard opened his top desk drawer and took out a folder in which he kept pictures of different rooms of the house.

"I've never seen you take a picture in my life," I said.

"I just took them a couple of days after the father died, to see if over time we started changing the way we organized objects, furniture. I'm not the best at noticing that kind of stuff."

"Did we change anything?"

"Not that I can see. I know Aurore reorganized her bookshelf alphabetically instead of chronologically, but I think that had nothing to do with her mourning. It was more of a post-PhD-defense ritual."

Jeremie put his second earphone back in. Our conversation must've disturbed his concentration without providing enough interest in exchange.

"But I guess my whole research has gotten to be more language oriented. Mostly, I look at how we changed the way we spoke of certain things," Leonard went on.

"But we never talk about the father," I said.

"That is actually one of my angles. How certain topics have become embarrassing, or how Mom and Aurore started talking like they're carrying heavy things—I call it *sigh-speak*—when they want to get off of a subject. You know, our avoidance strategies."

"Avoidance strategies," I repeated. "Is that what we do?"

"All the time. Defensive processes, protecting strategies, preventive avoidance . . ."

"I didn't know there were words for all that."

"Well I won't be so naive as to say there is a word or group of words for everything, but the beauty of being an academic is that you get to invent some for the things you're working on."

"Did you invent these?"

"Of course not."

"Did you invent any?"

Leonard looked either insulted or chagrined by my question.

"That's not the point," he said.

I didn't know there had been a point to our conversation or why we couldn't stray from it. I still didn't understand, at the time, that I had as much a right to decide what the point of a conversation was as anyone else participating in it. I looked at the picture of us some more, trying to find a question there that would be more in line with Leonard's view of our point.

"Did you notice any changes with me?" I asked. "After the father died?"

"I noticed you stopped rubbing the couch."

"That's because you guys made fun of me," I said.

"I noticed you started reading to Mom at night. I noticed you looked for a boyfriend for her. That gave me a lot to work with, by the way. Everyone's reaction to that guy . . . Daniel. That was really interesting."

I waited for Leonard to thank me but he didn't.

"Do your professors think you've got a worthy research topic?"

"It's wildly unconventional," Leonard admitted. "Most studies in micro-sociology are still pretty ill considered, and I'm sure I'll have a couple of assholes on my jury who will deem it scientifically irrelevant, but my adviser thinks I'm doing some groundbreaking work with this."

We heard Jeremie laugh in the background, but it wasn't at what Leonard had said. Jeremie laughed at music sometimes; certain arrangements of notes could be as funny as jokes to him, and he'd just heard one of those in his earphones.

"I can't believe Jeremie didn't know that's what you were

working on," I told Leonard. "You're practically living on top of each other."

"Are you kidding? No one in this house cares about what I do. And look at him!" Leonard lifted his chin in Jeremie's direction. Jeremie's shoulders were now moving to the rhythms he was controlling. "That's what he does all day. Never asks a damn question."

"He asked me if it was true I'd gotten laid," I noted.

Leonard didn't seem to think it counted.

"Aren't you the one who's supposed to ask us questions anyway?" I said. "I thought sociologists did interviews with the people they wrote about."

"My research is purely observation based. If I had told you that I was observing our family, your behaviors would've changed, and my work would've been compromised."

"So if we'd asked more precise questions about your dissertation, you wouldn't have told us anyway."

"Probably not."

"So why are you complaining that we didn't?"

"It doesn't matter now. The research phase is over. I'm almost done writing my first chapter."

"Can I read it?"

"No."

"Can I keep the picture?"

Leonard went through his file of photographs and laid out seven pictures on his desk that looked exactly like the one I was holding. He stared at them and at the one I was holding and then at the other ones again.

"I guess you can," he said.

Often, I dreamed the father wasn't dead—he'd faked his own death to protect us from the international villains he'd been secretly fighting his whole life, or they'd made a mistake at the hospital and we'd buried someone who looked like the father while the father had coincidentally been made a secret prisoner somewhere far away, or he'd been resurrected, no specific explanation for it. The scenarios varied but the conclusion was always the same: the father was back, and even though I was aware while dreaming it that a dream was all it was, I still enjoyed the chance I was given to see him again, and I woke up sad that dreams had to be so short, hopeful that in the next one (soon, if I was lucky), I would be better at controlling the setting and what the father and I would talk about. I'd read on the Internet that some people knew how to control their dreams. I don't really want to say it, but there was a part of me that thought that if I could control the dream, I'd maybe be able to bring the father back from there to real life.

Not long before I found out about Leonard's research, though, I'd started growing ambivalent about those dreams where the father wasn't dead. I'd started dreading them. See, the more time passed in real life, the more it did in dream life as well, and even in dreams, I'd gotten used to the idea that the father was dead, and the thought of his being resurrected had become discouraging, because if he wasn't dead, I thought, it meant he had yet to die, and I to go through all the steps of grieving him, and I didn't know if I could do it again. I felt guilty inside those dreams, selfish, and worse than that, obvious, like the father knew I didn't really want him to come back with me to real life anymore, the way sick people know, when you visit them in the hospital, that they don't look as good as you say they do and that you can't wait to leave. I was still sad waking up from these dreams, but the relief was new. I didn't tell Leonard about that. Maybe if he'd asked us questions, I would've. But I guess it wasn't part of the observable world he was interested in anyway.

———

The next time I saw her in the neighborhood, Daphné Marlotte confirmed she spoke German. I didn't ask her right away under what conditions she'd learned the language, if she'd been a Nazi or not. I wanted to save it for a lull in the conversation.

She understood what I meant when I talked about looking for a conversation partner and invited me for tea and cookies, or as she put it, *"für Tee und Kekse,"* which immediately made me realize how much I would learn from her, given how Herr Coffin had never thought it useful to teach us how to say *cookies* in German.

I'd walked by Daphné's building almost every day of my life but I'd never been inside her apartment. I'd caught glimpses of her living room now and then, particularly in the summer, when she opened all the windows looking out on the street—she lived on the first floor—but it had always been through her white lace curtains. Seeing those curtains, you'd think they wouldn't do a great job at concealing, with the hundreds of openings and the thinness of the fabric, but really they made it hard to discern much behind them, unless you stood by Daphné's window and picked a hole in the lace through which to look at her apartment and stuck your eye to it. Which was something I'd actually thought about doing, except I couldn't really find a valid reason to proceed.

Her place wasn't as crumbly and old as I'd expected. The kitchen had been recently remodeled, Daphné explained, by kind people from an organization that made sure older folks didn't give up on comfort and miss out on the newest home improvement technologies.

"It's very nice," I said, knocking on the imitation-marble counters as Daphné made us tea.

"I think it's too tacky, honestly," she said. "I don't like it one bit. But it was free, you know? Charity. I shouldn't complain."

She repeated the exact same thing in German.

It was weird being alone with Daphné. She seemed to have grown shyer inside her own home. She spoke more softly, like we might wake someone resting in the other room. I said I wasn't used to speaking everyday German, that my teacher was more into the nineteenth-century poets. She said it was all right, that I could speak to her in French and she would respond in German and that little by little, I'd grow confident enough to try out some words and, eventually, whole sentences.

We took our teas to the living room and sat there quietly for a minute, pretending that having to blow on our smoking cups prevented us from talking. It felt rude mentioning the fact that there were no cookies when she'd promised me some. I looked around the room for pictures to start a conversation about but there weren't any.

"You don't have pictures," I said.

Daphné smiled and said something in German that I didn't understand. I didn't know if you were supposed to have your conversation partner repeat what she'd said if you hadn't understood it, or just go with the flow.

"We don't have pictures either," I said.

She said something else, in which I recognized the words for *memories* and *sad* and *wall,* but I don't know if she said it was sad that she hadn't taken enough pictures to save and display good memories on her walls or if such a display would amount to building a wall of sadness.

"Maybe we should try the way we did it in the kitchen," I said, "when you first said the sentence in French and then repeated it in German?"

Daphné agreed to my suggestion but didn't offer a new topic of conversation.

"So," I said. "I've always wondered: do you still get excited for your birthdays?"

I had wanted to avoid the subject of her age, given it was what people always talked to her about, but apparently, I was no better than anyone else. Daphné had made good progress on the scale of old people over the past year: she was now the third-oldest person in the whole world. Two women had to die in India and she would be number one. People in town hoped that this would happen before her next birthday, to make it a national event, have the president come and celebrate with us, and I wondered if Daphné felt more pressure than usual to stay alive.

"It would be nice to meet the president on my next one," Daphné said, by which she admitted without actually saying the words that she wished those two old Indian women dead.

"Do you like him?"

"Not particularly. But I've never met a president. I don't get to have that many new experiences, you know?" She laughed a little and then translated what she'd said in German and laughed again. Her laughter was the same in both languages.

"Why do you want to learn German, little man?" Daphné asked me. "It is such a hideous language."

"It's pretty when you speak it," I said, which I didn't think was actually the case, but the father always said that those who believed German was an ugly language had probably never heard a kindhearted person speak it. I tried to remember other things the father used to say in defense of the German language, but nothing else came to mind.

"It's so rigid," Daphné said. "It's not a playful language. German puns suck."

"Well I was thinking I could be an interpreter or something," I said, ignoring her criticisms.

"For whom would you interpret? There are not that many German celebrities people care about outside of Germany, have you noticed?"

"I hadn't thought about that," I said, after trying to come up with names to prove her wrong.

"And most Germans know their language is useless anyway, so they all speak English nowadays."

"You don't think German is useful at all?"

"If you plan to live in Germany, it is most definitely useful," Daphné said. "Or if you fall in love with a German girl."

"Did you fall in love with a German boy?"

"I did," she said, "a long time ago. That's the only reason why I speak this horrible language."

"Was it your husband? People say your husband was a Nazi."

"I suppose those people you're talking about still haven't registered how old I actually am. I was *already* old when the Nazis started rising to power. My husband had died. He couldn't have been a Nazi even if he'd wanted to, poor Thomas darling. Not that he would've wanted to be a Nazi, of course, that's just a way of speaking. He was a German deserter from the *First* World War, that's how old I am. But maybe they don't teach you about the First World War in school anymore."

"They do," I said in a senseless attempt to defend my education, given I knew next to nothing about the First World War. "The First World War was with the trenches and the Second with the concentration camps."

"How specific," Daphné said.

"They do spend more time on the Second World War," I admitted. "We watched *Night and Fog* in history class."

"Well that didn't tell you much about the Occupation, did it?"

I'd fallen asleep during *Night and Fog*. I always fell asleep when we had TV time in school.

"Forget about it. I didn't mean to say you were poorly educated," Daphné said. "I apologize. *Entschuldigung.*"

"It's all right," I said.

"What I meant to say is that teachers probably make it look a little too easy nowadays, am I right? Especially around here. People take pride in the fact that there were a lot of famous members of the resistance in the area, but at the time, it didn't feel like it, I can tell you that much. Doesn't mean the rest of us were Nazis, but people have a great ability to go on with their lives no matter what, and I happened to be quite busy back then, with work, and my second husband dying on me. The Germans didn't come down here before 1942, but when they did, they came to my bar—I tended the bar at La Fontaine, did you know that? They came to La Fontaine because I spoke German, and I served them, what else could I do? I don't think that makes me a collaborator. They tipped better than the French. They were the ones with the money, I suppose."

Daphné had started telling her story, pausing after each sentence to translate it into German, but she got carried away at some point and went ahead in German. Reversing the order of the languages seemed to happen quite naturally for her, but not having the French version first made it harder for me to pick up new German words and match them with what I'd just heard.

"Didn't you meet a nice one?" I asked in French, hoping to put her back on the right track.

"Of course I met nice ones. You always meet at least one nice person in a bar, but that's neither here nor there. They'd ask how René was doing—René was my second husband—and when he died, they brought flowers and drank and tipped double. But they were still the enemy. That never once slipped my mind. Even when I laughed at their jokes."

"What was their best joke?"

"How old are you now?"

"I'll be fourteen soon," I said.

"I suppose that's old enough. So they had this joke about nuns. One morning in the convent, Mother Superior comes down to the commons to announce what the nuns will have for dinner that night. 'Tonight, carrots!' she says, and all the nuns are really excited and go, 'Ooooooh!' but then Mother Superior specifies, 'Grated!' and all the nuns go, 'Booooo!'"

"That was their best joke?" I said.

"It was a pretty good one in the forties," Daphné said. "Risqué."

The tea had infused too much and tasted like coins dipped in grenadine. I considered gulping the whole of it down and excusing myself—it was going to be dinnertime at home. Daphné must have felt her grated carrots joke hadn't won me over.

"Don't leave me just yet," she said. It was obvious she'd hoped to have come up with a reason why I should stay before she'd be finished saying "Don't leave me just yet" in two languages, but she hadn't, and I politely waited for her to figure one out.

"You could be a spy," she ended up saying. "That would be more interesting than interpreter. I thought about becoming one, during the war, but I didn't know where to go or who to offer my services to. I thought if they needed more spies, they'd find me, 'cause people knew I spoke German. But no one ever came, so I guess they weren't looking for spies in my corner of the world. But it's easier in times of peace, I would think, to make your ambitions known. You probably just have to send a letter to the DGSE and say you want to join their intelligence service, and they schedule an appointment. You would need to learn another language or two though, on top of German. Spies are polyglots. Maybe learn Arabic. Or Russian. I know a Russian lady who could be your conversation partner."

"My father knew many languages," I said. "Do you think he could've been a spy?"

"Your father? Your father's German was so precious, dear, it was like talking to a doily. When he spoke to me, I couldn't help but picture that horrible Fragonard painting, you know? The rosy-cheeked girl on her swing? All the pink taffeta and the layers in her dress? He would've needed to update his vocabulary and structures a bit if he'd wanted to make it into twenty-first century espionage, believe me."

I could picture a book spine that said "Fragonard" in brown letters on our living room shelves, where the art books were, but not a painting by him. If I could have, I would have been even more pissed at Daphné's words.

"And even leaving his German aside," she went on, "your father wasn't a double-life kind of man. He always looked so overwhelmed with just the one."

"What makes you say that?"

"Well, I saw him around. It seemed every situation made him uncomfortable. Wouldn't you say? Bumping into people, ordering a coffee . . . I mean, you can't be unsettled by a postal worker giving you a choice between regular and express mail and be a spy at the same time. It simply doesn't figure."

"Maybe that was part of his civil-life persona," I said.

"Maybe," Daphné said. *"Vielleicht."* She didn't believe it for a second.

"There was no need to say it in French first," I said, more angrily than I'd wanted. "I know how to say *maybe* in German."

"I'm sorry if I offended you, *mein Herr,*" Daphné said, but she wasn't. She thought I was overreacting.

"At least he loved German," I said. "At least he didn't just use his knowledge of German to get better tips from a bunch of Nazis."

"Oh yeah? And what did he use his precious knowledge for?" Daphné was done translating now. "Business meetings? Dinners? To bore an old lady stiff with his Goethe quotes just because she was nice enough to encourage him the first time?"

Drool started accumulating at the corners of Daphné's mouth as she spoke ill of the father, and I thought it was unusual considering how often she'd had to pause over the course of our conversation just to moisten her lips or sip some tea in order to go on.

"Are you all right?" I said.

Daphné said something in German, or maybe it was French and I just couldn't make sense of it—she could barely articulate. Her features, her whole face, seemed to be pulled down toward the ground by an invisible flesh magnet.

"Let me call 911," I said.

———

I left my argument with Daphné out of the story I told the paramedics. Not that they asked anything—I guess a stroke at Daphné's age was nothing unusual. They congratulated me for calling them so promptly. My mother did too, when I came home. She was convinced it had been too much emotion for Daphné, having a nice lively guest like me at her house instead of the routine nurse or a fellow old lady, and that it must've been the thrill that had caused her stroke. She told me I was a kind soul. I thought maybe she would reinstate my Internet hour, but she didn't mention it. She called the hospital every hour to get an update on Daphné, and when I woke up the next day, she told me that the doctors had been able to remove the clot in her brain and Daphné would only be partly paralyzed. She seemed to think it was good news.

"What a bunch of pricks," Denise said. "They only want to keep her alive to break some kind of record."

Denise had resumed meeting me on the staircase. She'd offered no explanation for her absence the previous days and didn't mention Porfi.

"You shouldn't have called 911," she went on. "You should've just let her die there. Poor woman. I'm sure she would've preferred that."

"I don't know," I said. "She sounded pretty excited for her birthday."

"She has to pretend she is, with the kind of parties the mayor has been throwing her. Can you imagine? Having to be grateful all the time? What a nightmare."

Denise was looking nowhere in particular, pulling hangnails off her fingers with her teeth. She usually flicked the little bits of skin down the stairs after tearing them, but that day she'd decided to swallow them. She asked what else was new and I told her about Leonard's writing his dissertation on us.

"So you guys are gonna be famous?"

"No one reads sociology dissertations," I said.

"But dissertations get published, right?"

"Berenice sold like forty copies of hers, I think. Aurore is supposed to edit her manuscript for publication, but I don't get the impression she's doing much of that lately."

"To be a character in a book," Denise said. "You must be pretty thrilled."

"Leonard says it's not really about us but about processes and strategies and language."

"That's just like when writers say one of their stories is about coming of age in a post-capitalistic world as well as an exploration of what it really means to get an education when all it is is a self-aggrandizing account of their first trip to a whorehouse."

"That's a very specific example," I said.

"Well I just made it up."

I wanted to tell Denise I was responsible for Daphné's stroke, that Daphné had compared my father to a Fragonard painting and that I'd gotten upset, but it seemed like a silly reason to almost kill someone, even by accident.

"The cool thing is," Denise said, still processing the news about Leonard's dissertation, "once your whole family is famous, you can build a career on that and write biographies for each one of them, not just Simone. And then you'll get famous both for being in your brother's book and for your own work as a biographer. You could write biographies of everyone you know after that."

"I see what you're getting at," I said. "You want me to write your biography too."

"That would be one very short, very boring book," Denise said, and I felt a wave of cold rush through my body.

"Would Porfi get his own chapter?" I asked.

Denise looked at her watch.

"Nine minutes," she said. "You held out nine whole minutes without mentioning Porfi. I'm impressed. I thought you would harass me with questions right away."

"Did you fall in love with him yet?"

"Honestly, I'm not sure I would recognize him on the street," Denise said. "He's so shy. He can't stand up straight and look at me. Although I guess there's a bit of progress: last time he spoke to me, he looked at *my* shoes instead of his."

"That's good," I said.

I thought about what Porfi had told me about people not liking Denise. Maybe Porfi was more embarrassed about being seen with her than shy.

"You should go out for coffee with him," I said.

"Why would I do that? I don't like coffee."

"It doesn't have to be coffee, you know? Maybe he's ill at ease courting you at school, maybe he wants the romance to stay private."

"There's no romance to speak of."

"But you like him."

"He's nice, I guess. He keeps asking if there's something he can do for me. He really wants to show me how good he is at repairing stuff, but I can never think of anything that he could help me with, so I asked him if he knew how to pick a lock and he said he did. I told him to come down here one of these days, open that door for you."

Denise turned her face to the door at the top of the stairs.

"Except I didn't tell him it was for you. I told him *I* was interested in knowing what was behind it."

"Why?"

"I'm always sort of embarrassed to admit I'm not interested in anything. I mean, I'm used to it, and I'm the person who should be most bothered by it, right? But when other people ask what I like and stuff, I feel like I should spare them the truth, that they couldn't bear it if they knew how little interest I had in life. And Porfi's so eager to find a way to make me like him, I feel like I have to pretend that there's something he could try, you know? Give him a glimmer of hope."

"Maybe if you keep pretending things interest you," I said, "you'll end up really caring about them."

"That's what my therapist used to say."

"And what does he say now?"

"He's clueless. I tried all possible meds. He says I should attempt meditation. That sounds like what you recommend when there's no hope left at all, don't you think?"

"I think if you're still able to lie to people in order to protect them, there's hope," I said.

"You should write for French TV."

"You don't want to go to Paris anymore?" I asked.

"Of course I do," Denise said.

"Are you lying to me right now?"

Denise looked at me like I'd asked a trick question when she was literally the only person on Earth who could've answered it.

"I'm not lying," she said. "I do want to go to Paris. I've never been."

"Have you thought about things you'd like to do while we're there?"

"We could go to a couple bookstores I guess. Porfi said he wanted to hit the Eiffel Tower."

"Forget about what Porfi wants. Bookstores for you. What else?"

"Maybe we could hang out in Juliette's neighborhood," Denise said tentatively, like she was ready to discard the idea right away if I found it ridiculous.

"Do you know where she lives?"

"Well I don't have her address or anything, but there's an interview on her website where she talks about how much she likes this one café on the Saint Martin Canal. I thought maybe we could check it out. Maybe she'll be there."

"That sounds great," I said, and it did. If we saw Juliette, we could finally ask her if she'd been an actress in the Let Them Sea video or a real kid who'd never seen the ocean.

"What do you plan on doing in Paris?" Denise asked me, just before the bell rang.

"I thought I would go see what the DGSE buildings look like."

"The intelligence agency? What for?"

"I've never seen a spy," I said. "I just want to see what the people who walk in there look like."

"Well those who just walk in through the front door will probably not be spies," Denise said.

"I know," I said. "But maybe one of them will."

Denise was unconvinced but humored me anyway.

"Whatever you want," she said. "You'll be our Paris guide, we'll just follow you around."

We got up to join our respective classrooms and I noticed as I walked down the stairs behind her that Denise was wearing perfume. The air carried whiffs of orange blossom after she'd passed through it.

"Do you think Porfi will let me watch how he picks a lock?" I asked.

"He'll do anything I ask him," Denise said, unfazed by the power she'd just recognized in herself.

———

On the second anniversary of the father's death, I received a letter from Rose:

Dear Isidor,

it said,

Two years already and the memory of your father's sodden death still haunts me.

After you left, my parents figured we had made love and you were not a penpal . . . it is ironic I think because you actually are! But I didn't tell them that. I guess I am the only one who writes anyway, you never answer (and it's fine, I mean, I'm writing to express sympathy and share your pain about your father) but anyway if you ever want to write me a letter, you better not do it here because they have me on close watch! They were really mad at me for lying to them, so if I were you I wouldn't come back to my house next time you runaway.

I broke up with Kevin after you left. I don't think I'm in love with you but I did like your penis more than Kevin's. Kevin's is very long but it is a bit too thin in comparison with yours, and it didn't feel right when we had sex the next time after you. He never gave me an orgasm. Not that you did either, I think we really didn't make love for long enough, but I think maybe if it had lasted longer it could've happened. I have never had an orgasm in my life and I am already 18 so I am starting to freek out a little. All my friends say they have orgasms ALL the time. Maybe they are lying. I feel stupid talking about your penis, but it is part of the things of life, so I should not be ashamed, and you, most importantly, shouldn't be embaraced that I talk about it, you should be very proud of it. It is important to be proud about things you have going for yourself. I am sure it is something your father would've told you if he hadn't died when you were so young.

Maybe when you grow up we should try to hang out more. I will go to university next year. I didn't get into med school but I will still study biology I think.

Cordially,
Rose

I wanted to be aroused by Rose's letter, but she made it very complicated. She was just mixing too many different topics in too few lines.

"Knock knock," I heard Jeremie say through the bedroom door, interrupting my rereading of Rose's letter. I said come in and asked him why he said "Knock knock" instead of actually knocking.

"I don't know," Jeremie said. "Why did you say 'Come in' instead of actually coming to the door to open it?"

"I would've had to get up from my bed," I said. "Knocking requires less energy."

"It still requires *some*," Jeremie said, and he sat on Simone's unmade bed and said nothing for a while.

"Did you come to see Simone?" I tried to guess. "She doesn't get off school before five on Thursdays."

"No, I came to see you," Jeremie said. "I just wanted to tell you that I think it was unfair of Mom to forbid you access to the Internet. I do think it was stupid of you to look for a boyfriend for her without taking her criteria into account, but neverthe-less, I believe it came from a good place and you shouldn't have been punished that hard for it. None of us ever got punished for anything before, as far as I can remember—none of us ever took any kind of initiative of that sort, either—and maybe Mom was disconcerted as to how to react to your mistake and ended up being a bit heavy-handed."

"Thanks," I said. "The whole Daniel fiasco was a few weeks ago, though, so why are you telling me this now?"

"Well, I wanted to come to you first thing to offer you access to my own computer—I wouldn't tell Mom you'd been on the Internet, of course—but I had very important work to do with it myself, so I couldn't just invite you to use it."

"But you're done with your work now?"

"For the most part, yes."

"So I can come and use your computer anytime?"

"Well, obviously not *any* time," Jeremie said. "When I'm not in my bedroom, say. You should feel free to use the computer then."

"But you're kind of always in your bedroom," I said.

Jeremie didn't respond to that. I said I appreciated his offer.

"You're welcome," he said.

I thought that would be the end of our interaction, but he just stayed there on the edge of Simone's bed, looking around our room like he'd never seen it before. Which in fact was not far from the truth.

"Have you read any of Leonard's dissertation?" I asked him.

"I look at what's on his computer screen when he goes to the bathroom sometimes," Jeremie confessed. Aurore had lent her own computer to Leonard for him to type his dissertation on.

"What does it say?"

"All I saw was a breakdown of the household budget before and after the father's death, reorganization of family expenses after the loss of the main source of income and with Mom's widow's pension, things like that. Nothing too interesting."

I'd never thought about the consequences of the father's death for the household budget. Since he'd died, we'd pretty much lived the same, I thought, except that we knew we'd never see him again. We ate the same things, rented the same number of movies.

"Are we poor now?" I asked.

"Of course not," Jeremie said. "If we were poor we would all be looking for jobs instead of getting PhDs or applying for second PhDs."

"Are you going to go for a PhD next year?"

Jeremie was just finishing his master's that year. He'd skipped one grade fewer than the others.

"I don't think so," he said.

"Why not? Are you just going to write music from now on?"

"Have you noticed that all of them, Berenice, Aurore, Leonard, went into getting a PhD thinking they'd get answers to all of their questions, but what it did to them instead is it made them need more and more time to answer simpler and simpler questions? Rather: that it made them need to break simple-seeming questions down to a multitude of subquestions in such a twisted way that they can never find their way back to the original question?"

"I don't know," I said. "I thought they'd always been like that."

"What I mean is I'm not sure I want to fill my head with more knowledge and theories at this point. It complicates everything.

I don't think it's good for the art. I think artists shouldn't be too smart."

"But you're super smart already," I said.

Jeremie seemed a bit insulted by this.

"What makes you say that?" he said.

"You're getting a master's in both physics and musicology," I said.

"Well that's just fun," he said. "Master's are for fun. PhDs require intellectual commitment. It's like dating versus getting married."

"And you don't want to commit to anything but music," I said.

"I don't."

"Because making music gets easier with time whereas academic research just gets more and more complicated."

"I never said music got easier with time," Jeremie said. "That whole thing people say about the hardest thing for an artist being his first novel, or first movie, or first opera, or whatever . . . well that's just nonsense. I believe if you're doing it right, the hardest thing to do for an artist should always precisely be the one he's working on."

"I don't see how it's different from getting a PhD then, if art doesn't get easier either."

"Who would want a thing that only got easier with time?"

"I wouldn't mind," I said.

"What do you know about difficulty? You're in tenth grade."

"Eighth," I said, and Jeremie must have detected a little shame in my answer—there was—because his tone softened.

"I guess certain things do get easier," he said, but he didn't give any examples.

"Do you know how to break up with a girl?" I asked.

"I don't think so," Jeremie said after thinking about it some. "I believe, when I'm with a girl, that it's always clear from the get-go that we're not engaging in any kind of relationship."

"Have you been with many girls?"

"Not that many, no. Ten, twelve."

"Do I know any of them?"

"The last one was Ohri's fiancée, Carla. I don't know that you ever met her."

"Did she and Ohri break up?"

"Not that I know of," Jeremie said.

"So how come you slept with her?"

"Berenice asked me if I could do it. I think she was trying to get back at Ohri for something without him having to know about it necessarily."

"How can you get back at someone if he never knows you did anything to get back at him?"

"It's just personal satisfaction, I guess. You get the satisfaction of having gotten back at the person without actually having hurt anyone. I think it's pretty healthy."

"So you had no interest in Carla but you slept with her for Berenice's satisfaction."

"You make it sound incestuous, Izzie."

"Sorry. What I meant to ask was if it was better to sleep with a girl when you were actually in love with her."

Jeremie plainly ignored my query.

"Who do you need to break up with anyway?" he asked.

"Just this girl," I said, tapping Rose's folded letter against my palm.

"The same girl you first had sex with? I didn't get that you were a couple."

"We're not, actually, but she still sends these letters and they make me uncomfortable."

"Letters? Aren't you in school together?"

"No," I said. "She lives in a different city."

"How did you meet her? We never go anywhere."

"She was Simone's pen pal."

"That girl Rose?" I was surprised Jeremie remembered her name. "God, she was thick."

"Well, don't tell anyone, okay?"

"I won't if you show me what kind of letters she sends you."

"I don't know which is more embarrassing," I said.

Jeremie gave me some time to think about it and started drumming on his thighs with his fingers. He had these very long fingers that people always said, as he was growing up, were perfect pianist fingers. Jeremie was indeed a very good pianist, but he didn't like to hear he had the hands for the job. He thought it minimized his achievements and all the hard work he'd put into mastering the instrument. I showed him Rose's letter.

"She does talk about your penis a lot," is all Jeremie said once he'd read it. He handed me the letter back. No question about my running away or mention that today was the anniversary of the father's death.

"So how do I break up with her?"

"Tell her you got into an accident and your cock shrank?"

"Seriously," I said.

"Oh, you're fine," Jeremie said. "She lives far away. You don't have to do anything. She'll forget all about you eventually."

"But if I were to write her a response, what would I say to suggest she shouldn't write to me anymore without hurting her feelings?"

"She can't even spell your name, how could you hurt her feelings?"

"Feelings don't depend on literacy," I said.

Jeremie didn't look convinced.

"Just tell her you fell in love with someone else then," he said. "Girls respect that kind of honesty. Better than boys at least."

Jeremie got up from Simone's bed and readjusted his pants at the waist. I wanted to ask him if he'd had or was still having problems finding comfortable underwear, like I did, but I thought he would just make a joke about the size of my penis.

"Do you know if Leonard is close to finishing his dissertation?" I asked him instead, as he went for the door.

"He talked about defending in the fall," Jeremie said, and then he made this grunt, this sort of maimed-animal grunt he had whenever our mother asked him to do something he didn't want to do but knew he had to, like renewing his insurance card at the beginning of a school year. "Sometimes I wonder if the father didn't die when he did just to avoid all the PhD defenses," he said.

⌒

In April, the two Indian women died within days of each other and Daphné Marlotte became the oldest person in the world. The journalist who wrote the article about it seemed to be walking on eggshells, though, not ready to cry victory too quickly. Daphné was still in the hospital recovering from her stroke and word had started to spread in town that the death of seniors of humanity went in threes and that Daphné might only have a few more days to live. I don't know if my mother believed that but she wanted to visit Daphné in the hospital and she wanted me to come along. I told her hospitals made me uncomfortable, even though I couldn't remember ever being in one. My mother didn't pick up on the discrepancy. She tried to convince me it was a once-in-a-lifetime opportunity, that we could pay a visit to the oldest person alive and then go down a couple of floors and see the newest newborns in the world, appreciate the greatness of the circle of life, and I said I didn't care, that I was good enough only seeing people in the middle of the life spectrum. She said I was starting to sound like my siblings. This seemed to worry her.

———

Denise and Porfi and I had planned to run away to Paris after school on a Friday, and for Porfi to pick the staircase-door lock before that, as a prelude to our adventure. I'd stuffed my backpack with the usual runaway accessories, and I'd made a list of useful items for Denise, telling her to share it with Porfi, but when he met us at the top of the staircase to pick the lock, his bag didn't look any more stuffed than usual.

"How come your bag is so slim?" I asked him. Porfi said there was no use in loading oneself like a mule when one knew where one's parents hid their cash and could just travel with a few wads and buy things whenever one needed them.

"Clever," Denise said.

I was uncomfortable with this. I didn't think running away with your parents' money counted, but I didn't say. I wanted to see how Porfi picked the lock before I'd engage in any kind of moral argument with him.

"Look what else I got from my mother!" he said, rummaging through his pocket to present us with a black bobby pin.

"Is that all you need to pick a lock?" I asked.

"Just watch and learn," he said.

Porfi opened his mother's bobby pin at a ninety-degree angle and placed the wavy side inside the lock.

"The key, if I may say, is to keep that part at the bottom of the lock," he explained, and then he started wiggling the flat part of the bobby pin left and right.

"Do you also know how to open dial combination safes just by listening to the mechanism?" I asked.

"Of course," Porfi said. "I'll show you if you want."

I just nodded, trying not to show my excitement too much. It seemed, from what I'd gathered in movies at least, that the spy apprentices who showed too much excitement didn't end up being as good as the placid ones.

"Okay," Porfi said. "I found the soft spot."

He looked nervous, and I thought it was because he was scared of what we would find on the other side of the door.

"How do you know you found it?" I said.

"You can tell the pin has slid between the latch and the plate."

"Can I feel it?"

"I'm scared if I drop it, I'll lose it," Porfi said.

Denise and I were holding our breaths, each leaning over a different one of Porfi's shoulders.

"What are you waiting for now?" Denise asked him after a minute where nothing had happened. Porfi let go of the pin and looked up at Denise.

"I'm worried that if I open this door for you now," he said, "you'll throw me out of the whole Paris thing. I want guarantees."

"Why would we throw you out?" Denise said.

"Because you would have gotten what you wanted from me."

"Are you kidding me? I don't even care what's behind that goddamned door," Denise said, and then she looked at me. "*He* does."

"What kind of guarantees do you want?" I asked Porfi, who glanced at me for a second before he went back to Denise.

"I want to know that we're a couple," he told her. "And to seal it with a kiss."

"To *seal* it with a kiss?" Denise said. "Who even says things like that?"

Porfi didn't let this get him down.

"I want a kiss with the tongue," he said.

"Are you going to add a condition every time I think something out loud?"

For a second, it looked like Denise wouldn't have minded Porfi's adding as many conditions as he wanted.

"Do you guys want some privacy?" I said.

"You're not going anywhere," Denise said, looking at me like everything that was happening was my fault, which I guess was the case.

"I've never kissed anyone," she told Porfi.

"Me neither," he said. "But I practiced on my hand, and I think I'm pretty good."

"Lucky me," Denise said, and she took a pack of gum out of her pocket. She always had gum in her pockets. She would chew one or two sticks at lunchtime instead of eating. She put one in her mouth and offered Porfi a piece.

"What flavor?" he said.

"Peppermint."

He took it and Denise offered me one too. The three of us chewed for a few seconds without talking.

"What now?" Denise asked.

"You have to close your eyes," Porfi said.

Denise rolled her eyes and shut them. Porfi cleared his throat. I didn't know if I was supposed to watch them or not. I looked down the stairs. I didn't hear their mouths touch but I saw a group of six or seven kids tiptoe over and form a line at the bottom of the stairs, Victor in the middle of them all. The way they laughed and pointed in our direction, I knew Porfi and Denise were at it.

"What are you looking at?" I yelled at Victor. "Get the hell out of here!"

Victor and his followers started clapping their hands and woo-hooing at Porfi and Denise, but I still didn't understand at that point that their presence down at the bottom of the stairs didn't owe to pure chance.

Then behind my back, I heard Porfi telling Denise he was sorry. She didn't ask what for, she'd put two and two together. Porfi was already walking down the stairs anyway, to meet his new crew.

There were a certain number of things one had to do to become a part of Victor's crew, and those things, I'd heard said, varied wildly, depending on Victor's inspiration on the day he gave his assignments, but all were aimed toward making the candidate feel lousy. Kissing Denise was supposed to be a ritual humiliation for Porfi, not her. I wasn't sure that she saw it that way. I was pretty sure I shouldn't help her to.

Victor high-fived Porfi as Porfi descended the stairs. Kissing

Denise with tongue must have been the last part of his hazing. All the kids went the way they'd come without another look at us.

"He didn't even open the fucking door," was the first thing Denise said.

"Are you okay?" I asked.

She was still chewing her gum.

"Of course I'm okay," she said. "That prick just took me for a ride, that's all. No need to dwell on it."

I could tell she was embarrassed to have been played like that, but it was hard to determine whether she was also hurt, because she always looked hurt. She was staring at the bobby pin Porfi had left behind, still dangling out of the unpicked lock.

"Do you still want to go to Paris after school?" I asked.

She did not.

———

Back home, I found Simone lying in bed on her stomach, swinging her legs back and forth at a pace I knew meant she was in a good mood. The leg movements drew half circles in the air, connecting her ass cheeks and the mattress—the knee joints being the center of the circle.

"Will you hand me the cold cream?" she said without even looking at me as I came into our bedroom. The cold cream was on the nightstand between our beds, closer to her than to me at this point, but for some reason, Simone always wanted me to hand it to her. I suspected she waited hours sometimes, in desperate need of the cold cream she could see but not reach without interrupting her reading, until I would come into the room and pass it to her.

Simone slathered her elbows with cold cream about a million times a day. Her elbows were constantly frayed and reddened from the amount of time she spent rubbing them against carpets and bedsheets while she lay on her stomach reading. She tried other reading positions now and then, to give her elbows a rest, but she always ended up on her stomach a few minutes later. She couldn't help it. For a whole month, she'd thought she'd solved the frayed-elbows problem altogether by buying a pair of those elbow pads that roller skaters and cyclists wear, walking around the house with them at all times, taking them off only for school, shower, and bed, but she'd developed an allergy to the neoprene that lined them. "There goes my roller skating career," she'd said after her dermatologist appointment, and resumed usage of the good old cold cream. I liked the way the cold cream made our bedroom smell, even though I pretended to find it too sweet and girly. I handed her the tube.

"I got a letter this morning," Simone said as she rubbed the cream into her cracked elbows, and for a second I thought the letter would be from Rose. "I got into the prep school I wanted in Paris."

"Congratulations," I said.

"Looks like you'll have the bedroom all to yourself next year."

I didn't know if Simone wanted me to be happy about that or start reciting a list of all the things I would miss about her constant presence. She had a way of making me feel like I was being tested sometimes.

"Looks like it," I said conservatively.

"What are we going to do about my biography?"

"I guess you'll have to send me written reports of prep school life," I said.

"What about calls? Do you think I could call you, like, every week or so?"

"I thought prep school was all about work work work," I said. "You might not have that much to report."

"Will you miss me?"

"Of course," I said. "I miss Berenice."

"But Berenice has been away more than half your life at this point," Simone said, apparently offended. "You're not as tight with her as you are with me! I think it is going to be way harder for you than you think when I'm gone."

I started unpacking my school bag on my desk, all of it, the cans of beans and the cookies and the kitchen knife. It didn't matter that Simone saw it.

"Did you run away for like five hours again?" she asked.

"I wish," I said, and then I crawled into bed, planning to only get back up when my mother called us down for dinner.

"What's wrong with you, Dory?" Simone asked.

I told her about how Porfi had made Denise believe he was in love with her only so he could kiss her in front of Victor and his minions as a dare and how humiliating it all was for Denise, even though she hadn't said anything about being humiliated. I said people like Victor were the dregs of humanity.

"Actually," Simone said, "the most horrible people really aren't the ones the majority would recognize as objectively horrible. I think the worst are those who *look up* to objectively horrible people." Then she thought about it a second and added that the same exact thing went for dumb people.

"So Porfi is the worst guy in this story?" I said.

"Well yeah. He didn't even come up with the idea to break

that poor girl's heart, he just thought it was worth his time and went along with it."

"But you could argue that because it wasn't his idea, and because he might never have come up with such a mean prank in the first place, then maybe he's inherently less bad than Victor, who was the brains of the operation."

"At least the other one had a brain," Simone said. "Even if a fucked-up one."

"So the problem with any dictatorship," I said, following Simone's argument, "is never really the dictator himself but the people who agree with him."

"Exactly," Simone said. "There could potentially be a good dictatorship—I don't see why the public could only be sheep for horrible leaders—but the problem is that good people never want to be dictators."

"That's a bummer," I said.

"All good people want is to be left alone and help those around them. The problem is good people lack ambition."

"You don't lack ambition," I said.

"Well, I'm not sure I qualify as a good person," Simone said, without any kind of emotion. "I don't have much patience."

She was still massaging the cream inside the cracks of her elbows. They were so red.

"Maybe *you* should be the dictator," she said, like it was the best idea she'd had in a while.

"I wouldn't know what to do with power," I said.

"I'd help you! I have a few ideas for a better society."

"I don't doubt it," I said, "but how would you telling me what to do be different than actually being the dictator yourself?"

"Dictators have advisers, you know? No one would expect you to come up with all the laws."

"What do you think should be my first measure as a dictator?" I said.

"If I were your adviser," Simone said, "I would make commenting on the Internet illegal. I don't think people should express themselves as much as they think they should."

"I'll keep that in mind," I said.

"Obviously, you should leave this exchange out of my biography."

———

Denise didn't meet me in the staircase the next day, or the one after that, but this time I knew she couldn't be flirting with Porfi and I got worried. I walked by the classroom where she had Chinese lessons in the mornings and took a look at the attendance sheet each teacher had to fill out at the beginning of their classes and stick outside the door for the monitors to collect and bring to the principal's office. Denise's name was in the "Absentees" column. I rushed to my own classroom before Herr Coffin would mark me as missing, but he hadn't yet taken attendance—he often forgot and the monitor had to interrupt our class for him to do it. Herr Coffin was trying to interest my fellow Germanists in a Hofmannsthal poem when I walked in.

"Who can think of another way the word *Erlebnis* could have been rendered by the translator of this poem?" he asked. No hands were raised.

Coffin was of the opinion that a translation, when well done, could be better than the original version. He said that the original contained the idea of what the poem aspired to but could never fully be, whereas a translation of said poem went straight for its essence and could carry out its potential while getting rid of the first empirical layer—whatever that meant—in the process, bringing it closer to its "truth."

To me, in German or French, Hofmannsthal made no sense at all.

"Herr Mazal?" Coffin asked as he handed me a Xerox of the poem we were looking at. "Do you know of any other ways to translate the word *Erlebnis*?"

I looked down at the sheet of paper in case the answer had been written on it.

" 'Adventure'?" I tried.

Coffin was pleased, and I thought he would leave me alone for the rest of the hour. Except I was the only one who had any interest in German, and when Coffin was tired of attempting to catch the others' attention, he pretended the class was just composed of the two of us.

"And why is it you think the translator decided to translate *Erlebnis* as 'experience' and not 'adventure' here, in the particular case of this poem?"

"I would have to read the whole poem," I said, "to get some context."

"Please do," Coffin said.

I scanned through the poem, trying to spot the verbs first. *Filled, seeping, glowing* (twice), *fathom, sailing, gliding*. Not a single useful verb. Not one verb that helped me see what Hofmannsthal was talking about. Then nouns: *valley, dusk, chalice, lilac.* That's why I wasn't making any progress, I thought. Daphné Marlotte was right. Poetry was of no help when you wanted to learn actual German.

"I think *adventure* would have implied that something in the poem was going to happen," I said, "whereas all the narrator talks about here are sensations and feelings and images. So the word *experience,* being more static, was more appropriate, I suppose."

"You do not think death could be referred to as an adventure?" Coffin said, and I read the poem again. I guess Hofmannsthal was indeed talking about dying, but he wrapped it in so many flower names I had been confused.

"I don't know," I said. "I don't know if death should be called an adventure or an experience. I guess the fact that one only dies once would tip the scale in favor of *adventure,* in a way, because the word *adventure* implies a sort of uniqueness, when an experience can be repeated many times. Potentially."

"I think *experience* is just more poetic sounding," I heard Victor say from the last row. "And Hofmanstool was a poet, so he had to use the most poetic words. *Adventure* sounds more like it would be for an action movie title, maybe."

"Action movies were not too popular in Hofmannsthal's time," Herr Coffin said. "And we're talking about the translator's choices here, anyway, not the poet's."

"Oh," Victor said. "Right. *Entschuldigang.*"

"Sure," Coffin said. "No problem. Let's take a look at the first verse now."

He went to the blackboard and wrote down a couple of words I knew from previous poems we'd studied but he thought maybe the rest of the class had forgotten.

"We've been over these words already," I said, and Herr Coffin turned and looked at me above his glasses.

"Repetition is at the root of all worthy pedagogy," he said, and he went back to *dusk* and *valley*.

"I just can't think of a way I could use these words in a normal conversation," I interrupted him. I felt a wind of energy rise in the rows behind me, as if my classmates had been woken from an enchanted sleep: something was actually happening in German class. Coffin walked to my table and took his glasses off, which I knew was something old people did sometimes to see better.

"And what words do you think might be more suitable to a normal conversation?" he asked me. I looked down at my table and proceeded to list what was on it.

"*Pencil,*" I said, "*pencil case, pencil shavings, eraser, graffiti.*"

"Well these sound like the roots of a very promising exchange, don't they?" Coffin said. The whole room laughed politely, which encouraged him to keep going.

"I didn't know you were such a conversationalist, Herr Mazal. You must have many friends."

"He doesn't!" Victor said, in an attempt, I assumed, to get my roast under way and waste a few more minutes of German class, but which had the opposite effect of putting Coffin back on my side (Coffin couldn't have had that many friends growing up) and his glasses back on his nose.

"Enough already," he yelled Victor's way. Herr Coffin never yelled, and I understood why when he did. Someone must have told him how his yelling sounded like an old lady's as she was being mugged. He turned back to me and forced his voice down to a deeper pitch than usual.

"And what do you suggest would be a proper vector to teach you more 'normal' words, Herr Mazal?"

"Maybe we could watch movies?" I said. "Movies in German?"

Coffin didn't reject the idea right away but didn't seem to know what I was talking about either.

"Movies," he repeated, as if the word represented some complex concept he was trying to remember from college.

"Yes," I said, "movies where people have everyday conversations."

"Like *Dirty Dancing*!" said Emilie, who sat next to me.

"That doesn't sound very German," Coffin said.

"Does it have to be?" Emilie bargained.

"I can't see what the pedagogical use would be otherwise."

"Maybe the movies would only have to be *dubbed* in German?" she said.

I thought this would ruin any chance we would ever have of Coffin's agreeing to show us a movie in class, but it got him thinking. He admitted he hadn't seen a new movie in a long time, and that he didn't even know who today's stars were (Coffin called them "idols").

Emilie started naming movie stars, and Coffin stopped her at Brad Pitt. He didn't believe *Brad Pitt* could actually be anyone's name. He thought we were pulling his leg. I wondered what Coffin did when he was alone. Several of my classmates confirmed Brad Pitt existed, but Coffin looked at me for confirmation. "It really is a name," I said.

"Has he been in any good movies?" Coffin asked.

"*Legends of the Fall*," Victor said, which surprised me a little. I wouldn't have gotten away with *Legends of the Fall*, but Victor was a popular guy, so no one made fun of him.

"Well I'll tell you what," Coffin said. "If all of you participate in class today, and by participating, I mean saying something not too dumb about this Hofmannsthal poem, and trying to do so in German, I will look for a version of *Legends of the Fall* dubbed in German."

Everyone suddenly had something to say about Hofmannsthal, and I thought they would all thank me for coming up with the watching-a-movie idea, but after class, the boys gathered around Victor and the girls around Emilie to show gratitude and share their excitement about *Legends of the Fall*.

———

I called Denise's house. Her mother said she couldn't come to the phone. I asked what was wrong, if Denise was sick. Her mother said, very politely, that Denise had anorexia and depression, like I might not have noticed. It felt insensitive to tell her I knew all that already and ask if there wasn't anything new with her daughter. It seemed like enough illnesses for one person already.

"Will you tell her Isidore called?" I said.

She said sure and thanked me for calling, and for my concern, which would make Denise very happy. I knew it wouldn't, and for a second I understood why Denise's mother drove her so mad.

I didn't like calling people. I was okay with picking up the phone (I liked it, actually; Simone said I'd make a great receptionist) but I thought I had to have a very good reason to be responsible for a phone ringing in someone else's house. I think it is because the ringing of our own phone seemed to bother our mother immensely most of the time. She'd sigh and say, "Who the hell?" when it rang, but then she always picked up with a warm hello. I thought a ringing phone had to annoy everyone as much as it did my mother, and that there would be no way to know that you'd annoyed them because, like her, they would always pretend they were happy to answer. I'd pondered calling Denise for a while. I'd decided that if I could come up with four questions to ask her and a story to tell that she might find entertaining, it would be enough to justify a call. I'd struggled to find four questions but I hadn't given up, which I thought meant I really wanted to call Denise. My story was going to be that of having convinced Herr Coffin to show us *Legends of the Fall* in German class. I'd written all of it down, the questions and the key story points, on a piece of paper. I wondered if I could reuse it as a model for future phone calls. I wondered if I was the only one who needed excuses to call a friend.

From the living room where I sat I heard Leonard come down the stairs and rummage through our walk-in pantry.

"I killed the Oreos," I said, in case that was what he'd been looking for.

He came into the living room.

"I thought you were watching your weight," he said.

"Not really," I said. "Berenice says I won't grow much if I diet in my teenage years. I don't want to be a midget."

"When did you drop the diet?"

Leonard asked this with what seemed like scientific interest more than sheer curiosity.

"Is that relevant to your academic research?" I asked. "Do you think my losing weight was a mourning strategy?"

"Forget about it," Leonard said.

"Are you going for a swim?"

"Yes," he said, looking down at the duffel bag he'd once let a wet swimsuit go moldy in. "I'm going crazy up there writing all day. I need to spend some energy."

I apologized about the Oreos and he left. I realized Jeremie was at symphony practice and that I could go upstairs and use his computer now—and without having Leonard watching over my shoulder.

The boys' bedroom smelled like old water in a vase. On Leonard's desk, one of his many notebooks had been left open. I knew I wouldn't dare to turn the notebook's pages—my siblings had a secret way to know if someone had been through their things—so I hoped Leonard had left it open to an interesting one.

study of symbolized/institutionalized relationships between individuals within more or less complex contexts, for which the groups studied by the first ethnology give us paradigmatic examples, or, to speak as Durkheim and Levi-Strauss after him, elementary. (Augé)

Role reassignment
[The family's father has been dead eighty-six days]
At a party the whole family is attending (a town event) (all minus my middle sister), my youngest brother tries to initiate a conversation with a young girl whom he's probably interested in on a sexual level. I spot him from the other side of the room. Our eyes meet, and before I can think about it, I give him the thumbs-up, which is not something I can remember ever doing before. As I do it, I

wonder about the reasons behind this unprecedented gesture. I can't decide whether I adopted a fatherly posture toward my youngest brother (encouragement of his attempt at establishing contact with the other sex) because our father's passing has made it my role to take certain of his duties upon myself, or if that was only me acting as an older brother. The rupture caused by our father's death has made salient certain things we had taken for granted so far; it revealed our previous routines and "ordinary" (cf. Chauvier's definition of the term) at the very same time that it made it an obsolete frame of reference. My posture within the family group has to be redefined.

TV night
[Same day]

Our predictions regarding the plot have become a less systematic exercise. I sense hesitation on my siblings' part now when the time comes to share their guesses relative to

I didn't turn the page. As I sat at Jeremie's computer, I tried to think about ways in which Leonard's "posture" had changed since the father had died. He hadn't become a more caring older brother, I didn't think. He hadn't started doing the dishes on weekends, like the father used to. He hadn't found God or a steady girlfriend. The only new thing he'd done was that he'd turned our family from a model of academic achievement into the subject of his own academic achievement. I guess, knowing him, it was the best he could have done with a family tragedy.

I logged in to my dating website account. There was a message from Daniel, apologizing for his performance at dinner with us a few weeks before, asking if we would consider coming to his house so he could treat us all to his specialty, duck in a raspberry-vinegar sauce. The date and time on top of the message indicated that Daniel had sent this a few minutes after having gotten back home from the condescension fest my family had held at his expense. I deleted the account. A window popped up to tell me Rare Pearl was sorry to see me go, and that they hoped this only meant I had found that special someone.

I wasn't comfortable using the Internet when my mother had expressly forbidden it, so I wanted to make it quick (she would be back from work soon) and efficient. I meant to fix all the mistakes I'd made. I took a minute to look up strokes, see if it was possible I'd made Daphné's happen or if she'd had it coming anyway. All three websites I checked seemed to agree that she'd had it coming, and maybe my presence at the very moment it had happened had been a good thing in the end. I hoped Daphné saw it like that. Browsing medical websites took a weight off my shoulders. As did getting rid of Daniel. The Internet was going to help me free myself of all responsibilities. Contrary to Leonard, who needed to see sociological problems behind everything, including the death of the father—as if it weren't in itself problematic enough—I wanted to simplify my thoughts. And my thoughts had been clouded by the idea that I might have caused Daphné's stroke and Denise's heartbreak. There wasn't much to do about Denise, though. I didn't know how to make someone fall in love with her for real, and I certainly couldn't fall in love with her myself, but I thought I could try to take her mind off school and the Porfis of the world for a minute. I went on Juliette Corso's website and clicked on the "Contact" tab. Juliette said she loved hearing from her fans and gave an address at which one could write to her. There was also a gallery of pictures from which one could choose a photo that Juliette would sign for a mere five euros plus shipping fees. I took note of the address, picked a picture of Juliette I thought Denise would like, wrote the reference number down, and walked away from my brothers' bedroom as my mother was coming home. I borrowed Simone's calligraphy set from her top desk drawer (it had, on top of deep black China ink and all sorts of quills, these thick sheets of paper like tapestry that I thought were very refined, and a line guide to help you not write all crooked on them) and applied myself.

Dear Juliette,

I wrote,

I am writing to you on behalf of a friend, who has been a big fan of yours since you appeared in the video for the Let Them Sea campaign when you were probably twelve to thirteen years old (we watched it in school at the time). The reason why I'm writing and she's not is because she has depression and can't find much interest in life, and when she does (she's interested in you!), she can't seem to get herself to do anything about it. So I was wondering if maybe you could send her (through me) an autographed picture (reference number 808578). I think this might help her see that life can be nice sometimes. I think it would make her happy, or at the very least less depressed. Her name is Denise Galet, but maybe if you just wrote "For Denise," it would feel to her more personal and warm.

My own name is Isidore. I wouldn't mind an autographed pic-
ture as well, but your website says you only send one picture per
fan mail, so maybe I'll write my own letter later. What I am
most interested in, actually, is knowing whether the Let Them
Sea campaign video that you were in was candid footage, or if
it was work for you as an actress. In other words: Had you seen
the sea before the day you shot the video? Did you have a little
brother who had never seen the sea either? If not, if it was all
"fake," can you tell me how you got the idea to look at your
brother/actor the way you did in the video, instead of looking
at the sea yourself like anyone would expect a girl who'd never
seen it before would do (and like all other kids in the video
did)? I thought it was very moving. You're either a very good
person or a very good actress. Maybe both!

Thank you for your answer,
Isidore Mazal

I felt good about the letter when I was done, as good as I felt
whenever I put some order into my bedroom. Or rather: my side
of the bedroom. I felt as good as I did whenever I put some order
into my side of the bedroom and *before* I looked at Simone's.
Simone's was always in disarray. Her bed was unmade at all
times. I don't think she'd ever folded a piece of clothing in her
life. I always hoped tidying my side of the room would inspire
her to do the same with hers, and since it kept not happening,
I'd once taken it upon myself to do it for her. I'd heard about it
for weeks. "What the hell have you done?" she'd complained. "I
can't find anything anymore!" She'd said her apparent disorgani-
zation was how she kept things organized, that she'd mapped it

all out in her head, and that I should never again mess with other people's messes. I didn't think I had messed with Denise's mess by writing a letter to her childhood crush. But the more I grew up, the harder it became to tell the difference between what was mine to organize and what wasn't any of my business at all.

———

Berenice came to visit for my birthday in May. She got me a bilingual edition of Thomas Mann's *Buddenbrooks,* which I knew right away I would never read and bequeathed back to her when I updated my will later that night. I also included Denise in the new version, extending my will to people outside the family for the very first time. Denise would get my backpack if I died. There was nothing special about my backpack. It was a black version of the same backpack almost everyone had at the time, but Denise had mentioned liking it once, and Denise never really mentioned liking anything. She'd said she liked that it was black and unaltered, when all the other kids picked weird colors or added stickers and pins to theirs to express their uniqueness. She'd missed school for two weeks already. When I'd called her house again, after mailing my letter to Juliette's fan club, Denise's mother had told me she might not come back at all the rest of the school year. They'd had to commit her to a clinic so she would gain a little weight, she'd told me. The teachers had stopped marking her as absent on their attendance-control sheets.

Berenice was supposed to only stay for my birthday weekend, but Monday came and went and she didn't head back to Paris. My mother asked if she didn't have a job to get back to. Berenice didn't say exactly what had happened with her contract, her school, just that she couldn't work there anymore. I assumed that meant her superiors had confirmed her suspension and cut away all forms of income, but she presented her situation as an affair that had everything and nothing to do with her at the same time.

"I might be too charismatic to teach," is what she said.

"Are those your superiors' words?" my mother asked. "Did students complain about your charisma?"

Berenice dismissed questions about her charisma by saying she was tired of explaining, as if she'd had many other people to explain her problem to over the previous days. If she had, we'd never heard of them.

At night, she often went out with Aurore, and they would come home tiptoeing and whisper-laughing in the wee hours of the morning and fall asleep in Aurore's bed. Aurore had defended her PhD almost six months before, but she didn't seem to be looking for a teaching job. I think Berenice was trying to convince her to get a second PhD instead.

In the afternoons, Berenice monopolized the house computer to look for an apartment in Chicago, where she wanted to move as soon as possible to familiarize herself with American English (hers was British English; I didn't know what the difference was) and American culture before school would start. She also looked forward to taking advantage of the University of Chicago Library, which she assumed would be deserted in the summer. I was secretly hoping she would never find an apartment and never move away from our house again. She had this mix of older-sibling sweetness and authority (I don't know if that's what she called her charisma) that made us all want to be on our best behavior around her. Everyone seemed less sad when she was home.

———

Denise missed about a month and a half of school and came back mid-June, a week before the end of the school year. She was fatter than I'd ever seen her, which was still not fat at all, but I knew it was too much for her and didn't comment on it. She had cheeks now, not just cheekbones, and I tried not to stare at them.

"You look good," I said, slightly worried she might find it insulting, but she thanked me. She sat on her usual step, but then got up right away and said it was nice enough out to go feed the birds. I didn't expect she would want to expose herself to all the kids on the playground on her first day back at school, but I thought maybe this meant she was cured and I followed her outside. We sat on the bench under the poplar, where everybody could see us, though some, like Porfi, pretended they didn't. Denise took a chocolate-covered candy bar out of her backpack. It was the first time I'd ever seen her holding such a thing. She usually brought day-old bread when she wanted to feed the birds.

"You're going to make these pigeons very happy," I said, looking at the chocolate bar.

"Are you crazy?" Denise said. "Chocolate *kills* birds. Don't you know that?"

Then she handed me some stale bread to crumble, unwrapped her chocolate bar, and started sucking on it, as if that was the way people ate them.

"I always wanted to try one of these," she said.

"What do you think?"

"It's pretty good. Although I'm not sure it's worth the amount of calories." She looked at the nutrition facts on the wrapping paper and informed me that three of those bars contained enough calories to get you through the day.

"You're supposed to bite through it," I said, "to get all the textures at once. Try it like that before you reach a final verdict."

Denise seemed hesitant, as if we were on a plane and I'd just asked her to do a parachute jump. She took the smallest possible bite. It wasn't even a bite, really, more a careful dissection of the outer chocolate that exposed the layers inside of the bar, none of which had met with her teeth.

"So?"

She brought her hand to her mouth and made a sign like she would answer me once she'd finished chewing, except I didn't understand how anyone could actually chew so tiny a bite of food as the one she'd taken. I saw Herr Coffin cross the playground, and Victor and Emilie run after him. I assume they asked him if he'd brought us a movie, and I assume Coffin said he hadn't, because both Victor and Emilie looked disappointed and went their separate ways to bring news to their respective groups.

"It *is* better that way," Denise said.

Coffin had gone weeks telling us he couldn't find a version of *Legends of the Fall* dubbed in German and that if we kept complaining about how he wasn't holding to his promise to show us a movie, he would cease looking for *Legends of the Fall* at once, or worse, bring us an actual German movie of his choosing. He didn't say "or worse," but people heard it anyway.

"You know what else is good?" I told Denise. "Ice cream."

"I remember ice cream," Denise said. "I think it's overrated."

She resumed sucking on her chocolate bar instead of really eating it.

"Have you talked to Porfi recently?" she asked. I said I hadn't and couldn't think of a reason to.

"Well I doubt he'll ever dare talk to me again," she said, "but if he comes to you, will you please tell him I never gave a shit about him? I would like him to know that."

"Why don't you tell him directly?"

"I tried to just catch his eye this morning on the way to class, but he won't even look in my direction. I think it would be more powerful coming from you anyway," she said. "Boys never believe a girl when she says she never cared. He would think it's pride or something."

"I would believe it," I said.

"You have many sisters. You don't count." She looked pretty certain I didn't qualify as a boy in this particular instance. "Will you tell him?"

"Sure," I said. "Whatever you want."

The birds at our feet didn't once look up to see where all the bread was coming from, as if crumbs falling from the sky wasn't a mystery worth investigating. But maybe they already knew that bread crumbs always came from humans and weren't too interested in figuring out in what specific ways I differed from the others. The monitor who had forbidden us to feed the birds before gave me a look from the other side of the playground but didn't come our way. The principal had probably instructed him to let Denise do whatever she wanted, and the small privileges her mental illness brought her must have, in his mind, extended to me.

When the bell rang, I told Denise I was glad she was back. I'd pondered telling her I had missed her but decided not to go that far, even though it was the truth.

"I'm glad too," she said, and then she dumped the rest of her chocolate bar, which was pretty much the whole of it, into the garbage can by the bench.

About ten minutes later, as Herr Coffin was going over the subtleties of the word *Geist,* I thought about how I should have told Denise to hold on to the chocolate bar. The garbage can on the playground didn't have a lid, and I feared the birds would dive in and have a taste of chocolate and die from it. I decided I would go down and retrieve the chocolate bar from the garbage can as soon as German class was over, but then I started to worry it might be too late. I was about to ask Coffin for permission to leave the room (at the risk of having everyone believe I had a small bladder) to sneak down to the playground and snatch the chocolate bar when we heard a thud, coming from the main hall. I didn't think it was a particularly alarming sound, but Victor took it as an opportunity to interrupt Coffin's class. "What was that?" he said, already up and ready to go out and check. Coffin said it was probably nothing and we ought to go on with the poem he'd brought us that day, but then we heard a woman scream and no one waited for Coffin's authorization to rush out of the room. Miss Da Ming, Denise's Chinese teacher, was holding on to the guardrail overlooking the school's entrance hall four floors down. "Someone call an ambulance," she said, but everyone wanted to see what an ambulance was needed for before they would do anything. "She just said she needed to go to the bathroom," I heard Miss Da Ming whisper as I elbowed my way through the students gathered around the rail. Denise was lying facedown on the tile floor thirty feet below, her arms bent at angles they shouldn't have been. For a whole minute, I think, I wondered how she'd managed to fall over the rail. It wasn't even a rail, more a concrete wall the height of a rail. "Check out that dent on the lockers!" a kid said. "She must've bounced on it on her way down!" "Maybe it softened the fall?" a girl said. I didn't understand how bouncing on the metal lockers could have softened anything. Denise wasn't moving, but there was no blood around her or anything. I thought it was a good sign. After the paramedics took Denise to the hospital (she was still breathing), I went downstairs and took away the chocolate bar from the top of the garbage can. It didn't look like the birds had touched it.

———

After Denise jumped in the atrium (which is what the teachers started calling the entrance hall that day, as if a suicide attempt created the need to use fancier words, or else, perhaps, to rename everything), classes were canceled for the rest of the day. Berenice was reading on the couch when I came home, and I startled her, as if I'd walked in on her in the middle of a very private activity. Which I guess was how she thought of reading.

"Shouldn't you be in school?" she said.

"No school today," I said. I didn't know how to explain that Denise had tried to kill herself after recess without having to have a whole conversation about it. I was still holding the barely eaten chocolate bar. It had melted a bit on the way home. Berenice folded her legs to make some room for me on the couch.

"I found an apartment in Chicago," she said.

"That's great news," I said. I felt like the projectionist had skipped a reel, like a whole scene was missing from between the last time I'd sat on the couch that morning and this one.

"I'll have to have roommates, though," Berenice said. "There was no way around it."

I knew how much the idea of sharing space with strangers made Berenice uncomfortable. "Maybe they'll be nice," I said.

"Well, at the very least, they should be smart. That's no small feat in this world."

"Are they all PhDs?"

"That's what they say."

Berenice picked up the book she'd laid open on her chest and started reading again.

"Do you mind if I watch TV?" I said.

"Of course I do. I'm reading."

"Maybe you could stop?"

"To watch daytime television?"

"We could go rent a movie or something. I'm sure we could find one that's set in Chicago. To get you in the mood. Or one where the hero has roommates."

"Why don't you go find yourself a book and sit here with me instead? We can have a reading workshop."

"I don't like reading," I said.

"You're too old to say things like that. It's not cute. Go get the book I got you for your birthday."

"It sounds a bit boring," I admitted, picturing all the shades of brown on the *Buddenbrooks* dust jacket.

"It's your fault for being into German culture," Berenice said. "I would've gotten you something less taxing otherwise."

It became clear to me at that point that I was about to cry. There was this pressure right behind my eyes. It burned, almost, while the rest of my body suddenly filled with a waft of cold air. I didn't understand how Berenice couldn't feel it. I always felt it when someone next to me was sad.

"Are you going to eat that?" Berenice was pointing at the chocolate bar in my hand.

I shook my head no and she grabbed the bar and bit through it like a normal person would.

"By the way," she said, her mouth full of peanuts and caramel and maybe some of Denise's saliva from two hours before. "There was a letter for you in the mail."

It wasn't really a letter. Juliette had just sent an autographed picture, the one I'd requested, of her in a baby-blue dress standing in a field of sunflowers, on which she'd written, "For Denise Galet, With all my ❤❤❤ Juliette Corso." No note, no answers to my questions about the charity campaign. I wasn't even sure Juliette had read my letter, or if she had assistants who opened her mail for her and only made lists of the pictures she would have to sign and of the names that should go on them. I put the picture back in the reinforced envelope it had come in, so it wouldn't bend. There was a tiny chance, I thought, that Denise would be back in school in a day or two.

When school resumed, we were told a psychological support unit had been set up, for those who needed to talk about what had happened to Denise. No one went, and so the day after, the principal made it mandatory for all eighth graders to go talk to the social workers, so they wouldn't have come all the way there for nothing. We would be called in alphabetical order throughout the next couple of days, the principal said. At recess, I heard two girls, Steph and Jess, go to Sara Catalano to inquire about her meeting with the counselors.

"What did they ask you?" Jess said, like it was all a big school test and Sara could help them score better results.

"They asked how I was dealing with all of it," Sara said, visibly proud to have had the psychological support unit experience a couple of hours ahead of most people. "They asked if I felt guilty."

"Really? Why?"

"What did you say?"

"I think I'm not supposed to tell," Sara said. "There's professional confidentiality."

"Well that's just for them," Jess said. "You're not a professional."

"I guess you're right," Sara said. "Anyway. I told them I wished I could've done something to help Sunshine out but—"

"Wait, you actually told them Denise's nickname was Sunshine?"

"No, of course I didn't," Sara said.

"Did they know about it, though?"

"I don't know. They didn't refer to her as Sunshine."

They all went quiet for a few seconds, as if they were about to understand something.

"So," Sara resumed, "I told them I'd tried to reach out to

Sunshine in the past, like, I'd tried to show her that life wasn't all about being miserable and all, so I felt like I had done whatever I could and I didn't think I was guilty."

"I didn't know you'd tried to be friends with her."

"I didn't try to be *friends*, just, you know, see what her deal was."

"When?"

"I don't know. Couple years ago. Like, after she took all those pills. She came to my mother's practice for cavities. I saw her come out of the building and I was like, 'Why did you do that with your mother's pills?' like, I really wanted to understand what had gone on, but she told me to mind my own business so I was like, 'Okay, fine, I tried,' you know? But then I thought maybe she was being defensive because she didn't trust me or something and so I told her that if she needed to talk to someone, I was available. Like, not at school, but after school, if she wanted. We live on the same block. She didn't like that either."

"What did she say?"

"She told me to go to hell and to take my condensation with me."

Jess whistled, to signify how harsh she thought Denise's response had been.

"My mother said her teeth were all fucked up anyway," Sara added.

"Well they sure are now," Jess said. "They say her jaw blew to pieces."

They paused again.

"Did you tell them all that? That she'd turned you down?"

"At first I thought it would be unfair to Sunshine to talk about how she didn't want my help, but then I figured, what the hell, the more I talk, the more these shrinks feel like their job is important, and the more French class I get to miss."

"You're so lucky they called you during French class," Steph said. "With my luck, I'll probably just miss civics, which is basically, like, not a class anyway."

"Can you actually make it last as long as you want?" Jess inquired. "Like, if I start crying or something by the end of the thirty minutes, they'll have to keep me, right?"

My turn came the following morning. The psych support unit had been set up in the auditorium's dressing rooms, behind the stage, at the end of a narrow, tilted hallway. I'd never been there before. I'd never even auditioned for a school play. The social workers, a man and a woman wearing jackets in different shades of corduroy, had laid their files on the long table attached to a wall of mirrors where I assumed tissues and palettes of cheap makeup usually went. For a second I thought the mirrors were two-way and that Denise hadn't really jumped, but that this was in fact a criminal investigation. Only the male social worker talked. I wondered if the woman took care of the girls. She just stared at me the whole time and didn't say anything.

"Are you close to Denise?" the man asked me.

"I don't know," I said. "I'm not sure what *close* means."

"I heard people say she was your girlfriend."

"I heard people say strawberry was the best flavor of ice cream," I said.

"Hmm."

He wrote something down in his notebook and underlined it decisively.

"And what do you think is the best flavor of ice cream, Isidore?" he asked. He waited to be done with his question to look back up at me.

"Is this a new school of psychology?" I said. "Ice-cream preference based?"

He wrote down something else.

"Would you define yourself as skeptical? Do you believe people generally have hidden intentions? That their questions cannot be genuine?"

"Denise told me once that I took things too literally," I said. "I think she meant I was dumb."

"Did that hurt your feelings?"

"Not particularly."

"Where were you when Denise had her accident?"

"German class."

"Do you like German?"

"It has a few good words," I said.

"Were you aware Denise was suicidal?"

"Yes. I mean, everybody is. Aware of it, I mean."

"Would you say you understood what suicide meant before she jumped?"

"Yes, I would."

"Would you care to expand?"

"I don't feel guilty, if that's what you want to know," I said. "Denise doesn't like life. Not just her own. In general. It pains her. It has nothing to do with me. Not specifically."

"Who said anything about guilt? Do you think you're expected to feel guilty?"

"I think it would be pretentious to feel guilty. It would mean there was something I could've done to change her whole world-view and I didn't care to do it, or just forgot to pull it out of my sleeve. But I had nothing. I still have nothing."

The social worker nodded.

He asked about a few more things, my health, what kind of lifestyle I led, if I liked team sports. I didn't understand how that related to anything, but I answered as best I could. When he ran out of random questions, I got up to leave the way I'd come, but the woman social worker stopped me and shook her head no. Her colleague explained the next kid was waiting and we were not supposed to cross paths.

"Why not?" I asked.

"That's just how it works," he said, and he pointed at a small door at the other end of the room. "You can exit through here. It's the artists' exit."

I pushed the door open and found myself at the top of the staircase Denise and I had spent two years' worth of recesses in.

———

Back home I fixed myself a bowl of ice cream with all the flavors we had in the basement freezer. Some pints had been there for too long and their insides were covered with that thin layer of ice crystals that tells you the ice cream will taste exactly like the cardboard around it, but I scooped some out of those anyway. Our freezer was big enough that we didn't really ever need to organize it or get rid of anything, even the things we didn't like. I ended up with thirteen different flavors, cherry, candied chestnut, chocolate chip, coffee, lavender, blueberry, pineapple, rum raisin, nougat, pistachio, speculoos, coconut, and licorice. All the flavors that sounded weird had been bought by the father and were therefore at the very least two years and a couple of months old. I went back up to the living room and turned the TV on. A reality show was playing, introducing people who wanted to be famous for nothing in particular, like Simone but not as smart. One of them was eating ice cream too, out of a pint that had been covered with black duct tape to hide the brand.

"Who do you think will be eliminated next week?" the ice-cream-eating guy asked another guy.

"Geez, I hope Cynthia goes home," the second guy said. "She gets on my nerves so bad, you know? She's so negative."

"Totally, it's like she doesn't even want to *be* here," the first guy said, "like she can't see how lucky she is to even *be* here."

I thought the audience would be shown a scene with Cynthia next, so they could make up their mind about her, whether she should go home or not, but the two guys remained on-screen and talked some more about how lucky they were to be there, what a great opportunity it was, to be there, to just *be*, really, and to get all that love from the fans by just *being* there, *being themselves*. I started laughing because I couldn't really believe how much they were using the verb *to be*. I must have laughed very loud because Simone came rushing down the stairs to see what was up, and in the process of laughing I had spilled some ice cream on the couch, and I thought that was the reason why she was staring at me judgmentally, but then when I looked at the spilled ice cream and invoked laughing as an excuse for it, Simone just said that I had scared her, laughing like a maniac, and who the hell laughed when they were alone anyway? Then she walked back up to our room. The thirteen ice creams in my bowl had started to melt and now swirled together in one of those tie-dye-T-shirt patterns. I considered slurping the whole thing but then I thought it was too pretty to destroy.

I went to the kitchen to get a bucket of soapy water and a sponge to clean the ice cream I'd spilled on the couch before it would dry. While I was at it, I tried getting rid of the old stain, even though I'd tried and failed many times before. I thought maybe old stains could be like people and decide to give up one day, without a reason, to just disappear. This one didn't. The couch was just big enough for four of us. It had often been a source of conflict, who got to sit on the couch, who took the chair, who had to sit on cushions on the floor. But Berenice was packing to move to Chicago, Simone couldn't wait to start school in Paris, and the father was dead. Occasions to plead for a spot on the couch had gotten scarce and would only grow scarcer with time, I thought. Yet the repeated fights over who got to sit on the couch had been the best arguments in favor of getting a new, bigger one. From now on, no one but me would ever see the need to get rid of it. I scraped the old stain until it became a hole. Maybe a hole would make my family see that it was time for a change. Probably they wouldn't notice. When the hole got big enough, I started pulling the wadding out of the cushion. By the time I emptied the cushion entirely, my ice creams had all melted together in a light brown puddle.

The V-Effekt

ONLY DENISE'S FAMILY was allowed to visit her while she was in the coma. "Denise's family" meant her parents. She got transferred from the ICU to neurology a few days before the end of the school year. The doctors had no idea when she'd wake up, but they suspected that when she did, her main problems would be for the neurologists to solve. When Denise's parents told me this, I asked them if that meant Denise was going to be paralyzed, because I thought that people in wheelchairs were all that neurologists dealt with, but they both shook their heads silently like no one had told them anything and they were afraid to ask.

Since Denise had jumped, it seemed her parents had been trying to morph into one single person. You saw them walking on the street side by side, each one enveloping the other at the waist with an arm, the two other arms intertwined and clasped at the elbows in front of them. Simone joked that you could put your groceries in the crib that their arms formed, that they had become a human basket, and I couldn't help but visualize fruits and vegetables and bread in their arms whenever I saw them.

I wanted to like Denise's parents, because they were going through something horrible, but I was uncomfortable around them. They always insisted on talking about something other than Denise—the weather, my sisters—and I always had to answer their questions politely and wait until we were done going over the subjects they pretended to be interested in before I could ask how Denise was.

"Oh, it is so sweet of you to ask," they'd say, like they hadn't seen it coming.

I saw them one day on my way back from school, and I contemplated pretending I hadn't. I always felt lousy reverting to that trick. I believed that the second you decided to pretend not to see someone, they could feel it, and that there was no winning because the person would either stop and chat with you knowing you didn't want to, just to make you uneasy, or pass you and be hurt by your attitude, which I didn't think Denise's parents deserved. I crossed the street to go up to them.

Denise's mother smiled when she saw me and said they had great news.

"Has Denise woken up?" I said, and Denise's mother's smile disappeared when she admitted that no, she hadn't. "But we saw Daphné Marlotte getting some sun in her wheelchair in the hospital yard earlier, and her nurse said they were releasing her tomorrow. Isn't that wonderful?"

I glanced at Denise's father to see how wonderful he thought that was before I would decide what to say.

"Wonderful," he said. He pulled his wife even closer to his chest. "If she can make a full recovery, at her age, boy, there's hope for our little girl."

I wondered if they'd been told that Denise's fall had been an intentional one. They seemed to believe all problems would be solved once her body was fixed.

"I wasn't aware Mrs. Marlotte had fully recovered," I said.

"Well . . . she's not exactly fully there."

"Apparently, she lost the ability to speak," Denise's father explained.

"To speak French, at least."

"But her German seems to be accurate, so they set her up with a bilingual nurse, for the home visits."

"I don't understand," I said, even though I thought I did. "Daphné forgot how to speak French entirely? I thought this only happened in movies."

"Movies are often based on truth," Denise's father said.

"Yes. *The Notebook* was a true story, wasn't it?"

"I don't know about that one, honey, we'll have to check."

"Either way, it's a beautiful story, on the theme of memory."

"I haven't seen that movie," I said. I was sure Denise hadn't liked *The Notebook*, since her parents had, and I felt sad for her that they were the only ones allowed to visit her.

"The brain is such a mysterious muscle," said her father.

I wanted to give them Juliette's picture. I'd had it framed and always carried it in my bag. I thought it would make Denise happy to see it on her nightstand when she woke up, if they gave you such a thing as a nightstand when you were in a coma. Maybe she would think Juliette had been there in her room to encourage her to live longer. I could never get myself to hand her parents the picture though. They would've had to break the lock of their arms to take it.

———

On the last day of school, Coffin made arrangements with our French teacher to keep us for three hours in a row so we could watch an entire movie. He hadn't found *Legends of the Fall,* he said, and what he brought us didn't have Brad Pitt in it but Lauren Bacall, but that, in his opinion, was better. I thought he meant to say that it was better because he was a man and Lauren Bacall had been a stunning woman while he had no interest in Brad Pitt physically, but the movie was recent, and Lauren Bacall was an old woman in it. It wasn't a German movie, it wasn't even dubbed in German—Coffin could only find it with German subtitles—but in spite of that, he explained, it would teach us something about German culture. The movie was *Dogville* and no one liked it. The class felt cheated because it didn't even look like a movie but like filmed theater, which was the worst thing they could think of as far as entertainment went, worse even than live theater.

"There's no decor, no nothing," Emilie complained. "The whole time, you're supposed to buy that those white lines on the floor are walls, or mountains or gardens or whatever . . . I don't get it. It's like there wasn't any budget for the movie, but then Kidman's in it, so you know they had bank.

"And it warns you from the beginning that it's going to be a sad story," Emilie said. "It tells you there's going to be nine chapters, and before each chapter it tells you what's going to happen next. Who wants to watch something when they know how it will end?"

"I thought chapters were only for books anyway," Victor said.

Coffin let everyone vent for a while. I didn't say anything because I had actually enjoyed the movie somewhat—I had only fallen asleep a couple of times and had, as a result, found the warnings before each chapter quite handy. Coffin was so still behind his desk, I thought for a minute that he might've died of a fussless heart attack, like the father had. People had only noticed he was gone when their board meeting had ended and the father hadn't gotten up to shake their hands. But Coffin was still alive. He'd just been waiting for the class to run out of disappointed comments to share his own opinions on the film.

"Who among you," he said, "has any idea why a filmmaker would resort to such a bare setting to tell his story?" Silence. "You all seem to agree that what we just saw was lacking some sort of magic—if you'll allow me such a word—a magic that you would usually seek in a movie, one that ensues from rich set decoration, nail-biting suspense, et cetera. Why would an artist consciously decide to do without such . . . magic tricks?"

"To alienate the audience?" Emilie offered.

Some in the back rows laughed, assuming Emilie's intent had been comical, but Coffin was impressed by her answer.

"Very good," he said. "Your classmate Emilie has just, without knowing it, I assume, taken her stand in a very long debate about the translation of the word *Verfremdungseffekt*."

Victor coughed the second Coffin finished saying *Verfremdungseffekt*, which is something he thought was funny to do every time he heard a German word more than three syllables long. There were a lot of those.

"See," Coffin went on, ignoring Victor's coughing, "specialists of performing arts theory have long wondered how to best translate this term coined by playwright Bertolt Brecht, the *Ver-fremdungseffekt*." (Victor coughed again.) "Some choose to ren-der it as *distancing effect*, some as *estrangement effect*, and some even, as your friend Emilie intuited, as *alienation effect*. Now let's go a little farther. Why is it you think an artist would want to distance—or estrange, or alienate—his audience?"

Emilie's whole demeanor had shifted from sniffy to scholarly the moment Coffin had shown interest in her comment. She was thrilled and trying, poorly, to hide exactly how thrilled she was, the way I had been in swimming class after I'd held my breath longer than anybody. She was now assuming a posture of knowl-edge and tried to give Coffin the answer he wanted.

"Maybe if the artist doesn't want the audience to get in-volved?" she said.

"Well, yes, Emilie, sure. But that is just another way to say he would want to distance his audience," Coffin said. Emilie pinched her lips sideways. I didn't know if that meant she was looking to elaborate on her answer or if she was just disappointed to have lost her knowledgeable pose. No one said anything for a while, and Coffin had to come up with a new angle.

"It sounds to me," he said, "hearing your comments on the film, like it has indeed failed to get you involved in it, at least in the way you're used to getting involved in the movies you would typically watch. It didn't *move* you. A certain number of elements were missing in order for you to really relate to the characters. Instead, you found yourself wondering: Why am I being shown this character in this unusual way? How am I supposed to believe that there's a wall there when it's obviously just a piece of tape on the floor? What does this all mean about our society? What if the characters could see through the walls the way the audience can? Would the story be different? And, side note: of course it would. All the while, you're not building an emotional connection with the characters, but an intellectual one with the art piece itself. The movie didn't move you the way you wanted it to, but it made you think. That is the *Verfremdungseffekt*, or, as certain people would call it, the V-Effekt."

The class was not as interested in this as Coffin had hoped. Emilie glanced at her watch.

"But that's not entertainment, then, if you have to think about it," Victor said.

Coffin was ready to counter that.

"What Brecht thought," he said, "was that all the illusions that a traditional narrative encumbered itself with were only building a hypnotic field between the play and the audience, that the hypnotic field only brought passive compliance and let the public fall under its spell, never encouraging them to interpret the work critically."

"But we have philosophy classes for that," Emilie said. "And history and civics and all that. Science, even. Art is not there to make us think critically, it is just meant to help us escape our lives and make us feel things."

"And Brecht would argue that there is a form of involvement other than emotional empathy, one that requires the audience to go into a play, or a movie, with an investigating eye instead of a passive one."

"Germans are so fucked up," Victor said, not loud enough for Coffin to hear. "Can't just let people enjoy themselves."

The bell to the last class of the year was about to ring and I knew the rest of the class would hate me for having us stay even one minute overtime because of the stupid question I wanted to ask, but I asked it anyway.

"Isn't there a way to have it—" The bell rang there and I let it ring before resuming with my question, indicating I meant to resume by not packing my bag the way everyone else around me was. "Isn't there a way to have it all?" I said. "To be, at the same time, intellectually and emotionally involved in a movie or a play?"

I thought this would get Coffin thinking for a second but his answer was immediate and foursquare.

"Impossible," he said. "You cannot have both the critical interpretation and . . . the magic at the same time."

I wanted to ask him if he thought the same went for life in general, if one had to make a choice between overthinking and truly living it, but Coffin seemed so satisfied that the words he'd just spoken should be the last of his teaching year that I let him have it.

"You all have a wonderful summer now," he said, and half the class was lined up at the door before he'd finished his sentence. Coffin himself looked eager to get away from us.

"Great job requesting we watch a movie in class," Victor said as he passed my table. "I think we all would've preferred an actual German class to this shit."

I said I was sorry, even though I didn't believe Victor's feelings on the movie were my responsibility at all. I knew my apology would destabilize him and send him on his way to bother other people. It did. As I packed my bag, careful not to break the frame with Juliette's picture under the weight of my German textbook, I wondered if Leonard knew about the *Verfremdungs-*

effekt. Deprived of magic. I wondered if that was how he saw us, how he *had* to see us in order to write his PhD dissertation.

"Well I thought it was interesting," I heard Emilie say on her way out. She'd waited to be the last person in the room to tell me this, so I would be the only one to hear, and she'd only said it in passing, maybe just to be kind, but I clung to her remark as if we were friends.

"You don't think Coffin is wrong though?" I asked her. "About art either being an intellectual or an emotional experience?"

Emilie stopped and turned around to look at me but she didn't come closer, staying on the threshold of the classroom.

"I don't know." She shrugged. "He's the teacher. He has to know, right?"

I thought about this, apparently a bit too long for her taste.

"Anyway," she said, "enjoy your summer, Isidore. I hope Denise gets better."

I wanted to thank her but I could only wave before she was out of my sight.

When I came home, my mother was waiting for me on the sidewalk in front of our door. She was sitting on our couch, reading the paper.

"What's the couch doing on the sidewalk?" I said.

"Well, it's waiting for the trash truck, obviously."

"Did you get a new one?"

"No, not yet. I thought we could go pick one together one of these days."

"Where are we going to sit in the meantime?"

"What's with all the questions, Dory? I thought you'd be happy about this."

I sat on the couch next to her and said nothing.

"It was about time we changed it, don't you think?"

—

Berenice moved to Chicago in July. Denise was still in a coma, and I kept setting deadlines to maintain hope. *She'll wake up before the new couch comes in,* I'd told myself. Then when they'd delivered the couch, I'd thought, *She'll wake up before Berenice leaves.* I had to come up with new deadlines all the time.

I was trying to decide when Denise would wake up when Aurore came into my bedroom to see if Simone had borrowed her old edition of Tommaso Garzoni. Simone was in the shower.

"I don't think she would've told me about it," I said to Aurore. "But you're welcome to look around."

I knew Aurore had waited for Simone to be in the shower on purpose. My siblings always borrowed books from one another without warning the rightful owner. That way, they hoped, they would get to keep the books. If the rightful owner realized a book was missing, they'd retrieve it without a word to the borrower. They couldn't officially complain—they all did the same thing. It wasn't stealing but *hopeful borrowing,* Simone had explained to me. I guess it worked and the borrowers got to keep the books sometimes, or else they wouldn't have kept doing it.

Aurore started scanning Simone's bookshelves, and as she spotted what she was looking for, or something else she could hopeful-borrow, she extended her whole body to grab it and her loose pajama top lifted and I saw that she was pregnant. Just a little, I thought, but then there was no such thing as being just a little pregnant. She didn't catch me looking, acted unaware, even, that anyone might notice, and I wondered if she herself knew what was going on.

"How have you been?" I said.

"What do you mean how have I been?" Aurore said. "I live in the bedroom across the hall from you, have you noticed? You talk like you haven't seen me in ages."

"Well you've been out with Ber a lot lately. We haven't seen much of you."

"You never see much of me," Aurore said.

She grabbed another book, flipped through it, and said something about Simone's horrible reading habits (dog-earing, underlining, correcting typos).

"Are you thinking about getting a second PhD too?" I asked.

"Maybe," she said. "Employment prospects for a history PhD in France are just dismal."

"I didn't realize you'd been looking for a job."

Aurore looked like she was going to respond to that but then she changed her mind and put the second book back on the shelves and I saw her round stomach again. Could it just be that she'd been drinking more than usual and what she had was what people called beer belly?

"Maybe *Berenice* left with my Garzoni," Aurore said, like we were both involved in solving a mystery.

I looked at her breasts, to see if they'd gotten any bigger. I thought I was being stealthy, only glancing for a second, and only on my way to pretend-look at the clock on Simone's shelf, but girls have an extra sense when it comes to people checking out their breasts. Aurore felt I'd been looking and held the first book she'd taken from Simone's shelf tight against her chest.

"I guess I'll just borrow this one then," she said.

"Sure."

"No need to tell Simone."

"Of course not."

She left the room and closed the door behind her, which was something I often complained no one ever did. Maybe she assumed, because she'd caught me looking at her breasts, that I needed some privacy. I was embarrassed by that. Mostly though, I was excited that I was going to be an uncle. I had no idea how far along Aurore was, but I started making plans for when the baby would arrive. I guessed he would sleep in Aurore's bedroom at first, but that she would get tired of his screaming fast, and then he'd end up with me, since Simone would've moved out by then. I tried to picture a crib where Simone's bed was. I wanted to picture other things but I didn't know much about babies. I pictured myself teaching him things—what, exactly, I would determine later. I pictured myself taking him out for strolls, introducing him to people, when people were interested. I pictured him smiling at Denise in a way that would show her that life was not all bad. Denise would be awake by the time the baby was born, I'd decided.

———

Denise awoke before Aurore's body really had time to show any more signs of pregnancy. Her mother gave me a call and said I could come visit Denise at the hospital whenever I wanted before eight p.m. I subtly tried to figure out a time when I could go without having to see her parents ("I don't want to be in your way," I said), and Denise's mother said that around five thirty, she and her husband would go home to take showers and watch *Questions pour un Champion* before they would return to the hospital to kiss their daughter good night. I said it sounded great, that if I went while they watched their show, Denise wouldn't have to be alone at any point. Except when I knocked on Denise's door, her room was empty and I was told a nurse was taking her through the hospital for various tests. A male nurse who walked around with what looked like Ziplocs full of blood showed me a place to sit and said I might wait awhile.

"Can't I just go meet her wherever she is right now?" I asked, but the nurse told me there was no way to know where Denise was exactly at this moment. I thought he just didn't want to take the time to help me, but then as I sat and waited, I heard people ask where their doctors were and saw doctors come by wondering where their patients were, and the nurses couldn't tell them anything either, and doctors and patients seemed to find that perfectly normal, like a hospital was by definition a place where no one knew where anyone else was.

On the wall between the waiting room and the nurses' station, someone had pinned a little piece of paper that read something like evryethnig one nedeed in odrer to undresatnd a mesasge was for the frist and last letrtes of its wodrs to be wehre tehy had to and the rset of the lettres colud be all fcuked aournd wtih it did not matetr becuase the barin rergonaized the lettres autaomitcally.

It didn't say that exactly, but that was the idea. I wondered if Simone knew about that.

I waited and waited until visiting hours were over, surprised and also relieved Denise's parents hadn't shown up. I'd read on the Internet that in some cases of depression, doctors opted for isolating the patient from anyone she knew, friend or family, in order for her to recover. I thought maybe that's what they were doing with Denise, except they'd warned her parents and not me. I waited another half hour and finally, a nurse I'd never seen before but who seemed to know who I was came to me and told me that Denise had died an hour ago, inside the MRI machine. She told me her parents were with the body, and she gave me instructions on how to go see the body myself. She kept saying *body*. I had no desire to see the body. I started to translate, in my head, all the words the nurse had spoken into German. *Body. She is dead. Der Leib/der Körper. Sie ist tot/Sie ist gestorben.* They had less power that way.

I asked if I could go inside Denise's bedroom instead of the morgue, and the nurse repeated that Denise had died and that it meant no one would bring her back to her room. No one—*niemand*; room—*das Zimmer*; her room—*ihre Zimmer*.

"I understand," I said. "I would still like to go in."

She considered my request.

"All right," she said. "You can go. But the cleaning team will be here any minute."

I went in and she followed me. "We had some cases of theft on this floor," she explained.

Theft . . . how did one say that . . . *Stahl*?

I looked around the room and saw nothing worthy of being stolen, and the nurse must have shared my opinion because she sighed and said, "I'll give you some privacy now," and left. The room looked like the cleaning team had been there already. I took

Juliette's picture out of my bag and set it on the nightstand, since there was one, and sat on Denise's hospital bed. I didn't think I was accomplishing any kind of meaningful act of mourning there. I just never wanted to see the picture again.

⌣

Denise hadn't left any kind of note, which I'd found okay as long as she hadn't died from her suicide attempt—I thought it meant she hadn't really *meant* to die, and therefore that she wouldn't— but once she did, I couldn't wrap my head around it. "Most suicides don't leave notes, actually," Simone told me, as if blending the specificities of Denise's case into a standard pattern would somehow make the whole thing more acceptable. When I asked Simone how she knew about the notes, she just said that she did.

Denise had left instructions for her funeral, though, saying she would "prefer" it if the ceremony could be held in the afternoon, although she wasn't sure that it was done. She'd written that all people wanted to do after a funeral was sleep, and that having to go to one in the morning just made for too long a day. Her mother booked the latest possible time slot, five p.m. I didn't go.

My mother thought the reason why I didn't want to go was that I was angry at Denise, and she tried to get me to attend by explaining or having my siblings explain to me that I would regret it if I didn't go say good-bye, that there was nothing in Denise's decision that I should take personally, that she'd made a choice and that no matter how horrible it was, I should respect it etc. Except I wasn't angry. I was just too tired.

At four thirty, Simone tried one last time to get me out of bed.

"We're all here for you, Dory," she said. "We're all going." I said I was glad to hear they were all going to the funeral because the only thing I really wanted was to be home alone. And also to be called Izzie, even though I was kind of starting to give up on that one.

They all left and I stayed in bed, hoping to fall asleep until the next day, but at five p.m. sharp, the telephone rang and woke me. I let the answering machine pick up but couldn't hear, from my bedroom, whether anyone was leaving a message. The phone rang again. I dragged myself to the closest handset, in my mother's bedroom, my duvet on my shoulders hanging behind me like a train. As I picked up the phone, I wondered what had made me bring my duvet along, given my mother had blankets on her bed as well. I suspected myself of making a show of my sadness, except there wasn't anyone around to see it.

"Finally!" Berenice said at the other end of the line. "Where is everybody?"

I said they were at a funeral.

"Oh, right," Berenice said. "Your friend. I am so sorry, Dory."

"How's Chicago?" I asked.

Berenice sneezed and I heard a man in the background say, "Bless you," and Berenice's voice stray away from the receiver to thank him.

"Is that your roommate?" I said.

"No, I'm not even home. It's just some random guy in the student lounge. Our phone doesn't work and I had to get a calling card and come down here to call. I'm not exactly sure how long I have."

"Do random people bless you like that in America?"

"They do," Berenice said. She made it sound like a terrible thing. "Listen," she said. "I'm horribly sorry about your friend. I actually started writing you a letter yesterday."

"Why?"

"Well, just to cheer you up, you know? Tell you that I think about you."

"Why wouldn't you tell me over the phone?"

"I'm not as good with direct speech," she explained, and then she stayed silent for about thirty seconds, as if to illustrate what she'd just said.

"So how's life with roommates?" I asked.

"I don't think they like me much," Berenice said. "They're a bunch of tight-asses, if you want to know what I think. They always have a complaint, like I let things rot in the fridge, or my hair clogs the shower drain."

"Don't they have hair too?"

"My thoughts exactly. They actually *do* have hair. But they always assume it's mine that causes problems. And I mean, they're probably right, they're such tight-asses, I'm sure they have personal hair traps that they bring with them in the shower for their own sheddings. I don't know how they manage to never forget to clean after themselves. They're impossible to foil. They're the kind that clean everything before the cleaning lady comes."

"You guys have a cleaning lady?"

"Of course not. What are you talking about? It's an image."

"Do you talk to them at all?"

"I try to be nice, you know, with them being all over me because of my hair. I offered to do their dishes the other day, for instance. First, it took way longer than I thought it would, and then they didn't even thank me afterward. And last night, Michelle decided she had to cook some kind of vegetarian something and she realized we were out of whatever sprouts and so I told her I would go get some, even if I hadn't been the one to finish her sprouts behind her back, and I went to the store and brought her what she wanted . . . she didn't offer me any of her dish when she was done cooking. I mean, it looked disgusting, but still. And this morning she complained about my hair clogging the drain again. I thought my being nice would get her to back off a bit. I'm trying here, trying to be selfless, but the responses to my selflessness never really match my efforts, you know what I mean?"

"Isn't that the principle of selflessness?" I said.

"I guess you would know that. You're the specialist."

"What do you mean?"

"Well, you're always nice. You always want to please everyone. I don't know how you do it."

Berenice took a bite of something crunchy and chewed it right into the phone receiver. She couldn't possibly have been aware of how loud her chewing was in my ear, or she would have been embarrassed.

"Do you know Aurore is pregnant?" I said.

"Yeah," Berenice said. She stopped chewing, although she probably still had food in her mouth (I hadn't heard her swallow). "I didn't think anyone else knew."

"You don't sound too happy for her," I said.

"Does she look happy for herself?"

"Well," I said, "no. Not yet. But she has to love the baby when it comes, right?"

Berenice swallowed.

"There's not going to be a baby, Dory," she said.

I don't know if it was the fact she'd stopped chewing in my ear or what she'd said about the baby, but Berenice suddenly felt less close to me. I actually pictured the ocean between us.

"Let's talk about something else," she said.

"You're the one calling," I said. "Is there something you wanted to tell Mom?"

"I wanted to tell her about the meeting we had yesterday, with the whole program's faculty and all the students who are going to be in my class."

"Do they look nice?"

"Hard to tell. I didn't speak to anyone really, but guess what: they're all only getting their *first* PhD and I'm still *younger* than any of them! Can you believe that?"

"That's great!" I said. I knew that kind of thing was important to Berenice.

She made a strange throat sound, like she was swallowing something too big for it.

"Are you withholding a sneeze so that the guy doesn't bless you once more and you don't have to thank him again?"

"What? No, what are you talking about?"

"You are!"

"It's just . . . it makes me uncomfortable. The familiarity."

"What else do Americans do that's weird?" I said.

"Well, I knew they wouldn't let me smoke anywhere but no one told me about the booze situation. It's a dry campus, can you believe that? How horrible does that sound?"

"I don't know," I said. "I've never had a drink."

"You're kidding, right? You got laid before you ever had a drink? How is that even possible?"

"How do you know I got laid?"

"Mom told me."

"How does Mom know?"

"I don't know, Dory. Did you tell Simone? Simone repeats everything. Anyway, your friend just died. Now is the time to start drinking. Have a cognac or something. Mom always keeps a very good bottle for the harder times. It's in the bottom drawer of her dressing table, with all the makeup and powders and creams she never uses, hidden behind them."

She sneezed and got blessed and thanked the person.

"What did your letter say?" I asked.

"What letter?"

"The letter you started writing to me."

"Do you want me to call you back and read it to you? It's just a draft so far."

"No, I want you to tell me."

"It was just ideas, an outline. I didn't really write anything yet."

"Give me the outline, then."

"I was going to tell you about this friend Lea I had in grammar school. I was like six years old and she was maybe eight or something? You weren't even born yet."

"What about her?"

"She was one of these people, you know, they decide to be your friend like it's only up to them? You mind your own business, you don't ask for anything, and the person just sits next to you in class, follows you around at recess, wants to know what foods you like, and colors and such?"

"Sure," I said. I couldn't tell whether that was what Denise had done—decided for the both of us that we would be friends.

"Well anyway, we became sort of buddies. I even went to her

house for playdates, and she came to ours a few times—I didn't like that too much, to be honest, but Mom said we had to reciprocate. She always messed with my stuff. Anyway. At the end of that school year, teachers recommended I skip the next level, and I thought Lea would be sad that we wouldn't get to be in the same class anymore, but all she said was that it didn't really matter, and I thought she would come up with ways that we could remain friends or something, but you know what she said? She said it was okay, because the only reason she'd picked me as a friend in the first place was that I always had the best grades and that if she sat by me in class she would get to copy from me during tests."

There was a silence there that meant Berenice's story had ended.

"I don't see how that relates to my friend's suicide," I said.

"Well I was really hurt by that."

"I'm not hurt," I said. "I'm sad."

"I can relate to that too. I just don't have as tragic a story to draw on as a parallel to yours."

"The father dying is a much more tragic story than the one you just told me."

Berenice cleared her throat and ignored my comment.

"All I aimed to say was that you never know exactly what goes on in anyone else's head, but then when you do get to find out and uncover a tiny little piece of it, it's very likely that it's going to hurt or make you feel horrible."

"I didn't find out Denise was suicidal the day she jumped," I said. "I knew it from before."

"There's nothing you could've done," Berenice said.

A gust of wind burst through my mother's bedroom window

and slammed the door shut. I got up from the bed to close the window and watched the branches of our cherry tree brush against the glass for a while. I was still holding the receiver against my ear, but I'd left my blanket behind. I don't think Berenice said anything.

"What happened to your friend Lea?" I heard myself ask.

"I don't know. Last time I saw her she was coming out of a meditation class on Main Street. I think she became new-agey in college."

"Did you talk to her?"

"For a minute, yes."

"Did she ever apologize for what she said to you in grammar school?"

"Honestly, I don't think she remembers any of it," Berenice said. "I think that, in the end, people's brains only pick something like five memories to keep from all of their grammar school years. This one mustn't have made the cut for her."

Five sounded like too low a number for the memories one kept of a whole period, one that had seemed so long to me, but then I thought about my own time in grammar school, not so long before, and very few images came to mind: the Let Them Sea campaign in fourth grade, Porfi's crying because I'd called him myopic, the teacher pulling my ear because I wouldn't stop singing "Au Clair de la Lune." The rest, hundreds of days and thousands of details, all gone, or rather, all balled up in a corner of my head under the label "grammar school," every specificity crushed and replaced by the sense-memory of what it had *felt* like to be in grammar school—clueless and uneasy. And I was supposed to be the one with a great memory.

"How many memories do people keep from junior high?" I asked Berenice.

"About the same as from grammar school, I'd say." She thought about it a little. "Actually, maybe even less."

The rain started to fall hard, drops ricocheting from the tree leaves to the window. I hoped Denise's funeral was still going. I thought she would've liked to know she'd had a rainy one, and decided right away to never think again in terms of what Denise would or would not have liked. I knew I could decide something like that and hold myself to it.

"What time is it by you?" I asked Berenice.

"It's about ten thirty in the morning."

"Is it raining?"

"No. It's been nothing but blue skies since I arrived. I don't think it rains much here."

"That's no good," I said.

"I fully agree. Sunny places make for overly optimistic people. I hope that the winters are horrible enough that it evens things out."

The leaves of our cherry tree seemed to be sorting the raindrops, which ones would get to pass through and fall to the ground, which would stay, which would bounce to the window and eventually dry and leave dusty smears on the glass.

"Did your friend Lea tell you why she went to meditation classes? When you bumped into her?"

"I must admit I didn't ask, Dory. Why do you care?"

"I don't really understand what meditation is for," I said. "Denise's doctors told her to try it, but I don't know that she ever did."

"Well, I tried it," Berenice said. "I didn't take a class or anything. I don't understand how it would be possible to think about nothing with other people around."

I knew Berenice was lying. Not about meditating but about the reasons why she wouldn't take a class to learn how. She would never risk taking a class in something she might not be the best at.

"How do you do it?" I asked.

"I just sit on the ground and I stare at something," Berenice said. "Then I try to visualize my own body, the inside of it I mean, organ after organ, the ones I know where they are at least, then tongue, muscles, nails, brain, etc., and then I try to have each part I visualize recede somewhere and disappear until I can't feel it anymore, and then I'm all light. At some point, my body is like an empty shell and I can feel currents of air gushing through it. It's very peaceful."

"What kind of meditation is that?" I asked. "It sounds unpleasant."

"It's not any particular kind," she said. "It's a mix of things I read in books. It's the Berenice kind."

"Why do you need to stare at something in the first place?"

"I don't know," she said. "I think some people just close their eyes."

She started saying something else but we got disconnected. I kept the phone to my ear anyway, as if Berenice's voice might just emerge again from under the dial tone and go on describing meditation or her new life in America. I went to my mother's dressing table and found the bottle of cognac where Berenice said I would. There was a little shot glass turned upside down over the tip of the bottle. It was a bit sticky, both inside and out. I wondered if my mother ever cleaned it. I poured myself some cognac anyway, because I'd never drunk straight from a bottle before and it felt too dramatic to start now, or like I was either too young or too old. I didn't like the taste. Rather, I couldn't taste anything, the cognac just burned the little cuts in my mouth, which I'd given up on trying to protect from the braces. I poured myself another glass to see if the cuts had been cleaned enough by the first shot that I could taste it better. I could. It tasted like marzipan set on fire. I hung up the phone and waited for the alcohol to have an effect, maybe make me a little less miserable. Because I was staring at something already, the branches and the leaves wiping the window, I thought I might as well try to meditate, but it was hard to focus. The image moved too much. I poured myself another shot of cognac and sat in what I thought was the lotus position in the middle of the bed, facing my mother's closet. The father's shirts and jackets were hanging in the same order they'd always been in, from black to light blue, going through grays and all shades of navy. I stared at the jacket in the middle of the rack and tried to visualize my body and then forget it, as Berenice had said. My mother never closed her closet door.

The next time I saw Aurore's stomach, the baby was gone, like Berenice said it would be. She was trying on clothes in front of the only full-length mirror we had, in the bathroom, and she'd left the door wide open so she could come and go between there and her bedroom, where more clothes waited to be rejected. Nothing seemed to satisfy her.

"What are you dressing up for?" I said, even though Aurore

wasn't trying anything fancy right then. The fact that she was giving any thought to what she was wearing was sign enough that she was getting ready for something special.

"Nothing special," Aurore said. "I'm just considering my options."

"Your options for what?"

"My options to not look like a history professor."

"What's wrong with looking like a history professor?"

"Men don't like it."

She said this angrily, like I was responsible for men's taste in general.

"Since when do you care what men like?"

"Why do you have to ask all these questions all the time, Dory? Is it because you miss interviewing Simone?"

Simone had just started school in Paris.

"I'm just interested in you," I said.

"Well, go ask Leonard. He's the foremost specialist on our family now. He must know why I do the things I do better than myself."

The night before Simone moved out, Leonard had broken the news to her, Aurore, and my mother that his PhD ethnographic study was about us. They hadn't taken it well. Aurore and my mother, particularly. Simone had just been worried that it meant Leonard would use episodes of her life that she therefore couldn't use herself in her fiction.

"Does Leonard know about your abortion?" I asked Aurore.

I couldn't see my own reflection in the mirror from where I stood, but because I could see hers, I knew she could see me. With her foot, she closed the door.

The reason Leonard had come clean about studying our family was that he was about to hand in the final draft of his dissertation and he suspected his professors would be interested in knowing what our reaction to his project had been. I suppose Aurore's anger was being disclosed and interpreted in the conclusion Leonard was crafting that very moment.

"I'm sorry," I told Aurore through the bathroom door. "I didn't mean to upset you."

Aurore didn't accept my apology, didn't say anything, in fact, and I hoped that it was because she was crying and didn't want me to hear it in her voice. Yet I didn't want to be the one who'd made her cry. I just didn't want to be the only one to be sad over there not being a baby.

"I'm sorry," I repeated.

I'd always thought of our house in the afternoon as a possible definition of silence, but now that Simone had gone away, I realized silence wasn't an absolute but could always go deeper. Simone, had she been home, might've done nothing more at this hour than breathe over some book in her bed, and it might not have sounded like much, but I could feel her breath missing in the acoustics of the house.

The doorbell rang and I thought for a second that I'd imagined it.

"Go get the fucking door," Aurore said. It didn't sound like she'd been crying.

I had to stand on tiptoe to see through the peephole. Herr Coffin's face was in there, his mouth wide open, in a yawn I assumed, but then it started closing and opening very quickly like Coffin was exercising his maxilla. He looked surprised to see me when I opened the door.

"Are you home alone?" he said.

"Everyone's here but my mother," I said. "Did you want to talk to her?"

"No, I came to see you, actually."

Herr Coffin didn't elaborate on his statement and I thought this meant I was supposed to let him in, so I did.

"I would offer you some coffee," I said, "but I don't know how to make it."

"That is fine. I do not drink coffee after two p.m. anyway."

We sat on the new couch, which was fake leather and squeaked whenever you moved on it even just a little. Leonard and Jeremie had complained about it, but I pretended I couldn't hear anything. Except I could, of course, and I knew Coffin could, and I was embarrassed.

"I have cognac, though," I said. "Would you care for some?"

"It's a little early for me," Coffin said.

I was trying to be as still as possible on the couch, and I imagined Coffin was trying to do the same.

"Are there specific hours to drink any drink?" I asked, only to cover potential squeaking, and Coffin must have figured I wasn't really interested in an answer because he just smiled and turned his whole body on the couch so he could almost face me. Major squeaking.

"So how have you been?" he said. "I didn't see you at your friend's funeral."

"I didn't know you'd gone," I said. "Denise was never your student."

"One doesn't have to be a Germanist for me to feel for them."

"Good for you," I said. "I guess it would be pretty lonely otherwise. There aren't that many Germanists around here."

"It's still quite lonely," Coffin said, and I didn't know what to make of that. I didn't want every sad person on Earth to see a confidant in me, so I didn't encourage him down that line. I wasn't too happy myself.

"Are you sure you're not alone here?" Coffin said after a long silence.

"I'm not. It's just very quiet around our house."

My mother came home from work and made for the kitchen without seeing us. We heard her open the fridge and throw some groceries in. By the sound of it, she'd bought way too much food. It always took her a while to adjust her grocery list to the number of children she had to feed whenever one of us went away. Since Simone had moved out, we'd had leftovers after every meal. She startled when she came out of the kitchen and saw us on the couch.

"Don't tell me you unearthed another bachelor online, Dory," she said.

"Mom, it's Herr Coffin," I said. "You met before."

"Oh yes, Mr. Coffin, of course. I am so sorry."

She almost ran to shake his hand.

"Completely understandable," Coffin said. "Out of context, one old man looks like nothing but another old man."

My mother didn't laugh or even smile at this. She must've thought Coffin had merely stated a true fact, and true facts were no laughing matter.

"Is Isidore in trouble?" she asked, and I tried to spot signs of excitement on her face, but it didn't look like she wanted me to be in trouble this time.

"Not at all," Coffin said. "Quite the opposite, actually. I came here to see if your boy would be interested in helping me with some work I've been assigned to do. I would pay him, of course."

"What kind of work?" my mother asked.

"Well, as you both know, Mrs. Daphné Marlotte's birthday is coming up at the end of the week, and I've been asked, since she only can express herself in German nowadays, to be her interpreter for her meeting with the president." Coffin paused there, to give us time to congratulate him, I imagine, but my mother and I just wanted to hear the rest of what he had to say and he went on. "Now, I remembered your son was interested in doing such interpreting work, so I thought he could assist me in this task. Daphné is scheduled to meet the president for fifteen minutes on Saturday at five forty-five, before the party."

Jeremie appeared on our staircase before my mother or I could say anything.

"I thought I'd heard voices," he said, and he came all the way down the stairs to salute Herr Coffin. *"Wie geht's?"* he asked him, and they started chitchatting in German and Coffin told Jeremie what he'd just told my mother and me, and Jeremie said it sounded like a great opportunity for me. Jeremie's German was infinitely better than mine.

Coffin stayed for tea but refused to impose on our family dinner. I thought my mother had only offered dinner out of obligation—he was going to introduce me to the president, after all—but when Coffin declined, she looked disappointed. She even insisted he share our roast, since she had bought too much anyway, she explained, and I tried to perceive romantic interest in her voice, but I understood she was only seeing in Coffin a distraction from the tension Leonard had raised in the house a few

days earlier. Coffin left and we ate in total silence. Aurore wore one of her many shapeless gray sweaters. She hadn't lied earlier. She had nowhere special to go that night.

———

I didn't think much of the president. All he asked Daphné was how she felt that day and exactly how many presidents had governed France over her lifetime, which was something he could've calculated for himself beforehand, I thought, instead of having the old lady—whose memory had not only been Germanized but also more broadly impaired by the stroke—make the effort. It took Daphné three whole minutes to go over the list, and she wasn't even sure she hadn't forgotten one or two names in the end. "All pretty useless anyway," Daphné said about the presidents she remembered, which is not something Herr Coffin translated back into French. I was only there to learn and take notes if I wanted, Coffin had said, so I didn't jump in to translate what Daphné had said about presidents' being useless, I just wrote down in my notebook that the things an interpreter thought could offend one of the parties present could be left out of the translation at his discretion. It is actually the only thing I took note of in the notebook my mother had bought for me specially for the occasion and that I would never use afterward. I had time to look at the president closely enough to notice he looked at people's mouths when they spoke. He was an expert at avoiding eye contact and I found that odd. I would have thought politicians to be masters of eye contact, that it was how they got people to believe they had a special connection with them and that their

voice mattered, but I guessed that now that the president was in office and wouldn't run for reelection, it was more important for him to not get caught in annoying conversations than to get approval, and you could always pretend you hadn't heard someone when you didn't look them in the eyes.

Simone, over the phone, had given me a list of questions for the president if I had a chance (she was mostly concerned about the latest draft of the government's secondary education reforms) as well as a selection of words she believed he would be inspired to look up in the dictionary when he had a minute (Simone had said if he actually only had one minute, he should just read the definition of the word *elitism*) because it was obvious to her he didn't precisely know what they meant. I had Simone's questions memorized, but I knew I wouldn't get to talk to the president at all. I knew he would just look at my mouth and pretend I either hadn't spoken or had said something different entirely, so I didn't even try. Also, I didn't like people looking at my mouth, with the braces and all.

An hour before the meeting, I'd been inspected by the secret service to make sure I wasn't planning on killing the president. That was something they did with anyone who was scheduled to be in a room with him. Coffin had explained this to me in a tone that suggested he was accustomed to such inspections, even though when I'd asked him if he'd met any other president before, he'd admitted he hadn't. When the secret service guys had asked me to confirm that my name was indeed Isidore Mazal, I'd thought they were only double-checking because they'd recognized the father's name and were amazed at the coincidence, for the father had been a dear colleague, a legend even, maybe, but when I'd confirmed my name, there had been no spark of

recognition in their eyes. But then if the father had really been a spy and these people had known him, I thought, they would've known better than to just reminisce with me about his many qualities and top secret achievements.

The meeting didn't go a second over the allotted fifteen minutes. On his way out, the president looked down at my notebook and asked me if I wanted an autograph. I said I was fine. His entourage laughed a little and a lady said, "Kids!" in a way that was meant to restore the president's confidence that he was still someone whose autograph any sane person would want and that also made it clear she had never spent too much time around kids.

"Who was that?" Daphné asked me once the president was gone.

I'd been nervous about seeing Daphné again, nervous that she would hold me responsible for her stroke, but she didn't seem to remember a thing about our last encounter, or to even understand she'd had a stroke. If anything, she thought I was her best friend.

"That was the president," I said.

"The president? What is he doing in town?"

"I'm not sure," I said.

Coffin was supposed to stay with Daphné 'til the end of her birthday party, in case people wanted to ask her questions and he had to interpret, but he asked me if I could take care of her for half an hour or so—he wanted to see if he could run after the president and try to raise his attention regarding a couple of flaws in his secondary education reform. I said I could manage Daphné, of course, but before he left, I needed to know something.

"Did the secret service people ask you to confirm your name?" I asked him.

"They did," Coffin said. I realized I didn't know his first name.

"It's Albert," he said, and he went chasing after the president.

Daphné and I were left alone in this small room behind the reception area of city hall. Through the door, I could hear people starting to gather and the sound of champagne corks popping. I wondered if Daphné had any idea this was all in her honor.

"Do you want me to bring you a glass of champagne?" I said, in German of course.

"Will you be sad when I die?" was her answer.

"I think so," I said.

"Will you really? Will you think about me? Or will you just find comfort in thinking that at least I will have had a full life?"

"I don't know what a full life means," I said.

"I know that that's what these people will think," Daphné said, eyeing the door between us and the reception hall. "That I've had a full life. Except I actually had more than a full life. It went way over the brim. And when it goes over the brim, all bets are off. Things that shouldn't happen start happening: you don't just lose one child, you lose all of them, you don't just have to learn about new technologies to keep up with the times, you have to learn about new technologies because the ones you were used to have simply disappeared. I knew how to send a telegram, for Christ's sake. What good is it to me now? I used to love so many people, what good is that to me now—now that they're gone? You know, when someone dies, it's not just the person that dies, but all the ties that that person had with those who survive them. Severed. It all just hangs loose in the survivor's brain and weighs, like a useless knowledge. I would just like it if I could weigh on someone's life, after *I* die, you know? Will I weigh on your life?"

I can't be a hundred percent sure that's what Daphné said

exactly—it was all in German. The way she stared at me after she was done speaking, though, her neck outstretched in my direction like a turtle's, it did look like she needed me to say yes to whatever she'd asked, and I thought about Berenice doing the dishes for her roommates in Chicago and how hard she felt it was to be nice to people. I didn't understand how anyone could find it hard to be nice. It seemed to me the easiest thing, pleasing people, strangers and friends. You only had to go with the flow, nod, agree, fetch, go do what they wanted you to. It made all the decisions for you.

"I can't promise you anything," I said to Daphné.

She said she understood.

―――――

Aurore was drinking wine in a corner with Ohri when I went into the reception room. She was laughing at something he'd said, but I knew it wasn't funny. We'd discussed how unfunny Ohri was a million times.

My mother wanted my impressions on meeting the president and all I did was shrug. I didn't care about the president, or Daphné's birthday. Maybe I didn't even care about German. Maybe German was useless. Hell, even the president didn't speak it. All I wanted was to find Porfi. I knew it would be giving him a disproportionate sense of his own power to put Denise's death on him, but if there was the slightest chance it would crush him, or at least make Denise one of the five or fewer prominent memories from junior high that would weigh on him forever, then it would be worth it.

Porfi and Victor were smoking in the parking lot. Their backs were to me and they didn't see me approach them until I was close enough that I could read the names on the soccer cards they were showing each other.

"Hey!" Porfi said as he turned to face me. "Don't sneak up on people like that. You fucking scared me."

"Have cards to trade?" Victor asked me.

They were both way taller than me, but I knew from watching Viet Vo Dao on TV that it didn't matter. I kicked Porfi in the knee, and as he bent to grab it, I punched his temple. He fell on his side on the pavement, wailing. I kicked him again, in the kidney, and pivoted, ready for Victor, but Victor went low, leaned over Porfi, struck him on the face.

"What the fuck are you doing?" I said.

Victor didn't respond. He kept smashing Porfi.

I sat right there, in the middle of all the soccer cards they'd dropped.

"Fucking pussy," Victor said, but I didn't know who he was saying it to. "Come finish what you started."

Victor helped me up. Porfi made a sound. I kicked him one last time and walked off.

———

I went straight home. There was nowhere else to go. I knew I'd left Aurore and my mother at the party, but the door to my brothers' room was closed—I didn't know if they were in there. I made myself a sandwich and took it to the living room. I knew exactly what would be playing on TV so I didn't bother turning it on,

I just sat there on the squeaking couch, kind of looking around for something to focus on other than Porfi. Halfway through my sandwich, I noticed that the printer next to the computer was blinking and got up to turn it off. There was an "out of paper" message on the screen, and I figured I could be a good citizen and fill the tray for the next user. The second I pushed the full tray closed, the printer started laboring loudly and spitting out pages of Leonard's dissertation, the last 16 of its 295 pages, to be precise. Leonard must not have seen the printer had run out of paper, and he'd probably taken the first 279 pages of his work upstairs assuming he had the whole thing. I knew he'd turned in his final manuscript the day before, four copies of it, bound and manically checked for page order beforehand, so this one was probably just a copy he'd printed for himself. I took the 16 pages to my room.

Simone called an hour later, from the cell phone my mother had bought her before she'd moved to Paris. She kept complaining that having a cell phone was a horrible thing because it made you reachable at all times, and being reachable at all times was the first step toward the end of freedom, but she still used the cell phone to call me every night. She also gave no hint that any human being other than our mother had ever dialed her number.

"So," Simone said. "Did you talk to him?"

"The president? No," I said, "I didn't get a chance. But I think Coffin had a word with him."

"About the education reforms?"

"What else is there to talk about?"

"Was he charismatic at all? He doesn't look too charismatic on TV, but sometimes it just doesn't translate."

"I think Coffin is actually more charismatic than him," I said.

"Ouch."

I'd picked up the cordless phone in my mother's room and brought it to mine. I was talking to Simone while lying on her old bed. I slept in it sometimes. I always made it in the morning when I did.

"What's new at home?"

"Nothing much," I said. "Leonard handed in his dissertation yesterday. Maybe we can all resume our normal lives now. It's been kind of tense here since you left."

"I'm certainly curious to see what he had to say about me," Simone said. I didn't tell her what I knew he'd written. "Do you know when the defense will be?"

"Sometime at the end of next month," I said. "But Leonard doesn't want us to come."

"Oh, I'll be there," Simone said.

"Won't you have classes and stuff?"

"If I can be honest with you, Dory—sorry: Izzie—I'm not sure I'll hang out here much longer."

"I thought this was your dream school."

"I don't know. I thought it would be. I thought it would be the perfect place for me because all they ask from us is to read a hell of a lot, and think, and write, but see, it seems to me I'm the only one who actually enjoys it. No one likes to read here. It's just something they're really good at."

"What do you care if they like it or not?"

"There's always a risk of contamination," Simone said.

"You went to school your whole life with people who didn't like studying as much as you did. I'd say it did the opposite of contaminating you. If there's a word for that."

"I guess most people would say *decontamination* is the antonym of *contamination*, but I see what you mean. It's not satisfying in our context."

"Whatever. That wasn't my point."

"The reason why it didn't contaminate me at the time was that I had you guys to come home to," Simone said. "I could see that Aurore took pleasure in her work, even if it drove her crazy sometimes. She read everything twice, and slowly. Here it's all about rushing and diagonal reading. I actually heard a guy boast that he'd mastered a technique that made him able to make out the contents of a paragraph just by *looking* at it a certain way."

"Is that even possible?"

"Don't know and don't care."

"What would you do if you quit school?"

"Well I'd come home, obviously."

"You can't stay home forever," I said.

Or maybe she could? Aurore and the boys weren't showing any signs of ever planning to leave.

"Not forever, of course," Simone said, "but for a little while. Until I write a book or something."

"Oh yeah? What will you write about?"

"I don't know . . . one doesn't write a novel *about* things, I don't think."

"I thought you wanted to write a novel about us," I said. "I thought you were mad at Leonard, for telling all our stories."

"Who would care for a novel about us?"

As I struggled to find an answer to Simone's question, I heard the boys' bedroom door open and close. Someone came down the stairs—Jeremie, I guessed, from the slowness of the steps.

"I'm afraid I did something wrong," I said to Simone. I was thinking of Porfi lying on his side, his fallen cigarette inches from his face, about to be extinguished by the blood spilling out from the corner of his mouth. That sound he'd made just before I'd walked away. Had he said my name? Had he coughed? Apologized?

Simone said, "You never do anything wrong, Dory. Izzie."

Jeremie started playing piano in the living room, the Chopin prelude the father used to sometimes request on Sunday nights. Leonard hated it, and Jeremie always complained it was too easy a piece, but he still complied. I couldn't recall his ever playing it since the father had died.

"You think Jeremie is playing that just to taunt Leonard?" Simone said.

"I don't know that taunting anyone would ever cross Jeremie's mind," I said.

She said, "You really think too highly of us sometimes."

I started saying something but Simone shushed me.

"Bring the phone closer," she said, "so I can hear him better."

"He'll stop playing if he sees me."

"Of course he will. Go sit on the stairs."

Our staircase was a complicated one, a squared spiral that turned twice. If I sat at the top, Jeremie wouldn't see me, but four more steps down and we would be eye-to-eye between the propped lid and the bare, silvery wires of his baby grand piano. I brought the phone to the top step and aimed the receiver down at the music. Leonard came from his room and sat a step below me. We stayed like that for a minute or so before I saw our dead bolt turning, and then Aurore and my mother tiptoeing into the hallway. They saw us sitting at the top of the stairs and both barred their mouths with their index fingers. We nodded our assent. At least I did. I don't know what Leonard did. I couldn't look at him straight, not so soon after reading his conclusions, what they said about me.

While the rest of the study's subjects have opted, after the initial trauma of their father's death, to retreat more deeply into tried-and-true behavioral patterns, presumably hoping that the wound that their father's loss has opened will, on its own, eventually reclose itself around the family unit, the youngest, Isidore, has labored to exploit the breach of said wound via investigating the possibility of relationships outside the family. Over the course of two years, while his siblings continued to pursue the same achievements they had already (i.e., prior to the father's death) been pursuing, Isidore, his sights now passionately set on a future career as a German-language pedagogue, sought and found a mentor for himself (Herr C.); lost his virginity (years ahead of the national average), possibly falling in love in the process; looked for a replacement of the paternal figure (via dating websites); and made a good friend at school (his very first).

By these means, and without (as far as I can tell) his being aware of it, his very role in the family system has changed: he has become the one the other subjects turn to for comfort and hope.

The prelude was just about to end. I could tell because it closed almost exactly the way it opened—the same motif repeated—except it didn't sound as light and heartening at the end as at the beginning because there was that big dramatic part in the middle that darkened and loaded and tainted everything.

Acknowledgments

This novel wouldn't exist without my husband, Adam Levin. His unwavering encouragement and constant support allowed me to see the book behind the book. I want to thank him for tricking me into believing I could finish it, for doing so for as long as it took me to finish it, and for helping me make English my second first language.

I'd also like to thank Christian TeBordo and Jeff Parker; your readings made the book better.

Thank you to my agent, Jackie Ko, for being the first person unrelated to me to think this book should be shown to other people unrelated to me.

Thank you, Tim Duggan, for being the second person to think that. Thank you as well to William Wolfslau and Aja Pollock.

Thanks to my brother and sisters: Jean-Sébastien, Florence, and Mélanie Bordas. And thanks to my mother, Marie, and her own trio of larger-than-fiction/stranger-than-life siblings: Pedro, José, and Juan.

About the Author

Camille Bordas is the author of two previous novels in French, *Les treize desserts* and *Partie commune.* Her short fiction has appeared in *The New Yorker.* She grew up in Paris and Mexico City and now lives in Chicago.